HOT STUFF

HOT STUFF

A NOVEL

DON BRUNS

LONGBOAT KEY, FLORIDA

ISBN 978-1-60809-061-7

Published in the United States of America by Oceanview Publishing, Longboat Key, Florida
www.oceanviewpub.com

2 4 6 8 10 9 7 5 3 1

PRINTED IN THE UNITED STATES OF AMERICA

Dedicated to The Food Channel, where so many of my friends spend their time getting fabulous tips from the great chefs of our time, and to the Bistro, a great restaurant that should have lasted forever.

ACKNOWLEDGMENTS

About thirty-two chefs around the country graciously opened their kitchens to me and allowed me to see firsthand how high-end meals are prepared. I thank each one of them and, although I love to cook, I wouldn't last five minutes in one their establishments. The pressure, the exact way that they prepare their food, and the hours they put in would drive me crazy. I got the idea for the tool chest full of knives from Chef Enzo and Chef Kane at Shawnee Country Club in Lima, Ohio. Thanks to Howard Koch for recipe ideas and Anne Decker, Don Witter, and Dave Bruns for reading the early draft.

A special thanks to Clayton's on Siesta Key, Alisa at the Fat Cat in Lima, Ohio, Duval's on Main in Sarasota, and Darwin's on 4th, also in Sarasota, where I had the author photo taken. To my favorite male cooks, Jim Gideon, Tom Biddle, Bill Lodermier, Mike Trump, and David Gutridge. I got some great ideas from Chip at The Main Bar Sandwich Shop in Sarasota. Dave Dorley from Keystone Meats in Lima, Ohio, gave me the butcher experience. Thanks to Doc Glidewell for the excellent photography and George Foster for the excellent cover. To my wife, Linda, for the first read and Bob and Pat, my publishers, for their continued support. David and Frank from Oceanview, thank you for your hard work.

Kelly Fields and Cheryl Deitering donated to the Rotary Foundation for a chance to be characters in *Hot Stuff* and I hope I treated them fairly. They are very nice ladies.

To the kitchen staffs around the world who create so many wonderful dishes, I salute you. May you never have a murder in your kitchen.

HOT STUFF

CHAPTER ONE

Two hours ago I hadn't even known what a sous chef was, but there she was, blood seeping from the wounds in her abdomen as she lay faceup in the alley behind L'Elfe, the famous French restaurant on Bayshore Drive in Miami.

You've heard of L'Elfe. It was featured on all the cooking channels, and the owner is Jean Bouvier. He and his wife, Sophia, own at least five restaurants. He's written ten cookbooks, owns lines of spices, pots and pans, cutlery, and you name it. This little guy, about five foot one, and his burly wife, had become a money machine, and my partner hated them.

James, my business associate, was a culinary major in college and now works for a fast-food chain in Carol City, just outside of Miami. He dreams of becoming a millionaire and is put off by anyone who has figured out how to actually become a business tycoon. So far the best we've been able to do is start a private investigating company. Which is one of the reasons why I was in the back alley of L'Elfe. Em dragged me back there, saying we had to find out who killed the girl, someone who had once been a good friend of hers.

You see, my girlfriend, Emily, was treating me to dinner this night. She'd landed a major construction deal for her employer, her father, and we were celebrating. Sous chef Amanda Wright had been a good friend of Em's all through high school. Em had even fixed her up with my roommate, James, for a couple of dates recently, and Em wanted to show her friend support by eating at L'Elfe. It seemed like a good idea at the time. And, I was getting a free meal at one of the hottest eateries in Miami. Now, staring at Amanda Wright's blood-drained face, I was having second thoughts.

"Jesus, Skip." The rescue squad had been called, but the pale body grotesquely sprawled on the concrete alley proved that there would be no rescue. "It's Amanda. I mean, it's really Amanda." She grabbed my hand and squeezed tight. "She was a friend. Someone I could count on." Em was trembling, her eyes focused on the corpse and the pool of blood that surrounded it.

I didn't know the girl that well, but looking at the pale, dark-haired young woman who seemed to have a brilliant future brought tears to my eyes. No one deserved to die at this age and be left to bleed to death in this dirty, vermin-infested, smelly alley with black vinyl trash bags lining the curb.

"What happened? We were talking to her just, what? An hour ago?" Over drinks and some type of scallops with seaweed.

I squeezed Em's hand back, sirens wailing in the distance, and the morbid curiosity seekers easing through the doorway from the kitchen. I was certain no one was left in the dining area. When our waiter ran into the restaurant screaming that there was a dead body in the alley, the place had cleared out quickly. Uneaten meals, unpaid bills, and undrunk drinks littered the tables as patrons hurried from their seats.

"Em, she's probably in a better place." The dumbest thing I could have said. She was about to be head chef at a South Beach restaurant. That was the place she should have been.

2

"She was so happy. An hour ago." Em was shaking. Not crying yet, but shaking as she buried her head in my shoulder. "She was so excited about the promotion. I've never seen her that happy."

Amanda Wright had stopped at our table, speaking a mile a minute about her new assignment. Hands waving in the air, she informed us that Bouvier had asked her to become executive chef at a brand-new restaurant he was opening on South Beach. La Plage. The Beach. An unbelievable achievement for someone of her age and background. Executive chef.

"It was her dream, her goal. Skip, she had so much to live for." I glanced at Em and tears were streaming down her face. I blinked, released her hand, and hugged her as purple lights swirled against the white building. Blue-and-red spinners from the police cars cast an eerie pattern down the narrow pavement, bathing everyone and everything in an unhealthy glow.

"Stand back." A uniformed officer stepped from the first vehicle, obviously ready to take charge as a white ambulance pulled up behind him. Two paramedics leaped from the white unit and rushed to the body, one carrying a black medical bag. I was reminded of a phrase my mother often used to describe our basic living conditions. "A day late and a dollar short."

"Em, they're going to get to the bottom of this."

She shook her head. "She's dead, Skip. Bad things like this can't happen to good people. They just can't."

I nodded.

"It's Amanda. She stood up for me when my whole world was coming apart." Em was shaking, quivering, and I wanted it to stop. "Skip, we've got to find out what happened. I owe her. I owe her, Skip."

I'd known Em a long time, and she was the most put together person I'd ever met.

"Skip, I never told you." The sobs were breaking up her speech. I held her tighter, wishing her some peace.

3

"Told me what?"

Em cleared her throat, taking some deep breaths as we stepped back from the crime scene. In hushed tones she spoke.

"During high school, before you and I started dating, I was charged with grand theft. Amanda and I—" she paused, trying to gain her composure.

My eyes shot open and I stared at her. Em was the most moral, decent person I knew. Grand theft?

"Explain that. Grand theft is a major charge." It was a whole lot more than a misdemeanor. "What could you possibly have—"

"I shouldn't have told you. It's just that—" She paused and stared back down at the body. "I don't want to get into it right now, but Amanda was there for me. I owe her, Skip. Please understand that."

"Grand theft? A felony? Em, what the hell did you—"

"I'm not going there, Skip."

Not going there? "You brought it up." Sometimes my girl-friend defied common sense.

The two young men in white jackets stood up, shaking their heads, walking slowly back to the ambulance as two police officers strung yellow tape around the area where the body lay, tying the ends off on a fire hydrant and a green Dumpster. A gruesome barricade bordered by alley fixtures.

"No one is to leave the scene." A potbellied, middle-aged uniformed cop with a squawking bullhorn shouted to the assembled. "We will want to talk to every one of you, and only after you're cleared can you leave."

"And Amanda stood up for you?"

Em looked into my eyes. "She did more than that."

"What, then?"

"She confessed to the crime."

"She committed the felony?"

"No."

I was more confused by the minute.

"She stood up for you, admitted to the crime so you could go free, and you're saying what?"

"She didn't do it." Em shuddered. "She confessed to get me off the hook."

CHAPTER TWO

It was after one in the morning when I finally got home and explained to James the evening's events.

"Dude, Em was charged with a felony?"

He'd known her almost as long as I had. My best friend and my girlfriend were long time acquaintances. Not always on the best of terms, but they knew each other pretty well.

"When? How long ago? I can't believe it. Em?"

He sat straight up on the old green sofa, his eyes wide open.

"I tell you that there's a dead woman in the alley behind L'Elfe, Amanda Wright, a dead woman you recently dated, and I tell you that Jean Bouvier is opening a new restaurant on South Beach called La Plage. I just explained that Amanda had been appointed executive chef at that restaurant, and I share with you that we spent an hour waiting to be interviewed by the cops and *this* is your only surprise? That Emily was charged with a felony in her past?"

He looked somewhat chagrined. "Skip, it's a scary story. I'm a little shook up, yeah. But, look, I don't know Bouvier. I can't afford to eat in his restaurants. And I feel really bad about

Amanda. My God, no one should go out like that. I mean it was months ago, and she was a nice girl, but I don't really have any feelings about her, you know? I mean she was—" He paused, searching for the right word, "She was out there, a little weird, a little clingy. Emotional, needy. Yes, I'm a little bummed. But then you tell me about Em? I know the lady. Emily being charged is hard to get my head around. That's big news, pal. What was the felony?"

"She didn't say."

I hadn't pushed it any harder. She sounded very protective about that part of her life.

"Actually, she *wouldn't* say. Once she gave me the outline of the story, she shut down."

"Well, it's a big revelation. She's starting to share the dark side of her life, amigo. Maybe a ring is in order?" He gave me a big-toothed nervous smile and brushed the hair from his face. Charming as ever.

I walked across the room to our small refrigerator and pulled out two bottles of Yuengling. Tossing one to James, I threw myself into the threadbare recliner with the broken handle. The chair remained permanently frozen in the reclining position.

"Amanda Wright." I took a long swallow of the cold beer. "She was good friends with Em, yet—"

"Yet you didn't know much about her."

James and I could sometimes finish each other's sentences. We probably spent way too much time together.

"Well, I knew a little about her. I mean Em would say Amanda this, Amanda that, but—"

She'd been a good friend. *Been* being the operative word. I think that they'd had a parting of the ways sometime back, some argument, disagreement, or something, but recently she'd fixed James up with the girl, and judging by what had happened tonight, Em still had feelings for Amanda. Apparently, very strong feelings.

When she dropped me off at my crappy apartment in Carol City, before she drove back to her twenty-third story condo overlooking Biscayne Bay, she'd once again warned me against bringing up the felony charges.

"Pretend I never mentioned it, Skip." Giving me a cold, hard look, she peeled away in her sleek sports car, without so much as a goodnight kiss.

"Dude," James was concentrating on the murder. "I haven't seen Amanda in a couple or three months. Hell, when was the last time we went out. I seriously can't remember. Didn't even know she was working at L'Elfe. You know, I picked her up, and we went to a movie the first time. She was a knockout, great face, body, but all she wanted to do was hold hands all through the flick. I mean, I believe in intimacy but," he paused for a moment as if the brutality of the crime had just hit him. "Stabbed, you said?"

"Multiple times in the stomach and lower abdomen."

"Somebody didn't like the beef bourguignon."

I didn't know if he was trying to be funny or mask his shock.

"At least we are out of it, James. The cops talked to everyone there, and I'm sure they're going to have some leads. They were very thorough. And, James, what exactly is a sous chef?"

"Come on, you should know that. You've watched enough of The Food Channel with me. A sous chef is a backup. Some guy—in this case some girl—who takes over when the executive chef isn't there. A sous chef is the first in line after the executive chef. They know the entire routine. They may be responsible for a menu. Maybe they come up with a special dish or sauce. Next step up, just like Em's friend, would be executive chef." James nodded smugly.

"Executive chef, right? Executive chef at L'Elfe? Wouldn't that be Bouvier?" The title threw me.

"Nah. Bouvier is the chef de cuisine. He *owns* the franchise.

8

He has the vision, conceives the menu, and gives the restaurant its personality. Bouvier, just like Paul Prudhomme at K-Paul's restaurant in New Orleans. Bobby Flay at Bar Americain in New York. They don't really spend time in those kitchens. They're busy running a food empire." I could see that elusive dream in his eyes.

James often talked about some of the famous restaurants that he'd studied in school. I had a passing knowledge of Prudhomme and his blackened redfish. James even made the New Orleans delicacy in our tiny kitchen. If memory serves, it was very good. And my roommate made smoked chicken and black bean quesadillas from a Bobby Flay recipe. James really is a good cook.

"Chef de cuisine really doesn't have much to do with the kitchen anymore. He'd have a executive chef and two or three sous chefs. And my thought is that he has somebody, maybe his wife, who probably runs the business side." He thought for a moment. "Somebody like Bouvier, he's the big-picture guy. Coming up with the next move, the next wave of his business. And his wife, Sophia, she's maybe the enforcer. She gets it done."

Too many titles, almost like royalty. Duke, duchess, countess. "So who would have become the next sous chef?"

"At L'Elfe? As I said, he probably has two or three of them. The fancy places usually have multiples. That restaurant puts out a lot of food, pardner. They need some serious supervision in the kitchen."

"Maybe it was somebody who didn't like Amanda's management style," I said. "What if it was—"

"Let's drop it, Skip. We're out of it. Not our problem. The cops can take this one and run with it."

Bruce Springsteen's "Born in the U.S.A." blared from my pocket and I pulled out the cell phone. Two a.m. It could only be Em.

"Skip, I'm a little freaked out."

"Hey, I understand. I didn't know Amanda that well, but—"

"Listen to me. I got a voice mail. I turned the phone off in the restaurant and forgot to turn it on until I got home."

"Who?"

"Jeez, Skip, it's very weird. The call was from Amanda."

"What?"

"It came in around seven thirty."

"We'd already talked to her by then. We were still in the dining room. What could she have wanted? I mean, she could have come out and—"

"She couldn't. She said she was under a lot of pressure and someone was watching her. She wasn't supposed to be using her cell phone. She wanted me to meet her after work."

"No mention of what the pressure was? I mean, she was upbeat when we saw her. I thought she was on top of the world."

"On my cell phone it didn't come off like that."

"What else did she say?"

"The creepiest part of all, Skip."

"Tell me."

"Someone had asked her to meet them in the alley. She didn't say who, but this person said it was a matter of life and death."

CHAPTER THREE

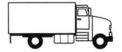

We were both quiet for a moment. James was staring at the TV, oblivious to the drama being played out on the phone.

"There's something else. I called Amanda's mother."

Pausing, I wondered how that conversation would have gone. Not a very pleasant thought.

"How's she doing?"

"Not well, Skip. Not well at all."

I took a deep breath. James lost his father when he was fairly young. I couldn't imagine how it would feel to lose a child.

"Jean Bouvier called her. She said he was very consoling, very concerned. Talked about how Amanda was almost a daughter to him."

"Glad to hear it." It showed there was some compassion in the little guy. Worried about the mother. "How are you holding up? Especially after the phone call."

"God, Skip, I didn't tell her about that. I'm not sure I should tell anyone. But when I talked to her mother, we could barely keep it together. Both of us tearing up. Gloria, her mom, she and

I were pretty tight when I was younger. We shared some stories and," her voice tightened, "it wasn't easy."

She was quiet for a moment, both of us picturing the grisly scene in the alley just hours ago.

"There have been several conversations back and forth between Mrs. Wright, Gloria, and Jean Bouvier."

"Several?"

"And with me."

"What?"

"Tonight, this morning. I've had some conversations with Bouvier and Amanda's mother. Simply put, the chef doesn't trust the police to find the killer. He's very passionate about this. He wants to investigate the murder on his own."

That sounded like James. He never trusted the police. It went back to the arrest of his father. He avoided cops at all costs.

"It just happened, Em. How is he going to barge in and do an investigation? He's got to give the cops a chance to start the process."

"I thought the same thing, Skip. But he feels this has to be brought under control immediately so that his reputation isn't hurt. Obviously some of it is damage control. Apparently his wife has been pressing him to go around the cops on this. Do some investigating on his own. He says that she has encouraged him to use an outside source. Bouvier says that he wants to know if anyone on his staff was responsible."

"The cops are pretty good at this. I still don't understand, Em. Why would they use an outside firm? The cops are not going to be happy about it. I mean, it makes no sense."

She took a breath. "Do you remember about two years ago, their kid who was killed in a drug deal that went bad? He was—"

"In Miami? No. There are no drug deals that go bad. I'm pretty sure there are no drugs in this city."

I could picture her rolling her eyes.

"I'm serious, Skip. Think back. Sophia and Jean Bouvier had a seventeen-year-old son, Jean-Luc, who was gunned down on Biscayne Boulevard. Middle of the day. It was a big story."

I concentrated, trying to remember.

"Middle of the street, Skip. Broad daylight. And dozens of witnesses."

"I've got it, Em."

I did remember. Not that I paid a lot of attention to the news, but this story had gotten some serious play. The kid had been in his Ferrari, driving down Biscayne Boulevard, when a Chevy Suburban pulled up alongside the sports car and, according to eyewitnesses, opened fire with a multitude of shots. The cops counted twenty-seven holes in the car. It took just one to kill the teenager.

"They never found the killer, am I right?" I seemed to recall that the press had a field day with the MPD. There was a rumor that some of the investigators were paid off by the coke dealers. Nothing was ever proven, and no one was ever convicted of the shooting.

"Never. The Bouviers spent hundreds of thousands of dollars trying to find the murderer, but they've had no success. They mounted an ad campaign, offering a big reward for anyone who supplied a lead. They hired a private agency out of Chicago and an attorney who looked into suing the Miami police department, but the case remains unsolved. The firm charged them a lot of money and came up with zilch."

For all of the Bouvier money, the drug guys apparently had more.

"And as far as the Bouviers are concerned, the cops are useless. The case remains open, but Sophia and Jean don't believe there is any real effort to solve the murder. Like Jean said, to the police it simply meant that one more drug user was off the street."

"If that is the way the cops approached it, it's pretty cold."

"Yeah. On the phone Bouvier told me his first reaction was that Amanda was like a daughter to him, and he wasn't going to let her death go unpunished like his son's. He was very passionate about that."

I took a deep breath. Again, I couldn't imagine the anguish someone must go through when losing an offspring.

James was obviously not paying any attention to the conversation, sipping his beer, feet up on the plastic coffee table, watching some stupid infomercial about hair replacement.

"So what are they going to do?"

"Are you sitting down?"

I was. Permanently reclined in our broken lounge chair. "Tell me."

"I've convinced him to interview James for a job."

"James?" I was stunned.

My partner turned his head, looking at me with raised eyebrows.

"Your roommate's got a degree in culinary arts, Skip. What better way to use his skills? Go undercover and investigate the murder from the inside. Also Bouvier knows that James dated Amanda. I filled him in on the relationship." She paused, letting me soak all of it in.

"Em, I think it's a terrible idea. And James never had a relationship with Amanda. It was like two dates."

"Anyway, Bouvier and his wife think this would be a perfect fit. James can keep his ear to the wall and get a feel for who might have been responsible. Chef is very interested in the idea."

"Jean Bouvier doesn't know James."

Now James was on his feet, slowly walking to my chair.

"Give him some credit, Skip. You and I work the outside, James works the inside, and we'll see if we can learn something."

"And the cops are just going to go along with this?"

"They don't have to know, Skip. We stay out of their way. This would be an internal investigation."

"This is crazy. This is something that James would come up with, not you. You do know that he's only had intern experience in a high-class restaurant? I mean, even that didn't go well." Half the kitchen staff at Jack's Half Shell had threatened to walk out unless James was replaced.

James stood over me, frowning.

"Skip, James spent four years learning how to cook and run a restaurant. A culinary arts degree. Think about it. He knows how it goes together. Maybe it wasn't L'Elfe, but he does work in a restaurant environment. I sincerely believe he could pull this off. And, Bouvier is willing to pay three thousand a week, two week minimum." She paused and I didn't say anything. I think I was in shock.

"Do you hear me? Three thousand a week. You could use the money, boyfriend. And I know your roommate could use it."

"What the hell are you discussing, amigo?" James drained the beer and pointed his finger at me.

I nodded to him. "Trying to figure out how you can get some time off at Cap'n Crab." A line cook at the Cap'n didn't make much money.

"And why would I want to do that?"

"Because for the next two weeks, you're going to be a sous chef at L'Elfe."

"I'll be damned," he said.

"Yes, you may well be." I gave him a grim smile. "Brush up on your cooking skills, James. This is the big league."

CHAPTER FOUR

"Joanne gave me the two weeks, amigo." James sipped his latte as we felt the morning sun warm the ceramic tile inside Starbucks.

"And how did you arrange that?"

"Threw her a couple of bones."

"James?"

"Yeah, well, she likes me, pally. Thinks that maybe we two might have a future together. So I promised her a date when I get back."

Maybe Amanda Wright had thought that she and James had a future together as well. It seemed that everybody succumbed to the charm and personality of my handsome roommate.

According to James, the interview at L'Elfe had been brief. Jean Bouvier had asked for help. When James asked about the actual position, the work, the employees, the format, the chef had shrugged his shoulders.

"This isn't a full-time position, Mr. Lessor. You are here for one reason and one reason only. To see if someone in my kitchen, in my restaurant, had anything to do with the death of the young woman. I will have my executive chef or our number two sous chef on duty at all times."

James had persisted, asking Bouvier about the actual duties. After all, he was a cook with formal training. He wanted to know what was expected.

James said that Bouvier's wife had interrupted the interview, walking into the tiny office and immediately asserting herself.

"She's a pain in the butt, amigo. This little short guy has an equally short, dumpy wife. As I thought, Sophia runs the business side of his company, and believe me, she was all business." He frowned. "Right in the middle of the interview, she marches in, stares at me for a second and says, 'This is who we're going to hire? I thought we'd find someone who appeared a little more mature.'"

"And?"

"Pissed me off. I can play mature if it means three thousand a week."

I studied him for a moment, his three-day beard growth, shaggy hair curling around his neck, dressed in ragged cutoffs and a Sheldon Cooper *Big Bang Theory* T-shirt that said, "Don't you think that if I were wrong, I'd know it?"

"I don't like someone judging me after they see me one time."

"There was a waitress the other day who judged you, and she actually asked you out, remember?"

"Yeah. Well, that's different. Anyway, this stubby little woman looks at her husband and asks, 'Are you going to hire him?'"

"And his answer was?"

"This titan of the kitchen, the one-man money machine of culinary arts, the little guy says, 'Only if you approve, sweetheart.'" James cringed. "If I ever get married, pard, please deliver me from someone who wears the pants."

Bouvier's wife apparently had made it clear that James and

his agency were being hired to scope out the restaurant staff. When he was in the kitchen, he would do the work, act as if the job mattered to him a great deal, but his main job was to see if the killer was on the premises.

"No thoughts about using this job as a launching pad to work for us," she had told him. James said Bouvier sat at his desk and didn't say a word.

"Did she say anything about Jean-Luc? The murdered son?"

"Matter of fact, she did. Very direct comments. She said the police had ignored her son's case. The lady even insinuated that the cops had possibly thwarted the investigation due to—"

"Payoffs, right?"

"She was on script. Same story she told two years ago, when they couldn't turn up anything."

"And?"

"She was a bitch, Skip. Rude, demanding, but I still had empathy. She's lost her only kid. And this time, with our efforts, she expects results. She was very clear about that. The two of them want to know if anyone on staff killed Amanda. That's our mission, to scope out the employees."

I thought back to what Em had said about the Bouviers spending hundreds of thousands of dollars to find Jean-Luc's killer. And we were offered six thousand bucks. There was some discrepancy there. No results for hundreds of thousands, but results expected for six thousand.

When she left, he'd received his orders.

"Chef told me I'd be working the broiler, under supervision. The line, under supervision, and once in a while working the," he cleared his throat, "the dishwasher." I could hear the disgust in his voice. Apparently, there was no supervision on the dishwasher.

"You have a problem with that, James? The dishwasher?"

"I don't know. He said any new hire would have to work the

entire operation to get a feel for how it goes. I get that. You need to know how the kitchen works. But I get the distinct feeling that I'm just decoration."

I rolled my eyes and drained my black coffee. "James, think this through. You are a detective, for God's sake. Give me a break. Why should they be interested in your culinary skills. He wants someone to find out if the kitchen staff was responsible for Amanda's death. That's the job."

"Skip, I'm aware of that. Still," James smiled at me over his cup of latte, "it would be nice to be appreciated for my cooking talent."

"Which, I will admit, is considerable. At least all the great meals I've had the pleasure to taste."

He nodded, almost taking his bow.

"But, interning for three months at a two-star restaurant and being a line cook at Cap'n Crab hardly qualifies you for running the kitchen at L'Elfe." Michael Trump, the chef at Jack's Half Shell, had actually liked James, and if I remembered correctly, he had bestowed upon him a kitchen knife that James had treasured. Maybe Trump had given him the present just to get rid of him. That also was a strong possibility.

We were both quiet, watching the patrons and the baristo as he blended the ingredients for the customers, his eyes glazed over like a robot.

Finally, James spoke, stating the obvious.

"Somebody in the kitchen could be a murderer."

"You think? That's the point of your hire."

James nodded and I saw one of the cute servers glancing his way. She smiled when she caught me looking at her.

"And if they think that I'm checking them out, if his staff realizes that I'm looking for a potential suspect—"

It was my turn to nod. "You could be in trouble."

"Yes, I could." He reached into his back pocket and pulled out two sheets of paper. "We've been in some serious trouble before, Skip."

We had.

"This sheet of paper is for you, the duplicate I'll hang onto."

Staring at the list, I saw names and titles.

"These are the suspects, Skip. This is the staff. If we can clear them all, we've done our job. If we suspect any one of them, I guess we follow that hunch. Let's hope that they all come out squeaky clean."

Names and titles. No personalities. A brief note as to how long each one of them had worked at the establishment. Nothing about relationships any of them may have had with Amanda Wright. Relationships were going to be our responsibility. James would have to find a way to ask some very sensitive questions.

He looked at me, hands flat on the table. "And what are you and the lovely Em doing all this time?"

"Following up leads on the outside."

"Give me an example."

I thought for a moment. "Okay, you come to me and say you're suspicious of a commis or an expediter and—"

"Whoa." James leaned back, giving me an admiring look. "What do you know about a commis or expediter? You're this guy who yesterday didn't know what the hell a sous chef was."

"This guy is paying us three grand a week, James. I figured I'd better get familiar with his world."

A commis is a chef in training. An expediter takes the order from the waitstaff, relays it to the different stations in the kitchen, sometimes puts the finishing garnish on the plate, and gets it back to the dining room. At least I think that's what these two people do.

I saw James's face light up as he sipped the coffee. "I think I've got it right, pardner. Let's see if I can remember this."

20

"What?"

He closed his eyes, and as if reading from a book he said, "The sous is responsible for the kitchen when the chef's not around. Saucier, in charge of sauces. Very important. Chef de partie, demi chef de partie, both important. Commis? Commis, they're the cooks. Very important."

"What? This is what you learned in culinary school? Something you had to memorize?"

"It's a movie quote, Skip. What did you think? We've watched it probably five times. You seriously can't remember?"

"We're trying to figure out who killed this girl and you want me to remember some movie quote that—"

"*Ratatouille*. You've got to remember that movie."

The Disney cartoon from 2007. "You spent how many years studying cooking, and the best you can come up with is a quote from a rat-infested Disney movie?"

James couldn't remember what he had for breakfast this morning, but he could remember a movie quote from five or six, or twenty or thirty years ago.

"Not just any Disney movie, amigo. The best."

Sophia Bouvier may have been right. James did lack maturity.

"What are we going to be doing? Let's say you tell me you think the dishwasher had it out for Amanda. Em and I run a check. We visit his home, the bar he frequents after work, we talk to his friends. That's what we're doing."

"While I'm sweating my ass off in the hot, stuffy kitchen, doing everybody else's job under the guise of training for a position."

"Three grand, James. Three grand per week."

"Yeah." He let out a long, slow breath. "All right, pardner. We'll take it. God knows we could use that kind of money." My partner closed his eyes for a second, folding his hands, obviously

21

a little concerned about the position. Then, turning his head toward the counter, he made a connection.

A shy smile from the girl and a grin from James.

"Be right back."

Walking up to the server, he talked in hushed tones. I turned and watched the traffic flow outside, South Beach vehicles with exotic emblems. Porsche, Ferrari, Rolls-Royce, and Bentley. I wondered what we were getting ourselves into. I was placing my best friend and roommate into a situation that could get him killed. What the hell, we'd done it before.

He walked back and I stood up.

"Ready?"

"Ready." The corners of his mouth turned up. "Got her number, so we're good to go."

CHAPTER FIVE

Breakfast outdoors at South Beach's News Café was an experience. James, Em, and I, working on an expense account plus the three grand a week, dined on omelets with smoked salmon, cream cheese, and onions, a Quiche Lorraine, and a vegetable quiche.

"Bacon, cheese, onion, light cream—"

"James." I nodded toward the sidewalk. A heavyset older couple walked by, the man in a Speedo bathing suit and his jiggling wife in a see-through cover-up. Nothing apparently underneath.

"I would use a little cayenne pepper and—"

"James, let us enjoy the food," Emily said.

"You should know what you're eating, Em."

"All I know is, I'm enjoying a free meal. Save the chef spiel for work, okay? Leave it alone."

They fought like little kids.

"Check this out." James reached down and picked up a plastic bag. Setting it on the table, he reached inside, pulling out a dark, polished wooden box. He opened it and held it up for us to see inside.

"A knife," I said.

Removing the shiny knife, he carefully placed it in the center of the table.

"Not just a knife. A Wüsthof nine-inch chef's knife. Forged from a single piece of carbon steel that will cut through veggies and meat like butter." He held it up, the sun glinting off the blade. "This was a gift from Michael Trump, head chef at Jack's Half Shell, when I graduated from culinary school. He'd had it for years, and, after I interned with him, he thought it was a fitting tribute to my culinary future." Shrugging his shoulders, he smiled sadly. "I've only used it maybe five or six times, but still—"

Trump obviously pictured a brighter future for James Lessor. The truth was, my roommate hadn't used the Wüsthof knife in years.

I had to admit it was a piece of art. The flow of the design and the curve of the steel along with the dark, triple-riveted handle setting off the silvery blade made it look as if the knife should be framed and hanging on a wall like some medieval dueling weapon preserved for the ages.

"It's got this little nick in the tip, right here, but other than that, it's a piece of work."

"You have to bring your own tools?" Em was intrigued as well.

"Any chef worth his weight has his own knife. Or knives. First thing Bouvier asked me. 'What kind of knife do you have?' He seemed impressed when I told him it was a nine-inch Wüsthof Classic."

"The guy doesn't really care what you do in his kitchen, but he's concerned about your tools?"

"I've got to look the part, Skip. A chef, a cook, needs his knives. I start with my chef's knife."

He was right. Even if Bouvier wasn't offering him an actual kitchen position, he needed to look the part. James needed to do everything possible to make his coworkers buy into his cover. It all started with his four years of college and a knife.

"Well, tonight's your first night," I said. "You've got your cell phone and your knife and—"

"Chef says no cell phones."

I swallowed a forkful of smoked salmon. "Screw Chef. If he wants results, we've got to have open communication, right? What if you need to contact us?"

"I explained that to him. Bouvier says I can take restroom breaks or sneak outside for a smoke and—"

"You quit smoking."

"Oh," James smiled, "you pay attention." James had tried for years to kick the habit for good. Now he had an excuse to start his habit all over again. The kind of luck James always had.

"What if someone comes out and catches you talking to one of us and—"

"I'll buy a pack. I'll look legit. My guess is that anyone in that restaurant who ducks out for a smoke break also checks their messages. It's the perfect excuse to use the cell phone. As for the cigarettes, I can light them and look like I'm grabbing a smoke. I just won't inhale." His smile was a dead giveaway.

"Right," Em rolled her eyes. "But I'm sure you'd consider taking up smoking again if it was part of the job."

"Anyway," James took a bite of his toast, "there are no exceptions in his kitchen. What happens outside during my pee breaks, or my smoke breaks, no one is the wiser. I'll find a reason to get out so I can call you guys."

A young man walked by on the sidewalk, sporting skin-tight lycra shorts and holding two leashes, black Doberman pinschers straining at the leather. I quickly looked back at Emily. Behind her a young lady in a micro bikini strutted across the street, her sculpted breasts bouncing with each step. South Beach.

"Guys," James affected a somber look. "As much as I like the

25

idea of three thousand dollars a week, and as much as we could use the money, I don't like the idea of being in that kitchen any longer than I have to be."

Em raised her pretty eyebrows. "James, I thought this would be your lifelong dream. Working in a celebrity kitchen."

He cleared his throat. "My dream, Emily, would be to have my own kitchen. I'm not ready to work in a four-star restaurant." James threw her a sincere gaze. "I can be an egotistical asshole sometimes, I am aware of that. But I am telling you, this shtick scares me."

It wasn't like James to acknowledge any shortcomings.

"I wouldn't normally admit this to anyone, but I'm not ready for sous chef. As much as I've thought about being in this type of position, I never really visualized it. In less than," he glanced at his cell phone, "six hours, I have to present myself to one of the finest restaurants on the East Coast. Let me tell you, friends, I am seriously not ready for this. I'm so sure they will find me out."

Honesty, brutal, total honesty was not a quality of my friend. So either he was lying to us, or he was petrified and had to tell someone. I believe it was the latter.

"I am woefully unprepared. I have no idea what I'm getting into. And, I may be working with a murderer."

"James," I looked him square in the eyes, "if you want to back out, we both understand. I mean, the people who work in kitchens," I hesitated, trying to find the right words, "they are a little strange. The pressure, the heat, the fast pace—"

"How the hell do you know all this, Skip? You've never been exposed to a commercial kitchen. I studied this for four years." James raised his voice and I could tell I'd touched a nerve.

"Yeah, you're right. But I read Anthony Bourdain's *Kitchen Confidential* in one sitting. Pretty brutal."

"Trust me," he almost whispered, "that guy didn't get everything right. It's not all yelling, swearing, sex in the walk-in, stealing food, and doing drugs."

"It's not?"

"No. The guy didn't get it *all* right, okay? Apparently working in a celebrity kitchen is also about a chef's kid getting killed because of a coke deal. It's about kitchen help getting murdered in dark alleys. It's about a dominating wife who runs the show." There was no smile. Just the cold, hard facts.

"Yeah, well, there's that too," I said.

My friend stared out at the sidewalk as South Beach woke up to the sun and fun of a new day. Tourists and locals mingled in a dance unlike anywhere I'd ever been. Beautiful women, chiseled men, and so many dogs I lost count. I couldn't imagine living in this crazy section of South Florida.

"James, just go with the flow. We'll be right there if you need us."

"I'm going to do it, Tonto, but I'm very apprehensive."

"I think you made that abundantly clear."

"Like Skip said, we'll be here. Whatever you need," Em said, hesitating, "within reason."

"You'll be on call."

"We will," I said.

I just had no idea how fast that call would come.

CHAPTER SIX

I drove him to work in the truck. It's a white Chevy box truck that barely runs, drinks oil like a bar lush drinks whiskey, and bounces over potholes like it has no shocks. Actually, the truck needs new shocks. Hell, it needs new brakes and new tires, but we can't afford everything necessary to make it a dependable means of transportation. What we needed was a new truck.

I diss his truck on a regular basis, but my rusted-out Taurus doesn't run at all, so we share the truck.

"How about we use some of the money we make for new shocks and to get you a new battery."

He agreed.

"So far, the cops haven't admitted to any suspects," James patted his shirt pocket, checking to make sure he'd brought his pack of Marlboros.

"No." I recited the brief information we'd seen on TV. "Multiple knife wounds to the abdomen. No immediate person or persons of interest. Friends, relations, and coworkers being interviewed."

The interviewer had been very interested in Em's relationship with Amanda Wright. He'd hung onto the fact that Em had been a good friend, then they'd drifted apart, then she'd fixed James up with Amanda, and finally that we were dining at L'Elfe largely because Amanda was the sous chef.

"Did you ever argue with the victim?" he'd asked. "Did your relationship with Miss Wright go any further than just friends?"

The whole question and answer thing had really upset Em. His final question was about James.

"You set your friend up on a date with a James Lessor. What's your impression of Mr. Lessor? Does he seem to be a stable person?"

"Damn," Em said after the conversation, "James? Stable? I hope I never get asked that question in court. I couldn't lie under oath."

I steered the truck by the MacArthur Causeway where two giant cruise ships were docked off to our right.

"I'd think that tonight you get a chance to listen, pick up some of the conversation."

"I was thinking the same thing," he said. "They're going to be discussing it. It's all over the 'net, TV."

"Should be a lot of rumors flying around. A lot of gossip in the kitchen, it's a given, right?"

"I'm sure the dining room will be buzzing too." He was starting to get into it, I could tell by the excitement in his voice. There was also some apprehension. Starting a brand-new job was stressful.

"There is going to be a lot of interest in you, too. People wanting to know why you were hired so soon. What magic ingredient you have that caused Bouvier to make the hire."

James nodded. "I thought of that. And since I don't have a good backstory, I'll go with what I've got. Four-year degree, brief internship, and Cap'n Crab. Bouvier thinks I have potential. Other than that, I'm going to attempt to do a whole lot more listening than talking."

"Good idea."

"There will probably be a lot of thrill seekers in the restaurant who can Tweet their friends and say 'guess where I am?'"

"You said the little guy will be there?"

"Told me that he needed to be the calming influence for the next couple of nights. I think it's a good idea. And Sophia, his wife, is supposed to be there as well. I'm not sure that's a good thing. I mean, the way she barged into the interview. I've been told she kind of brings the place down."

Sophia Bouvier. Arguably, one of the main reasons that Chef Jean was so successful. She ran the commodity side of the business, selling the spices, the pots and pans, the cutlery.

We'd researched the husband and wife team on the Internet. Besides the business venture, hundreds of full-time employees, the multimillion-dollar corporation with its various streams of income, besides the celebrity, the fame, and instant credibility, there was the death of Jean-Luc. The drug deal death of their son seemed to overshadow everything in the celebrity duo's life. Maybe Sophia's dour attitude was based on the price she paid for her position in this world.

"But remember," James said, "I'm just there for decoration. My job is to see if there's a killer in the house. They couldn't give a damn about my culinary skills." He was still miffed.

I'd only seen him on television. Jean Bouvier was a small guy with a big mouth. He had a shtick where he'd start preparing a meal, get to a certain point, then look to the camera. He'd point his index finger in your face, give you a cute little smile and, I swear, his eyes would sparkle.

"Any one of you can do what I just did," he'd say. "That part is simple. But can you do this?"

Then he'd whisk something or slice something or sprinkle something and supposedly the magic would happen. I'd seen him do it a half dozen times when James was watching The Food Channel. "But can you do this?" had become a tagline. It was even an answer on *Jeopardy* one night, and James found it in a *New York Times* crossword puzzle. "But can you do this?"

"You know," James was staring out the window, watching the water catch the late afternoon sun, "there's one common denominator in that kitchen."

"Common denominator?"

"Yeah. There's something that qualifies almost anyone on that kitchen staff to be the killer."

"And what's that?"

"They all know how to use a knife, Skip. They all know how to filet, slice, dice, chop. It's part of the culture."

I couldn't argue with that.

I saw his expression change, his eyes reflecting with a blank stare. "Well, that's not entirely true," he said.

It had made sense to me. "No?"

"The dishwasher. I mean, you start as a dishwasher. Bottom of the chain, you know? That guy, that girl doesn't have to know how to use a knife. Dishwashers are exempt. But everyone else—"

We drove the rest of the way in silence, and five minutes later I dropped him off at the rear of the small white-stucco building.

"You've got your knife?"

"Yes, Mother. And I'll play nice with all my new friends."

"Be safe, James."

He took a deep breath, slowly exhaled, and forced open the squeaky door. Glancing back at me, he folded his hands in front of him.

"Think about me, amigo."

"I will."

"And one more thing."

"What's that?"

"Both of these doors get harder to open every day," he said. "Get some WD-40, Skip. Oil the damned doors."

"Call if you find work," I shouted as he walked into the restaurant.

CHAPTER SEVEN

Em lives just down the street in a condo twenty-three stories over the water. I love waking up there in the early morning, looking out at the clear blue water and South Beach in the distance. I love going to sleep there, watching the tiny lights of South Beach, Star Island, and the causeways twinkle. I actually love waking up next to Emily. Most of the time I wake up at the crummy apartment where James and I live, where I can see a muddy dirt-brown ditch running behind the units. Not quite the same. I shared James's dream about one day being rich and famous. But the longer I spend time with him, I realize the way to achieve that dream is not always the same as my best friend's.

Em was waiting for me, and we'd decided to spend some time going over Amanda's past, seeing if there was anything Em might remember about her friend that would shed some light on the grisly killing.

I immediately thought about Amanda confessing to a crime that Em was accused of committing, but my girlfriend had told me that story wasn't going to see the light of day. Emily, being a strong woman, had laid down the rules long ago.

Her mom had died when she was eleven, a victim of breast cancer. Em had grown up an only child with a workaholic father who wanted only the best for his daughter. She'd taken on adult responsibilities at an early age and now practically ran the construction business for her father. She'd begged me to work for the company, I guess hoping that I'd finally grow up and be responsible for a change. But I couldn't convince myself to do it. Working for Em's dad would have been like working for Em, and that just wasn't going to fly.

When she was right, she was right. And, she seldom was wrong. If you didn't believe it, just ask her.

I was halfway to her condo, the white box truck sandwiched between an Escalade and a Porsche Panamera, when Bruce Springsteen's ring tone blared from my pocket.

"James, it's only been fifteen minutes. You've solved the crime?"

"Skip, there's a little matter here that I could use some help with. You know you said you had my back and all?"

I remembered that. "And we do. We have your back. Why would you even question that?" I'd told him that we were going to be approaching the murder from a different perspective. "James, tonight we're going to talk about Amanda and see if Em can remember—"

"Kind of a change in the plans, amigo." I heard him take a breath. I was certain it was a lungful of smoke.

"Got a smoke break already?"

"Chef Bouvier phoned me and asked me to go out and call you."

"Come on, James. What's so important?" Jeez, had something happened already? Fifteen minutes had passed and he was already either panicked or had the murder solved. Amazing, even for James. He was quiet for a moment, and my heart was racing. I had no idea where the conversation was going.

34

"Has something happened? It has, right?"

"I hate to ask this, Skip."

"Damn you, tell me what you need."

"A dishwasher."

I shook my head. "A what?"

"Dishwasher."

"And how can I help you with that? I don't know any—"

"You, Skip."

I was taken aback. Stunned. Taking my eyes off the road for two seconds, I about slammed into the back of a BMW. "Me?"

"Dishwasher didn't show up. With two of us back here, we can talk to a lot more people, put together a lot more scenarios."

"Oh, no. No. No. No."

It was a pattern. James would sucker punch me if it meant getting him out of a jam. "You volunteer to wash the dishes. Em and I have stuff to do. Research, doing background checks. You need someone on the outside. You know that and we've already discussed—"

"Em's on the outside, pard. You and me, we're a good team." I heard another intake and exhale.

"Come on, James, what am I going to do about my job? It's not as easy to ask for time off. I mean, you can date your boss. Ernie and I would not work out well on a date."

He coughed. It served him right.

"You blow that job off half the time anyway."

I did. I sold security systems to apartments and businesses in the urban community of Carol City where no one had anything worth securing. I didn't punch a time clock and I could make my calls any time I wanted. Anyway, it wasn't like I was setting the world on fire with my sales. Far from it.

"James, I didn't sign on to scrape plates and dispose of other people's garbage. That's not my end of the job."

"Skip, there's three thousand dollars a week on the line here.

35

Three thousand dollars a week. Minimum two weeks pay. Do you hear me?" I could sense the frustration in his voice. He'd been on the job for a quarter of an hour and already it sounded like he was losing it. "I told Chef you'd do it. The title of the job says it all, amigo. Dishwasher. You don't have to have any experience. So get your ass back here. Okay? We're going to solve this crime and we're going to become an agency that gets a lot of attention. And business. We're a team, amigo. A team. Got it?"

"I can't believe you're doing this. Hell, we just started this gig, and already you're pushing my buttons."

"Skip, the only buttons you have to worry about are on the dishwasher. The two of us are going to be a whole lot more effective. Will you do it?"

And like a dumb ass, I agreed.

"Give me twenty minutes." I was not happy.

"Fifteen, Skip. These dishes are piling up pretty fast."

CHAPTER EIGHT

James was busy scraping plates when I walked in. Tossing me an apron, he pointed at a box of rubber dishwashing gloves sitting on a stainless-steel counter.

"Glove up, pard."

I looked to my right as fire erupted under a cast-iron skillet. A young man with a white coat and Miami Dolphin cap deftly picked up the skillet and flipped whatever was in it, setting it back on the stovetop as the flame went out.

Looking back at James, I said, "You could have done the dishes."

"Could have, but they need me on the line."

I think James could have gotten along just fine without me, but I'd agreed to be the stooge.

"The runners bring trays of dishes, you scrape 'em, sort 'em, and put them in the dishwasher."

"Just like that?"

"It's not hard, Skip. It's minimum wage." James always had a way of making me feel small.

Minimum wage. That was about what the two of us were

making from our regular jobs. Not much more. For all the high-end dreams that we both had, for all the what-ifs, and mistakes that we made, we were still struggling. Maybe age would bring more maturity, but I doubted it.

The steamy sizzle of meat, the bubbly boiling of liquids, the clanging and banging of pots and pans, and the shouting back and forth between cooks when an order was placed and when that order was ready for pickup all filtered through the small kitchen as I tied on the apron and pulled on the rubber gloves.

"Chef Marty," James touched a white coat on the sleeve, "this is Skip. He'll fill in for the next few nights."

The man studied me for a moment. His irritation was obvious.

I turned and frowned at James. The next few nights? Nothing had been said about the next few nights.

The thin man nodded, his brief gaze ending when another burst of flames flared from a broiler. Wiping his brow on his jacket sleeve he walked over, picked up a pair of tongs, and turned a steak, checking its char with a seasoned look. He moved down the line, watching over the shoulders of several cooks as they stirred their pots. As busy as everything appeared, it seemed everyone was calm.

"Chef's name is Marty," James said. "I've read about the guy. He's been with Bouvier since the beginning."

"Good. You've already started sizing up the suspects." I realized I sounded a bit sarcastic, but I was genuinely pleased that James had already made some inroads on the staff.

"One other thing that would help here, Skip. If I'd only thought to take Spanish lessons. I'm missing about fifty percent of what's being said."

I eyed a tray of dishes and started scraping the scraps of what was an hour ago a delicious presentation on someone's table.

"Spanish, huh?"

"They go a mile a minute."

"A French American restaurant, where you have to know Spanish to survive? It doesn't seem right, does it?"

"I'll get by, pard. I will survive."

"You always do. Getting back to who knows what."

"Yeah?"

"Does this Chef Marty know?"

"What? Does he know Spanish? Or does he know who we are? No. He has no idea. At least Bouvier said he didn't." Speaking in a hushed tone, James said, "Chef Jean told the staff that he feels I have the talent to be a good chef, and he's taking me under his wing."

I'd always been a fan of James's cooking. I thought he had talent, but then almost anything beat Taco Bell or Macs, and that was about what we could normally afford. That and a cheap pizza and beer.

"Does anyone know who we are?"

He shook his head. "There's been no sign that this crew has a clue. I've got the college background, a culinary arts degree, and I would be surprised if more than one or two of these misfits even knows how to do a Google search. It wouldn't matter if they did. I've got creds, Skip, I've got creds."

He did. Even if he couldn't speak Spanish. And, if someone did research, if they conducted a background search, James came from working in a restaurant. A real restaurant. Not anything high-end, but his job had been in the Cap'n Crab kitchen. So if Bouvier pretended to have seen some talent, some potential in James, it was possible he found it at the fast-food restaurant. He could convince his staff that he'd found James at Cap'n Crab, and he'd felt that the culinary graduate had potential. I realized the idea was improbable, but possible.

"If they find out, James, we could be in a lot of trouble."

"Bouvier swore that he was keeping this a secret, okay?"

"Trust no one."

"Easy quote, Skip. *Doctor Strangelove*."

"No. I wasn't doing a movie quote. I'm simply saying—"

"I'm going to the line. Help where I can, talk to whoever I can. It's the only way we're going to get information."

"James," this was not the place to discuss our ulterior motives, but with the noise level at its peak, I figured no one would hear us, "when I called Em, the first thing she said was 'why didn't the dishwasher show up?'"

"Good question. Night after the murder."

"I think it needs an answer."

"You're right, we should look into it. But remember, man, these guys are gypsies. I mean they change jobs at the drop of a hat. Guy could have a drug habit, be running from the law, or trying to avoid an alimony payment."

"It's a place to start."

Over James's shoulder, Marty was motioning with his index finger. He wasn't trying to get my attention.

"James," I pointed toward the cooking line. "Marty, excuse me, C*hef* Marty wants you."

James looked at Marty and nodded. Turning back to me he frowned. "I'll get information on the dishwasher. Cell phone it to Em on my next cigarette break."

"Uh, James, do I get a break?"

"You smoke?"

I stared daggers at him as a runner brought another tray piled high.

"Better get scraping, pardner."

CHAPTER NINE

Half an hour turned into an hour, and I almost scalded myself with the one-hundred-eighty-degree water from the evil stainless machine. One of the runners in a white jacket and black headband stopped for a moment. As I grabbed his tray, he asked, "Where's Juan tonight?"

"Juan?"

"Juan, man. The dishwasher?"

"Didn't show up. You a friend of his?"

The swarthy runner glanced back at the cook staff, busily working at their stations. Roasting, broiling, boiling, baking, whatever it was that they did.

"Ain't nobody friends with nobody." He spoke softly as if this was a big secret. "*Yo conozco a ese hombre*. I know the man. You know? We used to go out for a drink after this place close down. Just wondered if something happened, man."

"If I see him, I'll tell him you asked about him. What's your name?"

He hesitated.

"Just asking, man."

"Carlos."

"Skip. Skip Moore." I reached out with a gloved hand but he kept his hands close to his sides.

"Don't have to mention this. *Yo no sé nada.*" He glanced again at the cook group, where James was slicing something with his prized knife. I hoped it wasn't his hand.

"Was Juan close to the girl who was killed?"

Carlos took a step back, a puzzled look on his face. "Why you ask something like that?"

"I just thought," I was winging it, "maybe he was upset about the murder and needed a day off to grieve."

"Maybe. He find her attractive. I don't think it went any further than that. Grieve? I don't know. Don't say nothing to him, okay? I never ask."

With that, Carlos spun around and headed back to the dining room. I saw him numerous times the rest of the night, bringing trays of dishes, but he never spoke to me again.

Halfway through the evening, I saw the baker, squeezing red icing from a tube onto a velvet cake, her long brown hair hanging to her shoulders. She had an amusing smile on her face, and I immediately thought of Em. You could almost put up with a kitchen environment when this lovely lady was in the room.

"Interesting crew, eh?" James appeared out of nowhere.

"Who is she?"

"Mrs. Fields."

"Not the cookie lady? Debbi Fields?"

"No." James rolled his eyes. "Kelly Fields. Pastry chef. She brightens up the place, doesn't she?"

"You know much about her?" I was intrigued.

"Apparently, she was one of the few people who really liked Amanda Wright." He gazed at the baker. "Somehow we've got to talk to her."

"Maybe Em can get involved. We could find a way for the two of them—"

"Maybe. But it wouldn't hurt for me to talk to her, you know, just tell her I'd heard that she and Amanda were friends and I was sorry for the loss."

"Maybe," I said.

Eleven at night and I was whipped.

Chef Jean had actually made an appearance in the kitchen with his equally short, stocky wife, Sophia. He'd shouted out a greeting to a couple of cooks, pulled Chef Marty aside, and had a serious talk with him. Then he came back to my station, saw the mess I was creating and he frowned. The little man walked away never to be seen again. The missus followed, with a sneer and huff. So much for his calming influence. So much for his wife's demure. She stuck her head in a couple more times during the evening, always with a drink in her hand. Like a little ghost. I'd look up and there she was, watching me. I never saw approval in her expression.

Bitterness rears its ugly head when things don't go your way. I'd been bitter once or twice in my short life, and I was certain the reason was largely because things hadn't gone according to my plan. My plan. But these plans were usually short-term goals. In the case of Sophia Bouvier, her future, the plans for Jean-Luc, her son, had not gone her way. Or his. And now someone had brutally murdered their candidate for head chef at their new South Beach bistro. I think she had a strong case for bitterness.

"Amigo," James walked up to me as I put the last tray into the washer. I turned and immediately saw his hands. They were adorned with three bandages, and he held them up as badges of courage.

"What the hell did you do?"

"I forgot. A chef and his knife become intimate, Skip.

43

Damn, that thing is sharp. And as far as my cutting skills go, I'm a little rusty."

"Thank goodness the knife isn't. We'd have to get you a tetanus shot."

"Skip, Bouvier was here tonight."

"For a minute."

"I noticed. But Sophia was here for several minutes. Did you get a look?"

"What a team."

"This is the future of American cooking, my friend."

James pointed his bandaged thumb in the direction that the couple had exited the restaurant. "Those two are the cream of the crop." He paused, then said, "The cooks fixed a little dinner for the staff. You get anything?"

"It's been a little busy back here, James. In case you haven't noticed."

Sheepishly, he smiled.

"You did get a late start, pard. Let's go back to the locker room."

So the cooks got a locker. The cooks had a dinner for the staff. The dishwasher guy got squat. It was no wonder that Juan had split and not returned.

As we walked, he untied his apron, tossing it into a laundry bag in the corner. I followed suit.

"You get a chance to talk to anyone?"

"I talked to one guy. Runner named Carlos. Aren't they usually called busboys?"

"At L'Elfe, busboy is one step up from the runner. He takes the plates from the table, politely asks the customer if everything is to their liking. He replaces a dropped fork, a spoon, and keeps an eye on the table, kind of troubleshooting. The runner, he just picks up the tub and brings it to you. That's pretty much his whole job. We've got levels of servers here, Skip. This isn't Cap'n Crab."

I was learning much more about the restaurant business than I wanted to.

"Anyway, this guy, Carlos, he's sort of friends with Juan Castro, the dishwasher. Says that Juan found Amanda attractive, but he didn't think it went any further than that. Sounded to me like a one-sided romance."

James nodded, brushing his hair back from his face as we walked into the locker room. "I never got information sent to Em, but I've got another name. The staff thinks they've got this murder figured out."

"Yeah?"

"Two of the cooks were talking when I got here. These two started it. Then it was like a fire, man. Seemed to catch on everywhere. Sous chef named Joaquin Vanderfield was ready to quit a couple of days ago when he found out Amanda was given the head chef job in South Beach. Guy was really pissed off."

"Guy was jealous? Pissed off? James, that's a breakthrough." The first real reason someone would consider killing Amanda.

"And it was the first real information that was offered."

Joaquin Vanderfield?

"Joaquin? That's his name? Really?" Who names their kid Joaquin? I immediately realized there had been an actor named Joaquin. He'd played Johnny Cash in a biopic.

"He probably would find the name Eugene a little strange too," James said.

I found Eugene strange. That's why I preferred Skip.

"You met this guy? Joaquin Vanderfield?"

"No. He called in sick tonight. But apparently he's a hot-head. Blows up when things don't go his way. The staff thinks he may be the culprit."

We now had a dishwasher and a sous chef who conveniently were not at work. It could mean something; it might mean nothing.

Walking into the employees' area, I saw a row of old battered metal lockers lining the wall. Half of them had locks hanging from their doors. Restrooms were at the end of the room. Two cooks were already leaving, dressed in street clothes. They nodded at James and me as they headed back down the hall. The rest of the staff who used the area must have gone or were still in the kitchen and dining room cleaning up.

"I've got number twenty." He pointed toward the gunmetal gray door. "I just put my personal stuff, credit cards, and cash in there."

James spun the dial on the padlock and opened the locker.

"What?" He shouted it out, stepping back and almost knocking me down.

"What?" I asked.

James moved aside, giving me a perfect view into the locker. An apparently blood-stained apron hung from a hook, a kitchen knife pierced through the fabric, the red liquid still wet on the white cloth.

"I thought you said no one knew who we were." I looked away from the props, watching him as he remained frozen on the spot.

My partner was silent, never taking his gaze from the apron with the bright red stain.

"James," I walked closer, inspecting the staged stabbing, "it's a joke. Just a knife and an apron. Settle down, man."

Finally, he shuddered and spoke.

"It was locked. Locked, dude."

"I'm sure there's an explanation."

"Like someone doesn't want me here."

"Hey, you can't make friends with everyone."

"This doesn't scare you? You don't look at this as a threat?"

James glanced around the room as a waiter and another cook walked in.

"Skip, maybe we should reconsider our commitment here."

CHAPTER TEN

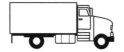

James and I left the truck in the parking lot and Em picked us up in her new car. Always a new set of wheels. So we'd have a drink, a little catch up on the evening's activities, and maybe we'd solve the case.

We kissed and she opened the door to the black Jag XJ as I crawled into the leather passenger seat. James sat in the rear, still a little shaken up, his knees cramped in the small space.

"Amanda was about to have the dream of a lifetime come true, guys. Can you imagine? Her own restaurant. Her own damned restaurant." Em had her daddy's company. There was no doubt she was going to be running it in the future. I think she was set for life. But her friend was about to realize a lofty goal that she'd apparently worked very hard for.

"She'd dreamed about it for years, guys. We've got to find out who killed her. I mean, really, can you imagine? Getting your own restaurant? And then—"

I knew James could imagine. He'd shared that dream for a long time. And now some girl he'd dated had almost done it. In a perverse way, I knew his ego was somewhat bruised.

Em reached into her purse. "Someone didn't want that to happen." She turned the key and the throaty roar of the engine reverberated down the alley.

"And we found a couple people who may have had a problem with that dream." I turned to her. "There's a dishwasher who may have found her very attractive, and there's a sous chef who was a little jealous of her promotion. He thought he was better than she was."

"So if she was gone, this chef might be in line to get the job?"

James spoke. "This guy, Joaquin something, he wasn't there tonight. But for five hours he was pretty much the topic of conversation. About every half hour someone would say something about him being upset regarding the appointment of Amanda Wright. And, the cooks agreed, she wasn't nearly the caliber that Joaquin was."

"She was a good chef. I'm sure of it."

"Well," James paused, drawing it out, "according to the kitchen crew, she wasn't that good. They used the word 'adequate.' Maybe she was good at something else? Business skills, personnel."

"She was a good friend, James. Don't push it."

"If we're going to get to the bottom of this, we've got to discuss Amanda Wright on every level, Emily. We may hear a lot of things about her, good and bad, but you can't put a roadblock up when we uncover a negative. You know what I mean?" He hesitated, waiting for a response. When there was none, he said, "I think all cards need to be on the table." She was quiet the rest of the ride.

Em pulled to the curb in front of Wet Willie's at Ocean and 8th in South Beach and an attendant in a black jacket opened her door.

As we walked through the throngs of locals and tourists up

49

to the second level deck I asked her, "Do you ever worry that the guy who's supposed to park your car may not even work here? He's just going to drive off in that new Jag?"

Em gave me a dazzling smile, her perfect teeth gleaming. "Skip, Skip. That's why I buy nice, expensive cars. They stick out. They're hard to hide. It's not hard to hide a Honda Civic or a Chevy Nova. Even a beat-up Chevy box truck or your twelve-year-old Taurus, but the black Jag? Nobody would dare steal it."

Every once in a while, she likes to rub it in.

We sat and ordered ice-cold margaritas, watching the steady flow of evening traffic down below, a solid stream of headlights. The humidity was thick enough we could cut it with James's knife and we could smell the salty ocean air.

"Okay, tell me about the dishwasher," Em said.

"Ah, the dishwasher. You know, for his first day on the job, Skip did okay." He grinned, his passion to bug my girlfriend having been fed. "Never got in the weeds, did you, amigo?" James said with a smug look on his damned face.

"Of course I'm talking about the old dishwasher, smartass. The one who didn't show up tonight." Em sighed, rolling her eyes.

"We're all hoping he shows up tomorrow," I said. At least one of us was.

"Skip, you said the dishwasher had a thing for Amanda."

I nodded. "One of the runners mentioned it."

"Runners?"

"Guy who brings the dishes back from the dining room. I saw the two of them all night long. I actually got a little tired of seeing them. Anyway, this guy Carlos said that he and Juan Castro would go out for drinks sometimes after work and apparently this Castro mentioned that he thought she was attractive. It's a little thin, but that's all that I've got."

Em sipped her drink, sensually licking the salt from the rim of the glass. "Amanda and a dishwasher? I don't see it."

"What about you?" James smiled. "You do realize that you're now officially dating a dishwasher, Em."

My girlfriend stared at him for a moment, then turned to me. "Maybe Amanda had higher standards than I do."

"And maybe he made his move and she turned him down." I wanted to drop the dishwasher putdowns. "People have been killed for less."

"We're starting a list?" James took a long swallow and tapped his fingers on the table.

Em pulled a pen from her bag. "We are."

"And we start with—"

"Juan Castro. Dishwasher. May have wanted a romantic involvement with the victim."

"It's Amanda, Skip. Not just the victim. Not some anonymous girl. Let's call her by her given name. Okay?"

"Noted."

We drained the sour drinks and ordered another round. It was good to be employed and on an expense account, just as long as the kitchen duty was temporary. Very temporary.

"Then we've got Joaquin Vanderfield, sous chef. Upset because he was passed over for the head job at the new South Beach restaurant." James was half done with his second drink, his bandaged hand holding the stem tight. "I think he's got some serious motive."

"And apparently the staff thinks so, too."

James nodded. "Joaquin Vanderfield may have been interested in Amanda. That was sort of an undercurrent in the conversations. He was upset that she got the promotion, partially because he felt he was a much better choice and partially because the two of them may have had an affair. But nobody came right out and said that. I got the impression it might have been a one-night thing, but it's too early to know for sure. Anyway, it was implied."

"Anybody else?" Em had two lines on her sheet of paper.

"Nothing else came up. Tomorrow's another day."

"Not much to go on, boys. I was hoping for a little more information."

"One thing we failed to mention," I said. "James had a message when he got back to his locker."

"Oh?"

"An apron, with a red liquid smeared on it to look like blood and a Wüsthof knife thrust through the cloth."

"Ooohhh. Gross."

"The knife appeared to be identical to James's."

James finished the drink. "Somebody broke into the locker and hung the apron on a hook. We're not sure if they know who I am, or if it was some sort of a warning. If someone thinks I'm a threat to their job or something."

Em nodded. "They could think you pose a threat. If they know you're investigating the murder or, especially, if they think you might be training to take the South Beach job at La Plage."

"So it could be either of our two suspects."

"Only one thing wrong with that scenario," I said.

"What?" They both said it together.

"Neither of them were at L'Elfe tonight."

We left Willie's and Em drove us back to the restaurant.

"How about James drives the truck back to your apartment and you and I have another drink at my place?" We'd stepped out of the car, standing by the white truck.

I liked the sound of that. "James?"

"Sure, pard."

I handed him the key.

He got into the truck and Em held out her fob.

"Want to drive?"

It appeared I was going to be lucky twice this evening.

"Emily?"

The male voice came from the dark place behind her Jag. I grabbed Em's hand and pulled her toward me.

"Emily Minard?"

"What do you want?" My voice was shaky. There was an empty feeling in my stomach and I realized I hadn't eaten. With two margaritas down there and no food since breakfast—

A shadowy figure rounded the car, a flashlight beam moving slowly over the two of us. As the body moved past our truck, I was startled by the loud squeak of the Chevy's door. It opened with a hard thrust as James leaned into it, hitting the man with the full force of the rusty metal.

The flashlight went flying as the dark form fell backward, cracking his head on the blacktop parking lot. Everything was quiet for a moment, then James stepped from the truck.

"Skip, Em, you guys okay?"

In the dim evening light I saw Em nodding emphatically.

"Dude," James's voice was shaking, "I almost didn't get it open. I told you to use some WD-40 on these doors."

CHAPTER ELEVEN

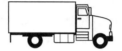

The flashlight battery was strong and the light was still on as I picked it off the pavement and focused the beam on the man's face. His eyes were closed and his breathing was shallow.

"I'll call nine-one-one," Em said as she searched in her purse for the iPhone.

Kneeling, James studied the form for a moment. Sport coat, green polo shirt, jeans, and a pair of white Nikes. James pulled the coat aside.

"Oh, shit." He shuddered and looked up at me. "We may have stepped into it this time, Tonto."

I saw what he was talking about in the ray of light. A shoulder holster with a gun tucked into the tan leather.

"Nine-one-one?" Em was staring at his weapon as well. "We've just been attacked by a man with a gun in the parking lot of—"

"Em. Hang up. Now!" James was rising, grabbing for her black phone.

"Never mind." Em pushed a button and as I swung the light to her, she threw her hands up in disgust. "What the hell was that all about? We've got an unconscious man with a gun who tried to attack us and you try to shut my—"

"Em, Skip." James opened his palm. "Look."

I focused the beam on his hand. He was cradling a gold badge with an embossed star in the center. The word "Detective" was at the top and "Sheriff's Office Miami Dade County Florida" surrounded the star.

"Uh-oh." I switched the light back to our uninvited guest and could hear his ragged breathing. "Guys, we've obviously got a serious problem. We've got to do something."

"We just assaulted an officer of the law," James said. "I've had dreams about that, but this time—"

Em played the cell phone back and forth, hand to hand.

"Skip, James, assaulting a police officer is one thing. Letting him die is something else."

"If we call the cops," I found myself breathing fast, taking shallow gulps of air, "we could seriously be arrested."

"Think, boys, think." Em was always the voice of reason. "James was getting out of the truck to see who was shouting out my name." She pointed to James. "That's all you were doing, right?"

"True," James said, the three of us knowing full well that he'd deliberately hit the man with the truck's door.

"We didn't mug him. We didn't threaten him or hit him with our fists. James stepped out of the truck and this guy, this detective, happened to be in the way." Em was trembling but sure of herself.

"Yeah. The guy walked into it. We cannot be accountable for that, right?"

"It happened that way. We had no idea who he was." I was in total agreement. We had our defense all ready for the trial.

"So we call 911? We tell them there's been an accident, and—"

"Right after we called and said we were being attacked?" James said.

"Right after we thought we were being attacked, James."

"What happened?" The voice was shaky and weak.

I swung the light back to the horizontal body, and his eyes were open. A puzzled expression on his face, the prone figure lifted his arm and felt his chest, searching for the pistol in his holster.

"What the hell happened?"

"James," Em pointed to my best friend, "James was getting out of the truck and it so happened you were walking by at the exact same time, and—"

He struggled to sit up. "That the way you remember it?" The cop looked at me as he worked himself into a sitting position.

"Exactly."

He nodded, still touching his chest and stomach.

"Where's my badge?"

James leaned down and handed him the shiny gold metal. "We were just doing an ID check," he said. "We didn't know who you were and we just wanted to make sure everything was all right."

Sitting on the blacktop, the man pointed at Em.

"You're Emily Minard."

The light was dim, the moon and a lamp from the rear of the restaurant throwing shadows on the property. The cop appeared to be in his forties, hair slightly gray. I was pretty sure I'd never seen him before, but he seemed pretty confident in his identification of Em.

"Do we know each other?" Em was studying him, and I flashed the light back on his face.

"We do," the man slipped the badge into his shirt pocket. "Get the damned light out of my face."

I did.

"And you're eventually going to tell me what our relationship was?" Em's voice projected her irritation. A minute ago she was worried the man might die and now she was upset about his gamesmanship.

"I arrested you about nine years ago."

There was no response. There was no sound. James and I had nothing to add and Em was stunned. So this was back when her world was collapsing around her. I'd never heard the story.

The detective pushed himself off the black pavement and staggered to Em's Jaguar. Putting his right hand on the shiny black metal, he rested for a moment.

"The diamond theft. From Kahn's Jewelers. The one your friend eventually confessed to."

No sound. Em said nothing.

"You walked on that one."

"So did my friend, Detective Conway. Amanda Wright walked on that case too. The case ended up with no conviction. Do you remember that? You didn't have a lot of luck with that case, did you, Detective?"

This time it was the detective who said nothing.

"Did you ever find the robber? Ever figure out where the ring went? I don't recall ever hearing that you solved that case. You just put two people through a lot of stress."

"No, we never found the perp." Leaning on the new car, he gingerly rubbed the back of his head.

"Sorry about that," James said. "Really, I was just getting out of the truck when you walked by and—"

The detective ignored him.

"We had a pretty good idea. We still think we know who lifted the ring." He sounded sullen.

"Statute of limitations run out on that?" Em was goading him.

"Five years, Miss Minard. If you did it, you're off the hook. However, I was looking you up for another reason."

She nervously ran her hand through her blonde tresses.

"You looked me up in the parking lot of a restaurant at this hour of the night? For God's sake, what for?"

"What for? Because I'm now working homicide, and I'm the lead on the Amanda Wright murder. And you're supposedly still a good friend of hers. Or you were."

Conway took his hand off the Jaguar and stood up straight. A good sign for him, and good sign for us.

"I'm looking you up because I've dealt with the two of you before and because Amanda's mother told me that you referred a private investigation agency to the restaurant. Lessor and Moore?"

I glanced at James who was shaking his head. The cover was blown in less than twenty-four hours.

"Is that against the law?"

"No. By law they can solve this damned case if they want to, but if they get in my way, if they interfere in any way with the investigation, it *will* be against the law, and I'll come down on them like a ton of bricks." His voice had an edge. "Do you understand?" Tough guy attitude.

"And you're telling me this because?"

"Because I can't find this agency in the phone book, online or—"

"They're licensed with the state," Em said. "How hard can it be? Is this another case you can't solve?" My girlfriend, sticking up for us. She sounded very frustrated.

We were licensed. With the Florida Department of Agriculture. Yeah, I know, what is FDOA doing licensing private detectives? I have no idea. This is Florida and Florida does some strange things. However, when they licensed us they misspelled James's name and we never bothered to correct it. Their letter said that "Moore or Less Investigations" had been approved as a private investigation firm, but James's name was spelled *Leser* on the official form. Not even close to the real spelling.

"Couldn't find them. This Lessor and Moore." He rubbed his head again. "I came to the restaurant to talk to the owner, and as luck would have it, they're closed. It was a long shot that you would be here, but since you recommended these guys I thought maybe you were involved."

Em said nothing.

"Anyway, I'm asking you to tell them for me—don't interfere. We'll find whoever did this and we don't need a couple of amateurs getting in the way. It usually makes things a lot harder. Okay."

He moved from the Jag, walked over to me a little wobbly on his feet, and grabbed the flashlight from my hand. Heading away from us, he looked back over his shoulder.

"I mean it. Those guys get in my way, I'll put them away."

"Detective, what if they could put someone in the kitchen? Someone who was a cook. Undercover?"

I was stunned.

He stopped and turned, the beam hitting James square in the face. The prominent frown on his face told me my partner was not happy.

"Who? This Lessor and Moore?"

"If they had someone who worked the kitchen, they could talk to the employees, get a feel for the inside of the operation. Would that help the investigation?"

The light was off James, but I knew he was pissed. There was no way he wanted to work with cops.

"They could do this?"

"Maybe." She was being coy, a little hesitant after his threat to shut us down. "This would be someone who has a culinary degree. Someone who knows his way around a kitchen."

"It's not something that we normally do. Asking someone who isn't in law enforcement to go undercover. I may have a hard time getting this approved."

"Detective," she said, using her most persuasive voice, "the one undercover has a culinary arts major. He's made a living working in restaurants, and he's a very good cook."

Conway seemed to weigh it for a moment.

"You think they could go under and make it believable?"

"I do."

"If they go under, they go under my supervision."

"I don't think it would work like that. A team effort maybe. These guys are pretty independent."

He was quiet. And I could hear James taking deep breaths. When Emily took control, he would usually go nuts.

"Then why would they work with me on this?"

"Because Amanda was a good friend of mine, and the two investigators would realize that we'd have a better chance of finding the killer if we worked together. You, Lessor, Moore, and me." She shot a glance at James, putting him on notice.

"No one else could know." The cop was quieter now, thinking through the idea. "I mean, if they pulled this off. Someone who fit in, who knows what goes on in a professional kitchen. I wouldn't tell anyone, you couldn't tell anyone. Undercover means exactly that."

"You wouldn't tell your supervisor?"

"Confidential informant."

"You can do that? You just said you'd have to get it approved."

"I'm lead investigator on the case. I can do anything."

"We could share information." Em was negotiating, while we were just observing. I knew it was driving my partner crazy.

"Some."

"We'd need a give and take." Em sounded confident. Like she was in charge. I wasn't so sure.

"We?"

"Mmmm, the investigators. Lessor and Moore. I mean, they would need a steady flow of your information. If you want theirs."

"They could get someone hired in that kitchen?" Cautious, but optimistic. The detective seemed excited about the possibility. "You think they could actually do this? Remember, we're dealing with a murderer here. I mean, if the killer really does work for that restaurant, that's a pretty dangerous place to be right now. This would have to be their call."

"They *already* have someone in there. Detective Conway, meet James Lessor and Skip Moore. James is a cook, pretending to be a sous chef, and Skip," she paused, obviously not proud of my station, "Skip is the dishwasher."

He looked at James, turned and looked at me, and took a deep breath. Glancing back at Em he said, "Oh, great."

CHAPTER TWELVE

"He is going to watch you like a hawk."

The three of us stood in the parking lot as we stared at his unmarked Chevy driving off, the red taillights winking in the dark Miami night.

"I don't care. We don't need to be sharing any information with the cops. You had no right to—"

"Listen to me, damn it." With an edge to her voice, she spoke to him in a firm tone. "Conway said you'd better stay out of the way. If he found you interfering, he'd nail you. He was ready to put you out of business. Shut you down. Do you understand that?" She was breathing hard, and I was somewhat worried about her. "Did you not hear him, James? Did you? I dealt with this guy. Nine years ago. He's serious, and he doesn't back down."

James was quiet, waiting for the tempest to subside.

"And what did I do? I gave you a free pass, Lessor." Now she was pointing at him, almost pushing her finger into his chest. "I gave you a chance to earn your three thousand dollars a week, no hassle from the cops. What the hell do you want? If your fragile ego is in the way of your earning power, then let me know. I'll call the detective and tell him to go ahead and hassle you all he wants."

Em took a deep breath, put her hand to her side, and kept her gaze on my partner.

"You want the money, James. I want Amanda's killer."

"Em," I very seldom saw her so riled, "we just didn't see that coming." I just wanted her to settle down.

"I want this case solved, Skip. I've got a very personal stake in the outcome of this investigation. This girl was a friend. She stood up for me. Usually, I look out for you. And sometimes, your partner. Actually, very seldom is it your partner. But this time, I'm looking out for Amanda, because she can't very well look out for herself. Got it?"

I nodded. James was still seething.

"Em, take it easy. We want the job." I glanced at James, trying to gauge his reaction. In the deepening shadows, his face was a curious mask of anger and awe.

"As I see it, we approach the situation just as we have. The only difference is, we now have some access to what the cops know. And that has got to be a plus."

After a long silence James spoke. "All right."

I'm certain my jaw dropped. The resignation surprised me. This was a surrender I hadn't anticipated.

"We have no choice at this point. However, I think we need to keep Bouvier out of this. He's paying for our service, but the reason he hired us was that he doesn't trust cops."

James paused, seeming to gather his thoughts.

"I understand that sentiment. I think you two know very well that I come down on the side of there is too much 'law' in this land. However—"

"However what?" I wasn't sure where he was going with this.

"As far as anyone else is concerned, anyone else, we're working undercover for Jean and Sophia Bouvier."

"James," I had to point out the obvious, "as far as anyone else is concerned, we're not undercover. You are a sous chef."

He gave me a grim smile. "It gets confusing, pardner."

Em and I nodded.

"Conway said we don't tell anyone. So that's settled."

"If we can trust Conway." The "Can-Can" played on Em's phone and she grabbed it from her purse and pushed the button. "What?"

Pausing, she gritted her teeth. "I'm sorry. It was all a mistake." Obviously. someone on the other end was grilling her.

"No, no. It was, it was a friend playing a prank."

Another long silence.

"Believe me, I would never—no, please. It was a mistake, someone was messing with me. Okay?"

She nodded and hung up. "Damn. Nine-one-one does not like to be fooled with. Not in the least."

James climbed back into the truck. I opened the passenger door of the Jag and Em got in. I was going to drive to Em's place in a brand-new Jaguar, a sleek, sexy sports sedan. Then I was going to make love to a sleek, sexy sporty young lady. Her fire, her passion had ignited my passion.

"I'm serious, Skip. There's only one thing I want from this investigation, from this job. I want the killer. I'll do anything that has to be done to achieve that end. Please understand that."

"I believe you."

"If your roommate, if your best friend screws this up, I'll have no mercy. I've never been so serious."

I'd seldom seen her so worked up.

"Em?"

"What?"

"You were accused of a diamond heist? They thought you stole a ring from Kahn's Jewelers?"

"I told you that was off limits."

"Look, there's you, Amanda, and this cop. For the second time in the last nine years the three of your lives are intertwined. And one of you isn't alive right now to discuss it. Don't you think it is kind of important that—"

"Drop it, Skip." Her tone was icy.

"You tend to call the shots a lot."

She crossed her arms and stared out the window into the dark evening. Finally, she spoke. "Look, I loved Amanda. She wasn't the easiest person to be close to, and in the end," she paused for a moment, a break in her voice, "in the end, she turned out not to be the nicest person in the world. But understand this. I place a lot of emphasis on loyalty. And even though we had grown apart, Amanda Wright was always there for me. It's a very personal thing, Skip, and I don't care to go into it with you. Please, work with me here. The diamond thing, it's not worth discussing."

"You said it brought your whole world down."

"It's in the past, Skip. My position in this world has evolved, okay? Let's leave it there."

I drove down the street, not even thinking about the automobile I commanded. I was always there for Em. We went to bed and never touched each other till morning, when she gave me a chaste kiss. James picked me up at nine and asked me how the night had been. I never gave him an answer.

CHAPTER THIRTEEN

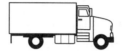

James was in the permanently reclined recliner. I sat on the beer-stained sofa sipping the last Yuengling beer.

"Maybe the cop thing is a good idea." I couldn't believe he was admitting that playing along with the cops was a positive thing.

"You? You're admitting that it might be a good idea to team up with the professionals?"

"I want to know the wound reports. Do you think that the cops might give that up? They have the information."

"Wound reports?" I had no idea what he was talking about.

"You know. Do the wounds telegraph what kind of knife was used in the stabbing? How deep were the cuts? Did it take some strong guy, or could a slight woman make those wounds? We need to know this kind of stuff, Skip, if we want to be serious investigators."

I nodded.

"You know, I've cut enough meat in school and in restaurants to know that flesh, muscles, and other organs are flexible. They contract, they expand. With that in mind, you could stab someone with a short knife, and as you push the blade, you could go in a lot deeper than the blade is long. I've done it. But I've never wondered what kind of a knife someone is using. We need to know if there's a science to stab wounds. At least that would make sense to me."

I'm sure he was right.

"What did they find in the alley? I mean, were there foreign fibers on the body? Was there evidence of someone else's blood? If this guy, this hotshot detective, really is willing to share information, we could learn a lot, Skip."

I nodded. There was a certain amount of maturity in his outlook. A maturity that wasn't there in the past.

"While you and I are in that kitchen—"

"While you're in that kitchen, James. I'm out of there. No more dishwashing. Please understand that."

"While *we're* in there, we need to be looking at knives, right? If I knew something about what kinds of wounds certain knives make, I could see what kind of knives the cooks are using."

It actually made sense.

My cell phone erupted with the Springsteen anthem, "Born in the U.S.A." I really needed to update the ring.

"Skip, I need the knife that James found in his locker." Emily sounded a little icy, matter-of-fact.

"We were just talking about—why do you need the knife?"

"Fingerprints."

"I'm sure James's are all over it." James had pulled it from the apron, and even passed it to— "Oops. Mine are on it too."

"So they'll take that into consideration," she said. I heard another voice in the background. "Listen, I talked to Ted, and he thinks—"

"Ted?"

"The detective, remember?"

"Oh, it's become Ted? Not Detective Conway?"

"He'd like to examine the knife, Skip." Cold, impersonal.

I glanced at James. "You got the knife?"

"Mine?"

"The one from your locker. The Wüsthof that was sticking through the catsup-stained apron."

"It's still in the locker. Along with my Wüsthof."

"Skip, I heard that. Can you get it?"

"If you and *Ted* think it's important."

"What I think is that the faster we resolve any questions, the faster we can wrap this up." I felt the icy chill coming through the phone.

"Yeah. We'll get it."

"The detective said pick it up with plastic wrap, okay? Plastic wrap, Skip. I'll meet you there."

And she was gone.

"The cop wants to check it for fingerprints. You and I picked it up last night so I'm sure ours are on it."

"So, she told him about our knife and apron." Surprisingly he smiled. "That's good, man."

"Why is that good?"

"We shared. We've given him some information. Now he knows we're serious. We're involved."

"And?"

"He owes us, amigo. It's his turn to tell us something about the case."

CHAPTER FOURTEEN

Twenty-five minutes later James pulled the white, four-wheeled oil burner into L'Elfe's parking lot. Two in the afternoon, and my partner still had the evening stretching out in front of him. I hoped that I wasn't pulling dishwasher duty two nights in a row.

There was no Jaguar waiting for us.

"Em's not here yet. You sure you can get in?"

He nodded. "Cleanup guy, setup guy, somebody'll be inside."

"And your excuse for showing up hours early?"

"I forgot something from my locker. Which, it so happens, is the truth. Sometimes, Skip, the truth is the best answer."

I'd never found James to follow that rule.

"Come with me. We may be able to talk to one of the guys for a couple of minutes. We've got to interview as many people as we can."

"Without coming off like an interview."

Walking up to the back door, James pushed it open. The heavy metal gave easily and we walked into the rear of the kitchen.

Holding the door open for a moment, I said, "Check this

out, James. A magnetic alarm system on the door. Do you know how easy it would be to disarm this? These guys are ripe for a break-in."

There was no fire-breathing grill, no pans banging, no knife artists wielding their shiny blades of steel and, thankfully, no scalding hot water or garbage cans of people's leftovers.

The rap music was loud, blaring through the kitchen and probably out into the empty dining room.

"I'll go back to the locker." James raised his voice several decibels. "You check out front and see who's working. Tell them you just came along with me for the ride, and say something like, I don't know, wasn't it too bad about the Wright girl and what do you think happened, you know?"

"I do know. I can handle this. Are we supposed to be friends?"

He nodded. "Yeah, we are. And you know you didn't exactly show that kind of confidence when you talked to the runner last night."

"I've got it under control now, okay?"

"You go that way, I'll go this way." James headed to the left toward the lockers, and I walked through the kitchen, past the gleaming stainless counters and took a right through the swinging doors into the dining area.

Black tables, stark against a ceramic white inlay, and a blood-red carpet that almost squished under my feet. The small bar, complete with granite top and twelve leather stools, was off to my left, and a glassed-in wine cabinet to my right. When Em and I had eaten here, it didn't seem so severe. The dining area was empty, except for the little guy in the far corner. He was wiping down the tables, bopping to the music.

"World Series attitude, champagne bottle life."

A song by Drake and Lil Wayne.

"You do the cleanup?" I shouted to him.

There was no response, just the heavy beat of the music as the man danced and took swipes with a cloth at the table.

"Hey, you."

Finally the dark young man lifted his shaved head and concentrated his attention on my voice.

"Whatchu want?"

"Just wondered if you do the early cleanup? Setup?"

"Is that what it look like?"

I nodded.

"Then don't be askin' stupid questions."

Smiling, I reached out to shake his hand. He didn't reciprocate.

"I'm Skip."

"You work here? Or you stealin' food from the walk-in?" Stepping back, he folded his arms and watched for my reaction.

"Stealing food?"

"Could be both. You could work here, and you could steal food. Believe me, it's been done. Just don't steal it on my watch, okay?"

"Who are you?"

Studying me for a moment, he wiped his hands on his apron.

"Mikey. Mikey Pollerno. Again, whatchu doin' here?"

"My friend, he's new here, he had to come early to get something from his locker and I—"

"He gonna walk some meat out to his car? Not on my watch. There be no food stealin' today."

"Nobody's walking any food out of here, okay?"

"Damn straight. There're two locks on the walk-in. Two padlocks. Ain't nobody walkin' free food." A grin broke out on his face. "Unless it's me."

"You take food?"

"No. Come on, man. It's a joke. No way. Two locks on the

cooler. And Marty and Chef Jean? They don't trust nobody. Understand? Nobody. Sophia had 'em install cameras, dude. Three of them security things mounted outside the locker, just waitin' for you to walk some food out the door."

I was thoroughly confused.

"I'm messin' with you, dude. You couldn't take the food if you wanted. Although, some people try when the walk-in open. Steaks, lobster, scallops, they have a way of just disappearin'. So now, locks and cameras."

I hadn't considered taking anything. My mission was to get information.

"So, lots of excitement here a couple of nights ago."

"Yeah. Your friend, he takes the Wright girl's place?"

I was the one who was supposed to be asking the questions.

"What exactly happened?"

"The girl was cut up. Out in the alley. You don't know? Like a side of beef, man. Pretty nasty stuff."

"Yeah, yeah, I know. I just wondered why?"

I found myself almost shouting over the loud music.

Mikey smiled. "Oh, there could be lots of reasons. Boy-friend—"

"Did she have a boyfriend?"

Glancing around the room, he said, "I got to get these tables wiped down and set. Cloths, candles, flowers."

"Yeah. Big job. Did Amanda have a boyfriend? Somebody who worked in the kitchen?"

"Look, man, I din't know her. There's talk, you know. And why are you so interested?"

Why was I interested? I manufactured a reason that wasn't far from the truth. "I told you, my friend is working back there. I'm looking out for him. I guess I wanted to know if it's dangerous."

"Is he gonna piss people off? Is he gonna promote himself

where he shouldn't be promotin'? Is he gonna play like his shit don't stink?"

"That's why she was killed?"

He stared at me.

"Is that what she was like?"

"I don't know nothin'. Okay?"

"Hey, I'm just asking. I heard one of the cooks say that maybe she was seeing Joaquin Vanderfield."

His eyes narrowed and he took a step back.

"I din't say that. Who would say that? What goes on in that kitchen I don't know nothin' about. *Yo no sé nada.*"

It was the second time I'd heard that phrase in the last two days. I know nothing.

"Just wondered."

"Maybe you shouldn't wonder so much," he paused and then turned away, picking up his rag and a spray bottle, and moving to the next table. The conversation was obviously over.

As I walked back into the kitchen, I wondered if I'd received a veiled threat. Or maybe I was just being paranoid. The walls echoed with Alley Boy's "Gonna Rob Me a Nigga." I couldn't say much for Mikey's taste in music.

Checking the parking lot, I saw no sign of the black Jag, so I ducked back in and strolled down the hall, past the walk-in with two padlocks on it. I glanced up and saw one of the cameras, the lens pointing right at me. Instinctively I smiled, ran my fingers through my hair and continued to the employee locker room. No James. His locker was closed, but the padlock was open.

"James. You back here?"

There was no answer, just the backbeat of the recording echoing down the hall from the kitchen.

"James?"

Nothing. And then I heard a cough. Faint, like the sound of

someone softly clearing his throat. There was no one in the locker room. Two restrooms were at the far end of the area, and I pushed open the men's door.

"James."

Stall doors were open and there was no one there.

Pushing open the women's door, I hesitated, then stuck my head in.

"Somebody here?"

One stall door was closed. There was no sign of anyone's legs under the door, and even though it was doubtful someone was there, I almost walked in. One night on the job probably didn't give me the right to intrude. Into the women's restroom or anywhere else.

"James?"

Then I heard the outside kitchen door open and footsteps, fast, coming my way. Someone jogging, running.

"James?"

He rounded the corner, breathless, his eyes wide.

"Dude, there's something very strange going on here."

"No shit."

"No. I come back here, the lock's in place, so I open the locker and guess what?"

I had no idea.

"Somebody's been in it again. That wooden-handled Wüsthof knife, the apron, they're gone. Somebody—"

"James. Where did you get the padlock?" I didn't remember him buying one. He just announced he had a locker.

"Standard issue. Chef Marty gave it to me as soon as I started."

"Think, my friend. Marty probably knows that combination. Everyone in the entire restaurant could know that combination. The lock belongs to L'Elfe. It's their property, right?"

I saw the surprised hurt look in his eyes. "No, don't tell me. I'm not that stupid, am I?"

I kept a sober look on my face.

"Damn. Skip, I swear, I never even thought of it. How did that get by me? Hell, I'll get my own lock."

"A little late for that."

He stared at the locker for a moment, then grabbed me by my shoulder, turning me around.

"Follow me, man. I want someone else to see this with his own eyes."

Giving me a push forward, he headed back out the door.

"What?"

James didn't say anything as we walked out the door into the parking lot. The black asphalt had soaked up the hot Miami sun and it radiated as we walked twenty feet where James stopped.

"You're not going to believe this, amigo."

Stepping up to an army-green garbage Dumpster, he grabbed a pole, and forced the top open.

"Look inside."

I stepped up on an empty plastic crate and stared down into the slimy empty cavity. Even with the garbage removed the stench of spoiled vegetables and rotting meat was overwhelming.

"Nothing there, man. It's empty."

"What? That's impossible."

James stepped up and looked.

"Damn."

"What did you see?"

"The apron, the knife, they weren't in my locker. So I'm thinking, where would someone put them?"

"The trash."

"Yeah. So on a wild hunch I looked in here. The apron was in there, covered with some boxes and stuff. Then I took this pole," he pointed to a long wooden rod propped up against the Dumpster, "and I pushed the boxes out of the way."

"You didn't touch anything?"

"No. No more fingerprints. I didn't want to contaminate anything. I was going to get some plastic wrap."

"And?"

"I saw a knife."

"You mean the one from your locker? The one the cop wanted to test for fingerprints?"

"Identical. Identical to mine and the one that was stabbed through the apron. The same one that my first boss, Michael Trump, gave me. The Wüsthof. I showed it to you at the News Café."

"Your knife was in the Dumpster?"

"I'll know in a minute. Mine was stashed in my locker. That top metal shelf. Along with the plastic holster."

He stayed on the crate for a moment, looking into the empty shell and shaking his head.

At that very moment Em's black Jag pulled up and she stepped out, pushing her Ray-Bans back on her head.

"That trash hauler almost hit me back there." She glanced back over her shoulder. "Just as I turned into the drive, here he comes."

"Trash hauler?" James looked at me. "Damn, Skip, that's where it went. Em, can we follow that garbage truck?" James pointed down the road.

"What?"

"James thinks he saw his knife in the Dumpster, but now it's probably inside that truck that almost hit you."

"What was your knife doing in there anyway?"

"We're not sure," James said.

Em frowned. "You want me to chase a garbage hauler so James can get his knife back?"

76

"Along with the apron and maybe the knife with finger-prints on it. The one that *Ted* was so interested in."

She took a deep breath. "Some things you just don't sign on for."

"Em—"

"Well, get in." The disgust was thick in her voice. "If we don't leave now we'll lose him."

Obviously chasing a trash hauler was low on her list of priorities, but if it was one more step in finding Amanda's killer, she was willing to take the ride.

CHAPTER FIFTEEN

The driver was a she, Maggie Juniper. About forty-five years old, a wide smile with laugh lines around her eyes. She and a quiet, young male sidekick ran the truck and the route, and we caught up with them about three restaurants down the road. I'll have to admit she was fast. They were in and out of those places in less than two minutes.

"It's not in my job description, but let's see what we can do."

Flipping a switch, she climbed out of the big blue refuse hauler, complete in her Carhartt jeans, Pendleton work shirt, and black rubber boots.

"Normally you have to engage the lifter and it just picks up the Dumpster, opens in the rear, dumps the load, and closes back up. Pretty slick. But I've got a manual override so I can open her up this way."

She studied James for a moment.

"You're sure you know what you're looking for? You're sure it's in here? We've got a pretty tight schedule."

Walking to the back of the truck, she and the boy leaned in

with gloved hands and started sorting through the garbage and trash.

"We loaded another establishment, plus this one before you ran us down. Quite a bit of stuff back here."

"I can't tell you how much we appreciate this. I mean, if we had gloves—" James trailed off.

Maggie spun around, smiling. "Oh, gloves are something we're not short on. Brian, get the man a pair of gloves."

James grimaced.

"Don't worry about it, James." I smiled at him. "I scraped it all off the plates just last night so not too much of it should be spoiled."

He muttered something under his breath and started spreading the garbage. Fifteen minutes later Maggie called a halt to the process.

"Kids, as I pointed out, I've got a schedule, and I'm already behind. I'm sorry. Obviously, I want to help but—"

"Here it is," James yelled, pulling the Wüsthof out by the blade with a gloved hand.

"I can't believe it. I knew it was in that Dumpster. This is the knife." He was grinning as he held it up.

"Crocodile Dundee, James."

I could tell he remembered the scene. Where the teenaged punk pulls out a little knife when he's going to rob Dundee. The Australian says, "That's not a knife," as he produces a huge Bowie knife.

"That's a knife," James said. "Wow, Maggie, thank you. If there's ever anything I can do for you, let me know."

Flashing her smile, her eyes sparkling, she said, "Honey, if I was fifteen years younger."

I swear he blushed.

"Hey, I know how it is. Those things are expensive."

She drove off and Em stood there shaking her pretty head.

"You guys are a constant source of amusement. A constant source."

"We should have found the apron too," James lamented.

"Let's get back to the restaurant."

"Can James walk?" she asked. "He stinks and, after all, this is a brand-new car."

James rode in the back and Em kept the windows down.

CHAPTER SIXTEEN

James's knife was missing.

"So what does that mean? Somebody stole your knife? Maybe you misplaced it, James."

"That didn't happen."

"Maybe somebody stole it, but this one, the one from the trash, isn't yours? Or is it?" I was trying to make some sense out of it.

"Should have carved my initials in the handle. This one, the one we found, I wish it was mine, but it's not."

"They look the same to me."

"No nick in the blade. Mine had that tiny nick near the point."

"Let me take it to Ted." Em reached for the plastic-wrapped knife.

Ted again.

"He can at least check it for fingerprints."

"See if you can get it back before tonight. I've got to have a knife. I can score some smaller knives, but I need the big one. I can't cook without it."

Em nodded. "But think about this, James. Someone who had access to this kitchen apparently stole two knives from your locker."

"And?"

"And if you show up tonight using either of those knives, after they tossed this and possibly yours in the Dumpster, it's going to tip them off that you are on to them."

He shrugged his shoulders. "I'm not made of money, Emily. Just get it back, okay? To buy a new one would cost over one hundred dollars. And until we get paid for this gig, I don't have 'over' one hundred dollars."

Juan Castro didn't show up for work, so Chef Marty told James to call me. I refused at first, but after several threats and James begging a great deal, I said yes to one more night as dishwasher.

This time I got fed. The meal is standard in upscale kitchens. It seems the cooks prepare a meal for the staff before the customers show up. It wasn't the gourmet food that customers would be served, but it wasn't half bad. According to Chef Marty it was a French beef stew with more vegetables than beef, but it was filling. And Bouvier showed up. After the last time, I hadn't expected to be impressed, but having seen him half a dozen times on television, knowing his marketing influence and branding power, I have to admit I found him to live up to his hype. He seemed charged up, in broadcast form as he stood in front of the assembled kitchen staff. Smiling, his artificially whitened teeth glistening, he faced the staff.

He addressed them by saying, "You people—you are what makes this thing happen. It's not just me, it's you. Don't forget that."

I was reminded of Danny DeVito on steroids. He was short, somewhat rotund, with a fringe of hair around his ears. He bobbed and weaved as his hands did much of the talking.

Wearing an apron that appeared to be somewhat soiled, he showed he was still a working man, yet he hadn't cooked a thing. Either he didn't wash his aprons, or he simply wanted people to assume that he was busy in the kitchen and had just grabbed a break.

"You do things that our customers can't do. When I say to the TV audience, 'But can you do *this?*' it simply means that they probably can't. But you, my loyal staff, you can do this. You are the magic. That's exactly why our customers are here. Because when they go home, it turns out they can't do what we do. In the privacy of their own home kitchens, they fall short. Whatever they try, it lacks a little flavor, it doesn't have the same presentation, the portions aren't perfect. They can't do it, but you can. Our customers are here to experience the supernatural. They come here for the magic of Bouvier and L'Elfe. Don't forget that."

He paused, smiling, watching the reaction of the cooks and waitstaff.

"I've worked hard to bring this dream to life. You, my wonderful staff, you are the bridge between reality and dreams. Don't forget that."

He kept repeating that phrase, *don't forget that*, as if we all had attention deficit disorder.

"Make it happen tonight. Make some magic, people. We've had a little setback, and I feel bad about that. I'm certain that the person responsible will be found soon, but in the meantime, there's no reason for you to let down."

Pointing at the assembled staff, he smiled, a mellow, fatherly kind of look on his face, his eyes twinkling.

"When I say, 'can you do this', your answer to me should be, 'of course we can.' Because you can."

I found "a little setback" to be somewhat trivial when it came to the life of a young lady, but Chef Jean was on a mission. A mission to rally the troops. I forgave him the understatement.

"I want the food to be excellent, I want the service to be superb. I want people to walk out of here tonight saying, 'I could never make a dish like they do.' Don't forget that. They should look at each other and say, 'no, I couldn't do this!'" Bouvier glanced at me. "From the dishwasher to Chef Marty. From our sous chef trainee, James," I couldn't believe he was addressing us individually, "to our head waiter Justine and our pastry chef Kelly. Astound our customers tonight. Can you do that? Can you? Make this an experience they won't forget."

There was a brief round of applause, and I saw genuine enthusiasm on the faces of his staff. I noticed a scowl on Mikey Pollerno's face, but for the most part Bouvier's speech was well received. These people were working a celebrity kitchen, part of a team that was revered around the world.

I remembered James telling me that a handful of French chefs actually studied under Bouvier. He was an impressive little guy, and here he was, inspiring us, telling us to astound his customers with great food and great service.

For a brief moment, that's exactly what I wanted to do. Astound our customers. It was easy to see why James was caught up in the moment. I wanted Jean Bouvier to be proud of *my* efforts.

That brief moment was very brief. I was a dishwasher, and nobody in that fancy dining room, with the tablecloths, the flowers, and the fine wines and food ever considered that someone was scraping the remains of their meals off of the expensive china in the bowels of this famous kitchen. But it was fun being on the inside. That didn't often happen. It was exhilarating having a celebrity addressing me. Actually talking about me. Well, not by name, but—

"Eugene, James, could I see you for a moment."

I froze. Chef Jean Bouvier had just singled us out. And I wasn't sure that was a very good idea.

CHAPTER SEVENTEEN

He motioned to us and we went down the hall. I glanced up as we walked by the walk-in and saw the second camera, directly pointing at the door. Just before we entered the employee locker room, he opened a door in the middle of the hallway and entered his cramped office. I would have thought that a celebrity chef would have a spacious office with expensive walnut paneling and a mahogany desk. We followed him in and he pushed the door shut.

"Damned handle is jammed on the inside here. Can't lock it from the inside," he said. "Need to call a locksmith." He glared at it, as if a look would free it up.

"So, what do you have?" He sat down behind the banged-up steel desk. We stood in a room with no other chairs. One desk, one chair, a filing cabinet, and a three-foot-high red rolling tool cart with five drawers. A video monitor was mounted on the file cabinet, a stack of CDs sitting beside it.

James and I looked at each other. I spoke first. "We have a dishwasher who had a crush on Amanda. He's not shown up for two nights."

"What else?" Gone was the charm, the warmth. This was business. Cold, hard, ruthless.

"Joaquin Vanderfield," James said. "He thought he should have been chosen as the head chef of your South Beach restaurant."

"And?"

I glanced at James. In his white jacket with L'Elfe embroidered on the chest, his light brown hair falling over his forehead, he should have been a celebrity chef. A younger Bobby Flay. Given the right circumstances.

"Somebody threatened me." James brushed back his hair. "Last night I found an apron with a catsup stain on it and a knife stabbed through the cloth. It was hanging in my locker. At least, I took it as a threat. And, today when I went to retrieve my knife and the one in the apron they were gone. It appears that whoever broke into my locker stole both of the Wüsthof knives." He paused. "Apparently, we've pissed someone off."

Bouvier looked away, studying a couple of his poorly framed certificates carelessly hanging from the wall. A *Time* magazine cover featuring the chef and his stocky wife also hung in a frame, with the title splashed on the cover, "Celebrity Duo Defines French/American Cuisine."

"You could say that somebody is afraid that I'm grooming you for the South Beach restaurant."

"That's what we thought."

"I know they think that," he said. "It's because I told the staff that you were the heir apparent."

"What?" I studied him for a moment, and he gave me a wry smile.

"Why would you?"

"I wanted to flush out the killer. So we're getting there."

James's eyes were wide open. "Are you trying to get me killed?"

86

Bouvier stared at James for a second, that faint smile still on his lips. "Mr. Lessor, if I hadn't said it, everyone would have assumed it."

"I don't think that was a very good idea." I felt the need to disapprove.

Squinting his eyes, he nodded at James. "I've made a very good living trusting my gut instincts. I tend to think it was a very good idea. Whoever killed Amanda is considering your immediate rise in the company. Don't forget that."

"Making me the target."

"Mr. Lessor, you were a target the moment you walked into this kitchen. That's why I hired you."

"How do you figure that?"

Elbows on the desk, he crossed his plump fingers under his chin, resting his head on his hands for a moment. "You're considered undercover right now. Am I right? You are assuming an identity that isn't entirely yours." He watched James, trying to gauge his reaction.

"Yeah. Sort of. I mean, I am a cook. I'm actually pretty good at it. I work fast and I understand kitchen protocol."

"But you're a detective pretending to be a chef. And I have to support that undercover role. I want people to pay attention, respect you on the job, and fear your position. If I don't throw my full support behind you, no one will believe for an instant that you are really my chosen head chef."

I had to admit it made sense. A simple background check would show that James lacked serious experience.

"You lack experience. You have almost none, at least not what we would expect for such a position. Do we agree on that?"

The guy was reading my mind.

"Thomas Keller, executive chef and owner of the French Laundry in Napa, was just a kid when he took over as staff chef at the Dunes Club. Early twenties. But," he held out his hands, "he showed promise. He had the magic that can be seen by other chefs. Keller owned his own Wall Street restaurant in New York by the time he was thirty, and when he opened the French Laundry, one of the fifty best restaurants in the world," he paused, "he hired a twenty-two-year-old girl as his commis. She impressed him so much, he gave her that job. Do you understand?"

We both nodded, although I'm not sure we did.

"I tell you this to prove my faith in James. As far as the staff is concerned, I believe he has talent that can't be ignored, regardless of experience. Someone saw the talent in Keller, and he in turn saw the talent in the twenty-two-year-old girl."

Pushing his chair back, he licked his lips.

"I see the talent in you, Mr. Lessor."

For a brief moment, I think James believed it.

"I don't hire people to fill a position. I hire them because of their gift. For two weeks we have to convince my staff that you have that gift and, more importantly, that I believe in that gift."

If Bouvier made the case for James being groomed for La Plage, the staff would believe that somewhere, buried ever so deep, James had the talent. It was obvious that Chef Jean had a better understanding of undercover than we did.

Bouvier slapped his hand on the desk, the sound reverberating in the tiny office.

"You see. I tell you about Thomas Keller, who had little experience, and that proves the exception. I want people here to believe that you are my handpicked head chef. If I don't tell them, then you lose believability. And if you lose that, you are no longer undercover and no longer of use to me."

And I knew he was right. I also realized we had probably jumped off the deep end. It was as if we were puppets and Bouvier was pulling the strings. I'd often felt that James tried to control our relationship, positioning himself as a leader and me as his follower. But I could walk away at any time. Chef Bouvier had alerted his staff about James, and the only way James could regain control was to quit. Walk away. I didn't believe he thought that was an option at this time.

"My staff out there, the right mix of people, it works. Like a well-oiled machine. Like a magician and his apprentices." The short man reached into a cardboard box on his desk and pulled out a jar. The label featured his photo and name. *Bouvier's Essence.* "This rub, these spices that are in here, people think they're magic. The mix works."

Setting the jar on the desk, almost as a barrier between us, he tapped his fingers on the metal desktop. "Nutmeg, rosemary, some garlic, sea salt, basil, and black pepper." He stared at the jar. "I'm good at mixes. Don't ever forget that. I brought you in as part of the mix and I believe you will be successful."

I shook my head. "I still think you've put James in jeopardy."

We heard footsteps down the hall and as the door opened, Sophia Bouvier stuck her shaggy head into the room.

"Jean, we have things to do. Come along." Her words were slightly slurred.

He stared after her as she retreated back to the kitchen.

"She drinks a little," he murmured. "But, she has reasons."

Pausing for a moment, he closed his eyes.

"She cries a lot too—we lost a child. You never get over losing a child."

Looking up, he raised his voice.

"You are private investigators, gentlemen. It's what you do. You put yourself in jeopardy by the nature of your work. I'm simply moving the process along."

"Still," I said.

James took a step back, surveying the small office. "What's with the red tool chest?" he asked.

Never the one to be confrontational, I knew he was thinking of the ramifications. The entire kitchen staff now thought he was the heir apparent, but James was deflecting the situation. Bringing up the toolbox. And of course, it was the first time either of us had been in the office of an important chef.

"Knives." The chef stood up, coming around the desk.

Five drawers of knives.

"Any other questions?"

We were silent.

"Knives?" James had touched on something the celebrity chef was proud of.

"Some I won in competition, some were gifts from other chefs, some I have used in past restaurants. There are thirty-seven knives in those drawers. Thirty-seven pieces. They are important to me. Those steel blades are the tools of my trade, of any chef's trade."

I held up my hand. "Chef," I was almost comfortable with the title, "I'm on record as saying you've really compromised James and his position. We may have some second thoughts about our position here."

"Second thoughts?" He chuckled. "You're being compensated, Eugene. Quite well, I believe, considering I have no proof you will turn up anything beneficial. And I've explained to you we need believability in your friend's position. I thought this was a professional relationship. But it can be negated. Think about this. Talk it over. If you want to quit, let me know by the end of the shift."

Bouvier walked to the door. Turning to us he said, "Be safe, gentlemen. It's a tough world out there."

CHAPTER EIGHTEEN

"I didn't tell him about the setup guy."

James and I were walking back to the kitchen, Bouvier having exited the building. A little pep talk, a casual threat, and he was gone.

"What about the setup guy?"

"Oh, he's the guy who puts the salt and pepper on the table, flowers, tablecloths, and—"

"I know what a setup guy does, Skip." James frowned and looked down his nose at me. "Mikey somebody."

I was impressed. James was actually paying attention to the staff.

"Well, I'm talking to him this afternoon, Mikey Pollerno, and he says something about Amanda having a boyfriend."

"Yeah? A boyfriend? I believe she needed a mate. Felt incomplete without one. My opinion."

"I understand. But the way Pollerno said it, it was like having a boyfriend was a possible link to the murder. And then he shut down. He was finished talking. So I kept prodding him, trying to get more information."

"Mmmm."

"And he insinuated that she was an overachiever."

"What does that mean?"

"He suggested he thought you might be taking over, and if that was the case, he wondered if you were a self-promoter. He wanted to know if you promised more than you could deliver. I didn't give you away. Although sometimes maybe you do promise more than—"

"And?" James said it sternly. "What's your point?"

"Come on, roomy, he was telling me that this girl you used to date was a prima donna. She was positioning herself where she didn't belong. That's what he said. He wanted to know if that's the way you were going to be."

"Really? What does that have to do with me? All I remember is she was cloying. She was all over me."

"You are all about girls being over you."

He nodded. "Yeah, yeah. You think you know me so well. But clingy girls don't do it for me, Skip. I don't want to even say this because I know you'll get pissed off, but here's a shocker. Something you probably won't believe. Em, your girlfriend, is the type of girl I'd like to meet."

"What?"

"Someone with a little backbone. Amanda was needy. She wanted me to give her affirmation. And until I know something about a girl, I'm not about to do that. But I never had the impression she was pushy or trying to be something she wasn't. I just didn't find her personality that attractive."

It was a shock to me. I'd always viewed James as an opportunist. A one-night-stand kind of guy. And here he was admitting to me that deep down inside he wanted to date—Em?

"Well, at least we know the staff has been put on alert that you are gunning for the South Beach job."

James rubbed his hands absentmindedly on his apron.

"Joaquin will be happy to hear that he's been passed over once again."

"If he ever shows up again."

James was quiet, as if thinking about the jeopardy he was in.

Finally, he stopped and looked at me. "Who do you think did it, Skip? If you just had to guess?"

"We've got little to go on, James. Gut reaction?"

"That seems to work for Bouvier."

"The sous chef. Vanderfield. He's got the most to gain."

"We don't know all there is to gain yet, do we?"

"We'd better get busy," I said. "A lot of ground to cover."

"And we'd better be safe."

The *we* thing didn't make sense. I didn't want to tell him that bumping off a dishwasher didn't get anyone anything. It was the head chef in training that was standing in the way.

CHAPTER NINETEEN

We got slammed by a party of twelve right off the bat and it seemed that every one of the diners ordered something different. I guess this must be a problem, because there was a lot of swearing and banging around as cooks had to double up on preparation.

"Lessor, Gonzales, get over here and chop. Spring vegetables, onions—" More bandages. "I need this bowl filled. Then get on the onion soup. Slice two reds, two sweet—" he motioned to two large pots, steaming on the gas stove top.

I'd emptied the dishwasher and was waiting for the first round of salad and appetizer plates to come back. I lived to scrape and wash.

As orders flooded the computer screen, Marty pulled meat from the refrigerated drawers and threw steaks and four chicken breasts on the grill, orange flames leaping from the grate. He sprayed something on them with a squeeze bottle, then dipped a white fish in egg batter and dropped it into a deep fryer. With the casualness of a seasoned veteran, he picked up a large spice shaker and sprinkled something on the chicken.

Two of the other cooks were pan cooking something in a wine sauce, throwing it up in the air like I'd seen James do with omelets and catching it on the flip. An industrial-sized bottle of white wine rested on the stainless counter next to the steam table.

Steam and smoke were caught in a spiral, sucked up by the large stainless steel hood exhaust system. Grease spattered, meat sizzled, and one of the line cooks expertly wrapped bacon around scallops, tossing them in a skillet with olive oil and what appeared to be minced garlic. The aroma was, for a moment, overwhelming.

Spanish words I did not understand were hurled at blinding speed, and it all seemed like organized chaos, but the food hit the plates, the lady making salads was creating visual masterpieces of red, green, yellow, and orange peppers along with tomatoes, and the waiters were picking up their meals in an orderly fashion. Kelly Fields was putting finishing touches on her baked goods.

"Still waiting for the tuna at three." A waiter shouted out. I was wrong. There were some complications.

"I had to catch it first." A Puerto Rican cook with a thick accent and a black bandana around his head slammed a china plate down on the shiny stainless prep table, tossing seared ahi tuna from a pan. "*El ojete.*"

I was pretty sure the term translated to asshole.

The waiter grabbed it and pushed his way through swinging doors, eager to get the delicacy to his table.

I caught the figure from the corner of my eye, just as a runner sat my first tray of dishes on the stainless counter.

"Vanderfield, I hope you've got one hell of an excuse." Chef did not seem pleased.

"Yeah. Later, okay. Don't give me any shit right now. Things look a little busy." He ignored the chef to his face, then flashed him a middle finger behind his back and walked to his station.

Joaquin Vanderfield wore his white jacket, a black sash

around his waist and a holstered knife on his right side. A six-foot pirate with a two-day growth on his face and his weapon of choice strapped to his body, he immediately walked up to the video screen, studied it, spun around in his station, and grabbed two pans. The hotshot with the questionable reputation of having banged Amanda Wright, the bloodied victim.

Chef Marty frowned, grumbled under his breath, and went back to his grill, tossing three more steaks on the hot metal. I saw him glance at Vanderfield with a cold, hard stare. Another suspect in the murder. Joaquin Vanderfield, spooning a large gob of butter and grabbing a spray bottle, set the cast-iron skillets on the searing hot metal.

"Dude."

I spun to my left. James stood there, a Wüsthof knife in hand, a Miami Heat cap hiding his thick head of hair.

"A little crazy, huh?" I figured he'd noticed.

"First sitting, man. After that, we settle in. Every night is showtime. It just takes a little while to get rid of the butterflies."

He was really getting into the act.

"But get this, amigo. Marty comes up to me earlier and says, 'Chef Jean said to give you this knife.' What's that all about?"

"Cool. James, Jean Bouvier has five drawers of knives. It's not like he's using them." It made sense to me. "So Em didn't have to bring a knife back?"

"No. And I called her and alerted her to the situation."

"You've got a knife, James. That's a good thing."

"Skip, I had my own knife. Someone put another knife in my locker. Same identical knife. Then I find a knife in the Dumpster. Wüsthof. And, finally, the chef gives me a knife, again identical to my original knife. I find this a little strange. I think somebody is messing with me."

He was right. "Bouvier said he's put the word out on you. I understand his reasoning, but, my friend, you are now a target.

Before, you were just a chef in training. I don't know where we go from here, but I suggest we keep on trucking and talk to as many people as we can."

He nodded. "One more thing, amigo." He pointed toward the door that led to the dining room. "Bouvier's wife walked back in about ten minutes ago."

I hadn't noticed.

"She seems to be here a lot. Anyway, this stocky, short businesswoman, she pulls me aside, grabs my arm with a death grip, and reeking of alcohol tells me that she wants this killer caught. At any cost."

"I had the impression she wasn't happy that you were the one hired to go undercover in her kitchen. Even though you've got credentials. Even though you have kitchen experience."

"I had the same impression. But I happen to be the guy, so apparently she felt the need to put a little pressure on the situation. And she was a little drunk. Just saying—"

I nodded. I knew nothing about her.

"Anyway," James said, "she tells me she has a lot riding on the outcome of this murder investigation. The reputation of the company, the product line, and restaurants. And all the time she's got this vicelike hold on my bicep."

"James, she does have a lot to lose if this murder causes any defection of their customers."

"Oh, she gave me the movie trailer version. Said that this all was happening just as Bouvier is getting the best ratings of his career. Kohl's department stores are getting ready to release a new line of pans, and there's a new cookbook coming out that's all about the magic of Bouvier's spices."

"I don't see how a murder of his sous chef is going to slow down any of those milestones. In fact, the restaurant seems to be doing fine, and my guess is more people will tune into the cooking show. Murders get ratings."

"Yeah, yeah, but you haven't heard the real reason for our rendezvous." He glanced back at the frantic activity of the cook staff. Flames erupting from a pan of lamb chops, the cloud of steam from a pot of clam chowder.

"When she's done giving me the bullet points of their business, she focuses on my eyes and whispers, boozy breath and all, 'my husband did not commit this crime.' She just hit me with that and I'm like—"

"No shit?"

"No shit."

"She thinks we're going after her husband?"

"Sophia said, get this, that she'd heard someone was looking very seriously at Jean. The lady was very concerned for her husband."

"What? We haven't considered him at all. No motive that I can see." I stopped, trying to rationalize the thought. "James, they're paying us. She can't possibly think we are considering him. We work for these people."

James glanced around to make sure we weren't being overheard. "Skip, he goes down, the money train runs out."

"Who told her we were looking at Bouvier? For God's sake, he's the one who hired us. He and the missus."

"She was pleading, amigo. It was like, someone is pegging Jean Bouvier as the killer. That never crossed our minds. Why would Bouvier kill someone who was going to head up his next restaurant?" James just shook his head.

I nodded. It made no sense to me either. Bouvier had too much going on to bump off a sous chef. Didn't he?

"Unless—"

"Unless what?" I could think of no "unless."

"Unless the cops are investigating him. What if it's Ted Conway. For some reason he may be looking into a motive. Maybe the MPD have something on him and are making inquiries. I mean, she might have heard that questions were being asked and she naturally thought they were coming from us."

I nodded. Sometimes James comes up with good ideas. Not often, but sometimes.

"And one other thought, amigo. Maybe she thinks he might have done the deed."

"What?"

"She's concerned he may be the killer and she wants to go on record as defending him."

I intercepted Carlos with a full tray and started scraping.

"James, watch yourself. Seriously. No smoke breaks by yourself, no ducking out back for a phone call. You're a target. Don't play Mr. Macho, okay? I'm serious. Play it safe."

"Yeah."

"I've got to get back to my station, washing the damned dishes, but did you see the Vanderfield guy?"

"Hard to miss. Now there's Mr. Macho." James smirked.

"Well," I was still thinking it through, "Bouvier must have told the staff he was hiring you last night, before you showed up. He only hired you yesterday so he couldn't have mentioned you any earlier than that. Right?"

"So?"

"This Joaquin guy, he wasn't there. Took the night off, unannounced. So he didn't know about you. He probably didn't know that you were hired to take Amanda's place. Am I right?"

"Yeah. So he wouldn't have left the apron and knife?"

"I'm thinkin'."

James glanced back at the cooks, each of them busy at their station. "I'm not going to get that position in South Beach if I don't get back to work."

"Yeah. And good luck with that promotion, roomie." As usual, he was delusional.

James walked back to the grill, giving the brunette pastry

chef a grin. He never turned it off. I just felt strongly that some-one in that operation wasn't all that swayed by his charms. I shook my head, feeling the sweat running into my eyes. It was going to be a long, hot night.

CHAPTER TWENTY

I was groggy the next morning. James and I had sucked down a six-pack after work and I had to force myself to crawl out of bed. A quick shower, a check in the mirror for my daily body evaluation, and a pair of faded jeans, sandals, and T-shirt. The body evaluation didn't go so well. I needed a couple weeks in a gym. I couldn't afford a gym, but it sure would help.

The new sous chef was still sleeping, sprawled on the stained couch where he'd passed out after his third beer, so I borrowed the keys to the truck and drove to the Purple Pelican mall, a small strip of shops on Miami's north side. The Miami heat and the absence of air-conditioning in James's truck was giving me a headache. I wiped the sweat from my forehead as I saw the mall sign ahead.

Pulling into the parking lot, I watched for store signs. The Purple Pelican Bar and Grill anchored the strip of stores on one end with a faded plastic pelican mounted on a pole above the saloon, and halfway down I caught the white flashing neon diamond. Kahn's Jewelers.

Parking the truck, I walked down the sidewalk, hesitating as I stood in front of the establishment. It appeared to be a middle-class operation. Nothing ostentatious, but the window display showed a decent selection of rings, pendants, and necklaces. Of course, what the hell did I know about jewelry? I wondered why Em would ever visit this side of town.

I took a deep breath and walked into the store, hearing the electronic bell sound in the rear. I knew the routine. One person in the back. The bell sounds and they scoot to the front of the store. I'd sold security systems to a couple stores like this one. No chance that I can break a glass case and get out with any of the expensive stuff. But then, why does my mind work like that?

He was moving quickly, behind the counter with Bulova watches and thin gold chains. Brightly colored gemstones decorated the third section of the case as he reached me.

"Hi there, what can I do for you? A new watch? Something for the girlfriend? Maybe a tennis bracelet?"

Sandy-haired guy, about my height and age. He was dressed in khakis and a lightweight sweater vest, and his eyes didn't quite focus on me, just looked off to the side, to his other displays.

"Yeah. I have a couple of questions."

"I can probably help," he said. "Kevin Kahn. Jim Kahn's son." He reached for my hand, and I shook his.

"Skip Moore."

"I've been in this store for over ten years. It's my dad's, technically, but I've been working here since high school, so fire away. You've got questions, I've got answers. I got my education in jewelry at a pretty young age." Lots of nervous energy and too much information. He smiled and raised his eyebrows, waiting for me to make the next move.

"You've got, uh, nice stuff." What are you going to say?

"Thanks. I do a lot of the buying. You tell me what you're looking for, and I'll bet we can find it. If I don't have it, I'll order it for you. Nothing is impossible." He spoke in quick sound bites, his gaze drifting around the store.

"There was a robbery here about nine years ago."

His eyes snapped to focus. On mine. And I could see a question mark. Maybe he wouldn't want to discuss it, but I could tell he remembered. I doubted if you could forget something like that.

"It was a diamond ring. Do you remember?"

His gaze went left, right, and out the door.

"Any recollection at all?"

"Maybe," he said. "That was a long time ago. I don't know. We've had two or three thefts here since Dad bought the place and—"

"Amanda Wright. She admitted to the theft and then it turned out she wasn't the one who took it. Emily Minard was implicated as well. Two young ladies were caught up in this theft and neither one was guilty. You do remember, right? I mean, what was that all about?"

"Look, who are you?"

"Skip Moore, like I told you."

"What's your relation to Amanda?"

"She was killed two nights ago. Were you aware?"

Now he stared at the floor. The guy was acting very strange.

"I saw it online."

"It's just that—"

"Who are you?"

"Skip."

"Why are you asking me these questions? Are you a cop? What gives you the right to come in here and ask these questions?"

"No. No. Settle down." He was obviously agitated. "I'm a private detective. I'm just following up a couple of leads and this robbery is one of them."

"That happened nine years ago. I hardly think that a theft in this store nine years ago has any impact on the murder of a girl in Miami."

"You're probably right," I said. I was actually thinking he really was right. I was fishing. But his nature, his defiance, his shifty attitude had me interested. Bouvier said he went with his gut. I was thinking that the celebrity chef might be on to something. Go with my gut.

"Did you know Amanda?"

This time he focused his entire attention on me. I could feel the heat, his eyes boring into mine.

"Get the hell out of my store."

"I'm simply trying to find out if—"

"Get the hell out of my store. Do it now and I won't call the cops." He stepped from behind the counter and approached me. "Wait another twenty seconds and I will call them and tell them you were trying to steal a diamond ring. I'm very good at convincing the local law enforcement agencies. Do you understand? Do you?"

I did. I walked out and drove out of the parking lot. I planned on coming back, but I had one more stop to make before I did.

CHAPTER TWENTY-ONE

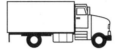

The small stucco block house on East 39th Avenue in Hialeah was sorely in need of a paint job. The once white exterior was a dirty gray color and the red tile roof was broken, with jagged pieces of clay lying in the front yard. The lawn was scraggly and the ground bore large bare patches of dirt and sand where grass should have grown. An overgrown bush pushed its way onto the front porch, barely giving me room to stand there and ring the doorbell. The place was a palace compared to where James and I lived.

I rang it three times. Even though a rusty Ford Ranger and a Volkswagen Jetta were parked in the gravel out front, it seemed that no one was home.

I considered walking around back, but waited another minute. Then I knocked loudly, knuckles pounding on the cheap, hollow door.

She answered it twenty seconds later.

"Yes?"

"Mrs. Wright?"

"Yes."

"I rang the doorbell, but—"

"Like most of the things around here, young man, it doesn't work."

"I'm Skip Moore. I'm a friend of Emily's. I'm one of the detectives who's working at L'Elfe to—"

"Oh, goodness. Please, excuse my manners. Do come in."

She opened the door wider, and I could smell the stale odor of fried fish.

"I am so glad to meet you. The thing about Amanda, it's just," she choked, and I just kept nodding. What can you say? I needed to get my information and leave. I wanted this to be brief.

"Please, sit down." She picked up an armload of laundry from the worn sofa and dropped it on the floor next to a pile of newspapers and magazines. It could have been dirty clothes or clothes just washed, but it was obvious that it had been a while since the room had been cleaned.

"Now," she dropped down beside me, between a sigh and a cry, "tell me what you've learned. The police won't tell me anything. Nothing at all."

I couldn't either. But the question had to be asked.

"Mrs. Wright, was Amanda dating anyone? Anyone from the restaurant?"

She shook her head. "She never told me if she was. But there was something about the way she acted, a little giddy, that made me think she might have someone she was interested in."

"Did you talk to her about it?"

"Well," she paused, "she didn't live here, you know. And we didn't talk that much. Occasionally she'd stop over or call me on her cell phone. Do you think a boyfriend might have—"

"I don't know."

"The police asked me the same thing."

At least I was doing it right.

106

"They asked me to list all of the friends that she kept in touch with. We found a lot of them on her phone and on her Facebook account."

We'd been hired to find out who from the restaurant might have wanted her dead. Thank God we didn't have to worry about everybody else in her life. To sift through someone's Facebook account. And phone. It just seemed to me that the process could take weeks.

"She never mentioned anyone from the restaurant?"

"Skip, was it?"

"Yes, ma'am."

"My Amanda, she was a beautiful girl. Men were drawn to her. She'd tell me about guys who, as she put it, hit on her. And just about everyone on that staff, every male, seemed attracted. She even thought the chef was interested."

"Marty?"

"Maybe. He was the head chef. Am I right? There might have been some flirting going on."

Tears sprang to her eyes and she wiped at them with her hand.

"Everyone liked her. She was such a good girl. Even Mr. Bouvier. I mean, he did offer her the South Beach restaurant." She started choking again and the tears were streaming down her face.

"But nothing serious? She didn't volunteer anything else?"

"I told you—"

We were both silent for a moment.

Finally she sniffed, "That boy, James, the one that Amanda dated, he's working in the kitchen now, right?"

"Yes, ma'am. You apparently told the detective about him."

She looked at me, teary eyed. "I hope that wasn't a wrong thing to do. It just came out. I so want them to find who did this to her."

"I have another question. This may be painful as well, but nine years ago Amanda was somehow involved in—"

"Yes, yes. They asked about that, too."

"Did they ask about Kevin Kahn?"

"What about Kevin?"

"Did your daughter know him well?"

"She dated him. They were very close."

I nodded, recording every word, every thought in my mind.

"At her age," she said, "I thought she might be a little too close to him." She sniffed again, and wiped at her moist eyes. "They were just teenagers."

"Mrs. Wright, were they dating when the ring was stolen?"

"Yes."

"And did they stay together after the incident?" It seemed like a likely follow-up question.

"No. Amanda thought that Emily was going to be blamed for the theft. Emily had been the last one to touch it. The diamond ring, you know. So Amanda confessed, to save Emily. It was a stupid, childish thing to do. Neither of those girls stole that ring. But when Amanda confessed, Mr. Kahn, Kevin's father, told him he could never see her again."

There was something I couldn't put my finger on. Something that brought Amanda, Em, and that cop together again. It was eluding me, but I was going with my gut. I kept pressing.

"I don't mean to impose, but when the ring came up missing, I assume this theft happened in the store. Somebody who was in Kahn's Jewelers walked out with this ring, right?"

"My understanding. I don't know why the girls were looking at a diamond engagement ring in the first place, but it was supposedly on the counter. There was no way Amanda could afford anything like that. Emily, with her family money, could have bought ten of them, I suppose."

She stood up. "Can I get you a cup of coffee? I'm going to have one."

"No, I've got to get going. Can I call you if I have any other questions?"

"Oh, heavens, the police are calling three and four times a day. I'll try to help anyone who can find out who murdered Amanda."

"By the way, when Mr. Kahn showed the girls the ring—"

"Mr. Kahn?"

"Yes. Kevin's father. When he showed them the ring, did Mr. Kahn leave the room for a moment? I mean, the ring was on the counter or the girls were trying it on and—"

"That's my understanding. But Mr. Kahn wasn't there."

"Who waited on the girls?"

"Kevin. Kevin Kahn, Amanda's boyfriend, was the one who was showing the girls the diamond."

CHAPTER TWENTY-TWO

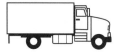

I drove back to the mall, past the once colorful, now faded, purple pelican that stood on top of the bar of the same name, and down to the jewelry store. Riding past the storefront several times, I decided to bag it and headed back to our apartment. I just didn't have it put together yet. Something was bothering me. I felt that Em knew more than she was willing to share, and it had something to do with Amanda's murder. What, I couldn't put my finger on. Somehow I was going to have to push Emily.

James was on the back porch, a tiny slab of stained and pitted concrete that looked directly into the back bedroom of the apartment fifteen feet across from us. He was texting someone and laughing as his two thumbs punched the keyboard.

"What's so funny?"

"It's the girl from Starbucks. Janine. She's sort of interested in going out this weekend, but—"

"But you've got to work. Long nights, late hours. Right?"

"Wrong." He gave me a wry smile. "Nothing on South Beach even starts until after we're closed, amigo."

I nodded. He was right. It's just that I didn't do the nightlife. If I wasn't with Em, I usually went home. To this crappy place. And besides, I couldn't afford Miami nightlife. Drinks, meals, and cover charges were way beyond my financial means. If we went out to anyplace fancy, it was Dutch treat or Em paid. I was in the heart of a huge entertainment center, but I never participated. Sooner or later, one of our schemes needed to pay off.

"The but is she wants to know a little more about me. Like maybe I'm a serial killer or something."

"She's probably going to Google you."

He grinned. "That's my thought." Looking down at his phone, he said, "Let her. No big deal. I mean, there's not much on there about me. Facebook information, and there's stuff about my degree and Cap'n Crab. You know, some credibility about my cooking prowess."

If you're going to enter into a relationship, it made sense to do a background check. The girl was smart. And as simple as a Google search was, I was reminded that we still hadn't checked out everyone from the staff. I'd have to get Em on that.

"Speaking of killers," and we were, "did anybody call about the knife? The forensic unit or Ted, the cop?"

"Mine? You're talking about my knife, or the one that appeared with the apron in my locker and ended up in the Dumpster? Or are you referring to the knife that Bouvier had Chef Marty give me last night?"

Obviously, I was talking about the knife in the locker, but there were a lot of knives in play.

"The one from your locker, James."

"No. I haven't heard anything. I'm not that concerned, Skip. I figure if they want my explanation, I'll hear from them."

I sat down beside him on a worn webbed lawn chair and explained my morning travels. I described the confrontation in the jewelry store and the emotional conversation with Amanda's mother.

"Busy guy."

"Two nights in the kitchen, James, and we still don't have any idea what happened. We've got to get more aggressive. Ask more questions. We can't just wait until something falls in our laps."

"And people will start to get suspicious. It's tricky, my friend. I agree, we're not where we need to be, but like Chef Jean said, we've got to convince the staff of our cover story. We start asking too many questions and—"

"But the positive side is we're getting there, man. I talked to the setup guy, Mikey Pollerno. He got me looking into the boyfriend angle. We know the dishwasher has disappeared. We also know that Joaquin Vanderfield took a hike the night after the murder, and he is pissed that he was passed over for the head chef job on South Beach. I think they all need a background check. We can get all of that online." We really did have a lot of loose ends to work on. "Plus, we should find a way to interview Kelly Fields. Reportedly, she was one of the few people Amanda was close to."

"Ah, the beautiful pastry queen. I may have to take that on myself."

"Keep it professional, James."

He smiled. "I'm a sous chef, Skip. Got to stay in touch with my staff. Oh, and by the way, while you were out harassing a local retailer, I called Em this morning and asked if she'd look into background checks on these guys."

He could read my mind. "Really? What did she say?"

"She was already on it, doing some computer stuff. Some outfit that charges by the name, but she says you can find out if somebody spit on the sidewalk. Pretty thorough."

"I guess you've got to spend money to make money."

"And the sous chef Vanderfield?" A question he was going to answer.

"I don't know what background checks will find, but this guy is brilliant. I don't like him, Skip, but he seriously knows his way around that kitchen. And he can throw a plate together that would be acceptable at Buckingham Palace, in a matter of minutes. I hate to admit it, but this guy would shine as a head chef."

"Really? Because I was getting some seriously bad vibes."

"Last night, he's doing this sauce, and it's like he's almost making it up, calling for butter, sliced button mushrooms, ground nutmeg—"

"James, fine. He's a great chef." I really didn't care about the recipe.

"But this thing with the jeweler, Kevin Kahn, I think you're off on a tangent." He stared out toward the brown water that floated in the ditch behind our complex. Waterview complex. "It's a coincidence that the detective gets involved a second time with Em and Amanda. Just that. A coincidence. There's no way some sixteen-year-old kid whose dad sells diamonds is responsible nine years later for a murder at L'Elfe. No way."

"I'm not saying he killed her, James, but there's something more to it. This thing goes deeper than we're digging. I'm going with my gut on this. And Em refuses to discuss it because she's still protecting Amanda. I can't explain it, but I feel certain that's why she won't share what happened that day."

"Em is protecting a dead girl's reputation. That's your take on this whole thing?"

"It is."

"And you think that if she spills the beans, tells us why she's so secretive, it will be a big clue as to who killed Amanda Wright?"

"I do."

James shrugged his shoulders, hit send on his phone, and stretched out his legs.

"Want to wager?" he asked.

"James, we're talking about Em's friend. Somebody you dated."

"We went out twice, amigo. That's hardly dating."

"You know damned well what I'm saying."

"The jeweler and the stolen diamond have nothing to do with this murder, Skip. Obviously Em doesn't think so either. If that story has anything to do with the death of Amanda Wright, I'll buy beer for a month. If it doesn't—"

"James, I'm telling you, it's not something you can just—"

"Beer for a month, Skip."

I let out a slow breath. "Done."

CHAPTER TWENTY-THREE

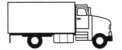

The call came at noon. We'd cracked our first beer of the day when my ringtone jangled and I answered with, "Hi, Em."

"Ted has information on the knife." Just like that.

"Yeah?"

"Yeah. He wants you two to come to the forensic lab and talk to one of the investigators."

"I thought this was an undercover operation. Now we're meeting investigators?"

"Skip, all I know is he wants to meet with you. It's east of the Miami Airport in Doral." She recited the address, and I concentrated hard. Enough to remember it and enter it in my phone.

"When?"

"Now."

James was watching me intently.

"Any chance it was James's knife?"

It was quiet on the other end.

"Meet us, Skip. He'll explain everything." She hung up.

"They've got information, right?"

"They do. And I have no idea what that information is, but you know what I don't like?"

"What?"

"It's Ted. All of a sudden it's Ted instead of Detective Conway or Conway. And she said, 'meet *us*,' like they're a couple. It's just a little strange."

"You're jealous of a cop?"

"A cop who has a steady job, probably a pretty good pension, is a good-looking older dude? Yeah."

"That's his future, Skip." James sipped from his bottle. "It's bland, predictable, and boring."

Slamming the bottle down on the cheap vinyl table, he stared at me, eyes opened wide.

"You, on the other hand, you've got a blank canvas in front of you. The colors, the textures, the patterns, and lines, they haven't even been invented yet. That's what Em finds attractive about you."

"You're crazy. You do know that, right?"

"You, pard, are a work in progress."

He chugged the beer, stood up, and walked into our abode.

I wondered if she had taken a liking to the detective. She was very businesslike in her attitude toward me, showing a different side. Or maybe it was Amanda. Em was still protecting her dead friend. Or her reputation, whatever that was. And maybe that was what was at stake, Amanda Wright's reputation. It hit me that in addition to background checks on the dishwasher, the setup guy, and the pissed off sous chef, I should do a background check on the victim. It would take some extra work, especially considering that there was someone in our group who already knew much of Wright's background. Emily.

As I sat there, I thought about what James had said. My life was like a big blank canvas. That's what I felt like at that moment.

•   •   •

Thirty minutes later, after adding two quarts of oil and ten dollars' worth of gas, we drove to Doral, famous for its golf and spa resort. We passed big homes, lush green lawns with towering palms, and luxury cars parked in circular driveways. The truly elite lived behind tall stucco walls, protecting them from the occasional belch of black smoke that shot out the back of our ancient Chevy truck.

Pulling into the parking lot of the sprawling complex, we walked into the entrance. Conway was standing in the lobby, glancing at his watch and frowning.

"We don't live right around the corner, you know," James said.

The detective simply motioned to us and we followed him down a series of hallways.

"In there," he said.

We walked through a door into a room that reminded me of the kitchen at L'Elfe only much more sterile. Two long stainless tables ran the length of the interior with benches surrounding them. Bottles of colored and clear liquid lined the shelves on the far wall, and Em sat on a stool at the end of the first table. My heart jumped.

"Hi, guys." She gave me a faint smile.

James looked around the lablike room.

"For the experiment to be a success," he said in an eerie voice, "all the body parts must be enlarged."

I knew the movie. *Young Frankenstein.* I gave him the last line. "He's going to be *very* popular."

We both laughed. Em and Conway just stared at us.

"So what's the news?" James had a job to go to this evening. He wanted to get in and get out.

Before Conway could answer, a tall, attractive woman with waves of golden hair walked through the door. Probably early

forties, she gave us a nod and a smile, her lab coat hiding her figure. She laid a clear plastic bag on the table and nodded toward
Ted Conway.

"Gentlemen," the word didn't seem comfortable coming
from his mouth, "this is Cheryl Deitering. She's one of the sci-
entists here at the forensic lab."

She smiled, flashing her perfect white teeth. "As Detective
Conway is lead investigator on the Amanda Wright murder, he
has cleared it that you three can receive privileged information
regarding the findings here."

With gloved hands, she removed the Wüsthof knife from its
plastic bag and motioned for us to come closer.

"This German knife is made from a single piece of forged
steel." She glanced up at me and smiled. "It's a wonderful piece of
craftsmanship and Wüsthof has a sterling reputation." She balanced the knife in her right hand. "It also holds its edge quite well."

I saw James nodding. He knew a little about kitchen knives.

She addressed me. "Do you know what the tang is?"

"Powdered orange drink?"

The smile turned to a frown. "In this case, the tang is the
part of the steel that attaches to the handle. As you can see, it ex-
tends the length of the knife handle and is secured to the handle
with three rivets. This gives the knife weight, balance, strength,
and durability. A cook will find that important when chopping,
slicing, butchering."

And stabbing, I thought.

James was nodding again. The cook who did all those
things, except stabbing.

"As I said, Wüsthof makes a very durable knife, and they go
to great lengths to make the tang and the handle as seamless as
possible. They don't want food to get into the seams, as it will
cause bacteria to grow."

"So," Em spoke up, "there's no way any blood could get between the tang and the handle?"

"Theoretically, no. Especially on a new knife. I've tested brand-new knives and it's almost impossible, after being sterilized, that a Wüsthof or most other commercial kitchen knives would retain any waste products. However—"

She held the knife by the blade.

"This knife has been around the block."

"Used hard?" James asked.

"Very hard. It's probably ten or twelve years old, and what happens is that these rivets and that seal give a little. Every time you cut a lamb chop, cut up a chicken, rock the knife to cut carrots or celery on a wooden cutting board, there's wear and tear on the seal between the tang and the handle. Even with a thorough cleaning, there's a chance to trap food."

"And blood?" Em was looking very closely at the nine-inch weapon.

"And blood." She nodded. "Did you know that forty percent of the murders committed in the United States are done with a kitchen knife. Forty percent."

Shaking her head, she said, "People need background checks to own a gun, but everyone has access to a kitchen knife." Deitering pointed to the handle. "This composite handle will hold fingerprints. And palm prints."

"And you found fingerprints?" I'd assumed as much. After all, that was the original reason for the police to take the knife.

"We did. But in order to find out whose prints they are, those prints have to be in our database. Unfortunately, we only found one set that we could match."

"Who?" The three of us said almost it in unison.

"James Lessor."

He'd been arrested in Islamorada on a suspected murder

charge. He was let out almost immediately, but there it was. His prints were on file and the Miami PD had easily identified them.

"Of course, they were on the handle," he said. "I pulled the knife out of the apron that was hanging in my locker. No big deal."

"Ah, but it is a big deal." Conway finally spoke. "The big deal, Mr. Lessor, is that this knife appears to be the murder weapon. A minute amount of Amanda Wright's blood was found where the tang meets the handle."

CHAPTER TWENTY-FOUR

Once Cheryl Deitering had left, Conway gave us his scenario on what happened. He informed us that the police had totally cleaned out every Dumpster for five city blocks, the night of the murder. It seems that that's where killers throw their weapons. Dumpsters. Go figure. Instead of tossing the knife into the Dumpster, the killer had stashed it in James's locker the next night. Whoever had committed the murder had shoved the Wüsthof through a catsup-stained apron, and stored it there until the following evening.

Now came the tricky part.

"What I can't figure out is why they did that," Conway had said. "I think it was to scare you off. But here was the actual murder weapon planted prominently in your locker. So maybe he, the killer, wanted you to pick it up, get your prints on it, and we'd consider you a strong suspect. And that's exactly what happened. A pro never would have picked up the knife."

Once again, reminding us that we didn't know what the hell we were doing.

"So I'm thinking," Conway said, "maybe the killer wanted

prints on the handle so James would be considered a suspect." He smiled at Em, and I got a cold chill down my spine.

"Except," I pointed out, "James didn't even know about the murder till I told him that night."

"Except," Conway pointed out, "James Lessor is an ex-boyfriend. And James Lessor owns an identical knife. And does James Lessor have an airtight alibi? Where was he the night of the murder? Can anyone back up his story? And maybe he's got motives we may not be aware of."

"What the hell does that mean?" James protested.

"Probably nothing."

"Give me a break. I was home, watching TV."

He couldn't prove that he was by himself that night, and he couldn't deny that Amanda had gone out with him. Within the last several months. But to make him a suspect in a cold-blooded murder? No way. I could tell that Conway wasn't buying it either, but there was that little doubt that still hung in the air. They couldn't convict James. I understood now how someone who was totally innocent might have to defend himself against circumstantial evidence. It wasn't a comforting thought.

"But why did someone throw the knife in the Dumpster? By rights it should never have been found. The trash haulers were going to dump it in the landfill." Em had been puzzled as we all had.

Conway pursed his lips, his eyes sweeping over the three of us. "I wondered the same thing. It was as if they almost knew that we'd check the Dumpsters the night of the murder, so they kept the knife out of sight. Then, after threatening Lessor, they tossed it away the next night. I know, it doesn't make a lot of sense, does it? Hell, if I had all the answers, we'd solve the murder."

James asked him what his next step would be, James actually being agreeable and laid-back in the presence of a police officer.

"Look, I agreed to bring you information in this case. You've now got a lot of what we have. We are going to fingerprint every-one on staff at the restaurant, well, everyone who is still working there. And we're going to put out an all-points bulletin on the dishwasher, this Juan Castro. I think his implication in the mur-der is a long shot, but we're going to find him. We'll print him and question him."

The meeting seemed to be over, and we'd gotten more than we'd given. At least that was my angle.

"One more thing, Detective."

He raised his eyebrow, glancing over at Emily. I didn't like the look.

"Is there any chance you've put Jean Bouvier on your suspect list? As the possible murderer?"

Now he studied me, cautiously weighing what I'd asked and how he should frame his answer.

"As much as I can share with you, which isn't much when it comes to our possible suspects—"

I assumed that was largely because they didn't have any sus-pects, just like the three of us.

"Everyone in that restaurant is a possible suspect. Are we pursuing the chef? At this point we are simply trying, as you are, to define who was there the night of the murder and who may have had a motive."

It was a cagey answer, giving us nothing. They were still eliminating staff members, but why did Sophia think her hus-band was a suspect? I didn't trust Conway. The guy was just a little too slick.

"While you're here, Mr. Moore, why don't we fingerprint you?"

It wasn't a request. It was an order in the form of a request.

I turned to Em and asked her if she'd driven, but she just shook her head and looked away. And then I got it. The detec-tive must have picked her up and brought her here.

"Need a ride?" I asked, already knowing the answer.

Conway didn't stick around for the paperwork. I knew he wouldn't, and I was seething inside.

After my printing, James and I drove back to the apartment by ourselves.

"Not a pleasant situation no matter how you slice it." James smoked a cigarette, flicking the ashes out the window on the driver's side.

"I thought you quit."

"Now's not the time, amigo."

I should have been more worried about the case. Instead, "What the hell was that all about? Ted. Is he going out with her?"

"You two have never been committed. I don't mean to be cruel, but she's taken off before, Skip. She plays by her own set of rules. You know that, but you keep going back for more."

"Yeah." James was right about one thing. Em had taken off before. And I had no idea where or even if she was with someone. But he was wrong about the commitment. Em wasn't committed. I had been committed since high school. If Em had ever shown any sign of a full-time commitment—

"Sometimes I think I should *be* committed."

He looked sideways at me, then understanding I meant to an asylum, he gave me a broad grin. "I've thought that about you too, amigo."

We were quiet for a moment.

"Talk to her about it, Skip. She's apparently going through some emotional thing since Amanda was killed."

And I'd decided that her concern about Amanda was part of it. I concentrated on my conversation with the baker babe and how I might approach her tonight. Screw James. Forget Em. If my girlfriend could play nice with the cop, I could flirt a little with Amanda's kitchen friend. And maybe I could get some answers on this boyfriend thing that kept coming up. Had the dead sous chef been dating someone on staff? The inference had come up a couple of times. And there was the teenage incident with her jeweler boyfriend.

"I'm talking to Kelly Fields tonight. I'll find a way, and I'll get whatever answers there are. I'm the one who's going to talk to her. Got it?"

James glanced at me, and I guess he saw that I was very serious.

"Got it. I'll leave her alone."

CHAPTER TWENTY-FIVE

At our small kitchen table, I pulled up Amanda Wright's Facebook page, staring at the profile photo and the cleavage she displayed. Long brown hair and what almost looked like a pout on her lips.

"Good-looking woman, James."

"Not my type, Skip."

"Hey, she went to our college, Samuel and Davidson." I hadn't known that. "What the hell, dude, she was in culinary arts with you. She was your classmate and you didn't tell me?"

"Yeah." He walked up and was looking over my shoulder. "It's no big deal. I didn't even remember her. She reminded me about it when we went out the first time. Said she dropped out after the first year."

James had done the full four years, barely graduating with a bachelor of science degree in culinary arts.

"She did a year? That was it? A year? Wow. What exactly did your four-year degree cover?"

"On top of culinary arts? Baking, pastry, food service management, and other assorted crap."

"So this girl dropped out of culinary school after a year, and yet she's working a high-end restaurant, given a chance to be the chef in her own kitchen?"

"I know. I know." He buried his head in his hands. "And I'm stuck as a line cook at some fast-food dump. But, Skip, you know how I feel. I don't see the future in it. There's way too much work involved, and we stand a much better chance to strike it rich if we keep our options open."

"Really? You really feel that way?"

I had a business degree, James the culinary background. It had been an early dream of ours to open a restaurant on South Beach, and now we were investigating the death of someone who had come damn close to our dream.

"It doesn't bother you that she was about to be at the top of her game, at her young age?"

"Seriously?"

"Yeah."

"Does that bother me?" James stepped back and looked out the window, staring into the parking lot.

"It does, doesn't it?"

"Yes, it bothers me. Now drop it. What else about her?"

I didn't want to push him any more.

"She's pretty vague about the rest of her background."

"Photos?"

I clicked on photos, and there were just two. Her profile, with the low-cut top and a group picture of the kitchen staff. Dressed in their white jackets, they were all smiling. Bouvier was in the center, his right arm around Chef Marty and his left arm around Amanda.

"Just Google her name. Put cook after it."

I ran it up on the screen and there were three Amanda Wrights. One was a cooking instructor, not our girl, and then there was an Amanda Cook Wright. The third reference was a newspaper article from a suburban journal called the *Dade Gazette.*

I read it out loud.

> *Nathan Brandt, instructor at Samuel and Davidson University, was arrested last night for sexual battery. A student at the institution, Amanda Wright, filed a complaint, claiming that Brandt had taken advantage of her during a student-teacher conference in his office. He remains in Dade County jail on fifty-thousand-dollars' bond.*

We were both silent for a moment.

"I didn't see that coming," James said.

"She was only there one year, and then she dropped out."

"Maybe that's why she dropped out." He was right with me. "Damn, look up the guy and see what happened to him."

I keyed in Nathan Brandt, Samuel and Davidson University.

"There're over one hundred references."

"Check one."

I moved down twenty and clicked it.

> *Nathan Brandt, business ethics instructor at Samuel and Davidson University, will be lecturing at the Junior Service League of Brandon—*

"When?"

"About one year ago."

"Okay, they couldn't prove the charges. He's still there." James straddled one of our two rickety kitchen chairs.

"Or she dropped them."

"You know, there's this growing list of people we need to interview." James was tapping his foot. Checking his cell phone, he stood up. "We've got to go, amigo. Almost showtime."

"*You've* got to go, amigo. I'm not washing dishes for a third night."

"Six thousand bucks and a missing Juan Castro says that you are, friend. And remember, you're talking to the lovely Kelly Fields tonight."

He was right. I was. And I did.

CHAPTER TWENTY-SIX

It started off slow, and I got a chance to share a moment with Carlos, the runner. He walked back into the kitchen and eyed me for a moment. I was leaning against the stainless counter as he approached.

"Juan's not coming back?"

"I haven't heard."

Carlos squinted his eyes. "What I tole you, it was not serious."

"Have you talked to him?"

"No." He was quick with his comeback. "I realize that when I say to you he was interested in the sous chef, you might think—" Shrugging his shoulders, he turned away from me.

"Carlos," he looked over his shoulder, "was there a boyfriend? Was Amanda seeing someone here?"

"You a cop?"

James was right. Asking questions was a dead giveaway.

"Definitely not a cop. I just wondered." Damn, it was hard to ask questions in a nonchalant manner. If you asked a question, it immediately became an inquisition. He turned and addressed me.

"If you're not a cop, Juan was jealous."

"Of what?"

"Of someone in the kitchen who was seeing her."

"He knew that?"

"He ask her if she would go for coffee one night. It took a lot of courage, but he wanted to do it. So he ask her. He's separated from his wife, broke up with his girlfrien' and—"

"And?"

"She told him she was seeing someone."

"It could have been anyone."

"She then tell him it was someone on the staff, and she was very sorry that she had to say no."

"Who was it?"

"Maybe no one. There was no real sign that she was involve with anyone, and Juan tole me that he thought she was just makin' an escuse."

He paused. "There was a rumor. Maybe she got caught outside with someone, but only that. A rumor."

God, I wanted to pursue this. Carlos was giving me some really solid ideas, but I couldn't give us away.

"You said, 'if you're not a cop.' What if I was?"

"This conversation never happen." He walked into the kitchen, and I looked around for the pastry chef.

Five minutes later I heard the commotion. A rise in the volume of voices. James walked back and grinned.

"Staff is stressed. Chef is barking out orders in case you haven't heard."

"Why?"

"The singer Enrique Iglesias and twenty of his entourage just walked in. Chef Jean is apparently on his way down to personally welcome them and apparently Iglesias and company are expecting some extras that are not, I repeat, *not* on the menu."

"That's not a good thing?"

"It's not a good thing, amigo. Stuff that's not on the menu is never a good thing. We earn our pay tonight."

The dishes were slow in coming back, and until the dinner party was finished, I didn't have much to do.

Bright-orange flames erupted like a volcano under pans laden with sauces, vegetables, and meats. I could smell chicken or some fowl roasting in the oven. The staff was scurrying back and forth, barely avoiding each other in the narrow confines. The aroma was that of Thanksgiving, with turkey and stuffing.

Kelly Fields was using a hand torch to brown the tops of a number of crème brûlées and I sauntered over to her.

"Dessert for the star?"

Her gaze never left the fifteen ceramic cups. "He's just another customer."

"I haven't been here very long—"

"Two nights," she said with attitude.

"But I can't believe Chef Jean would leave his home and come down here for 'just another customer.'"

"What do you care?"

"Are you kidding me?" I was getting my courage up. "I'm going to be scraping garbage from a plate used by a very famous person. Pretty exciting stuff."

Finally she glanced up. I saw the corners of her mouth move upward and I knew I had her.

"You are involved in the creative process, Mrs. Fields, but I get what's left over. It may not be glamorous, but—"

She laughed. "You're really a dishwasher?" She gave me a sidelong glance. Somehow I knew that she didn't believe it. It was as if she knew.

"I am. For two nights, as you pointed out. And now, for number three."

"I've met a lot of dishwashers, but you take the cake."

It was my turn to laugh. "Baker's humor?"

"Oh, my God, I didn't even realize—"

I hesitated. I didn't want to push this too fast, but the moment seemed right so I asked.

"Kelly, is there any chance you'd have coffee with me after our shift tonight?"

"Coffee?"

"Just."

"I'm married."

"Coffee. Nothing more."

She stared down at her torch, browning the desserts.

"I'm married. We're separated. Temporarily, but still—"

"Coffee."

"Kelly," Marty shot me an angry look, "where the hell is the brûlée?"

"Right here, Chef." She picked up the tray and walked it to the prep table. Turning back to me, she smiled. "Coffee, right?"

"I couldn't be any more clear."

"It's not that I'm class conscious, but—"

"I get it. Coffee with the dishwasher? Look, I plan on moving up the ladder very soon. You can always say you knew me when."

"I can't." She turned away. "Sorry. If I have coffee that late I can't sleep."

Damn. I'd struck out on the first try.

"Warm milk?"

She gave me a sidelong glance. "Maybe I could do that. Warm milk. That would help me sleep, right?"

"It's a date." I'd actually pulled it off. I was going out with Kelly Fields, and I was going to learn a little more about our victim, Amanda Wright.

James walked over and I could see sweat on his brow.

"Try making duck leg confit and sauce from scratch with a

complementary salad for nineteen and a Chicago-style hot dog for one. First of all, you need raw materials, and frankly, we didn't have them."

"You survived?"

"We did. We had one of the runners, Jimmy Gideon, hitting every restaurant within a five-mile radius. But, he got the stuff, so—" James shrugged his shoulders, obviously elated to have been a part of the excitement. "The sad part is that so far I haven't picked up much information."

"I think you're enjoying this," I said.

"Maybe just a little. But I know it's going to end, so I can revel in the moment. Know what I mean?"

What I knew was this. We needed a lot more work to solve this case.

"And you?" James asked.

"Got some very interesting information from Carlos, the runner, and—"

"What information?"

"Amanda told Juan Castro she was seeing someone on staff."

"Who? For God's sake, who, Skip?"

"The dishwasher told Carlos that he thought she made it up to get rid of him after he asked her out on a date."

"Shit."

"But, there's a rumor she got caught out back with someone, so we can pursue that story."

"Damn. All I got was a slice on my thumb from chopping asparagus."

"And James, I've got a warm milk date after work."

"A what?"

"Warm milk date. I'm having coffee, she's having milk."

"Tonto, you've got a question-and-answer session with the cookie lady. Tell me I'm wrong."

"You're not wrong. I do have a question-and-answer session with the lady. I'm quite excited."

"Ask her about Amanda's sexual battery thing from college. See if that ever came up in conversation."

"James, I'm going to ask her about everything I can think of."

CHAPTER TWENTY-SEVEN

I saw Bouvier and the ever-present Sophia before I left the restaurant. They'd apparently spent some time with the singer and his group, and Sophia had come back to the kitchen just before closing. Dressed in a long black dress and a string of pearls, she seriously reminded me a little bit of Miss Piggy, her eyes somewhat sunken in her plump face, and her wide nose sucking up all the available oxygen.

As she emerged from Chef Jean's office, I caught her looking at me as I walked out the back door with Kelly Fields. She didn't look happy. Maybe there was a policy about dating the help, but apparently Amanda Wright had done it. Oh, yeah, and maybe that's what got her killed.

The coffee and milk date happened three blocks away at a restaurant on Bayshore Drive called NoVe Kitchen and Bar. They are open until three a.m. and the food and drinks aren't bad. Em and I had eaten there before, and when I walked in with Kelly, the waitress acted as if she knew me. Of course, it wasn't the same waitress we'd had, so it was all fabricated.

"Do you have warm milk?" I asked her as we eased into our chairs.

"If Chef accidentally left it out all day."

That was not an option. "Very funny. Can you get me a cup of coffee and my friend a warm milk?"

"Actually," Kelly looked over at the bar, studying the selection, "bring me a beer. Yuengling draft."

I knew we were going to hit it off. "Make that two."

"So, Skip, you're working this profession because you plan on making it big in the dishwashing business someday?"

"There are bigger restaurants than L'Elfe. If I master dishwashing here, I could move to Twenty-One in New York, or Commander's Palace in New Orleans. Maybe the French Laundry in Napa or a Bobby Flay restaurant in New York." James and I had talked about the big guys, we just hadn't visited them yet.

"But you'd miss the warm climate and the friendly staff. Like the pastry chef." She gave me a broad smile, and I felt like I could ask her anything.

"You were good friends with Amanda?"

Her smile disappeared, and as the waitress set bottles on the table, she grabbed hers and squeezed it.

"I'm sorry, if it's not comfortable—"

"Did you know Amanda?" she asked.

"No," I said. "But I've followed the story. James, my friend who's the new sous chef, he went out with her twice. I guess they decided it was not to be."

The lady put her lips together and nodded, as if she understood. Again, I thought she might have figured it out. Then I saw the look collapse.

"Oh, Jesus. What a terrible end to a life with such promise."

"I agree. And you know what's funny?" It wasn't funny at all, but I wanted to ease into the Q and A. "One of the runners came up to me tonight and said that he thought the former dishwasher, Juan Castro, had asked Amanda out. He insinuated she told him she had a boyfriend on staff. Was that true?"

Kelly Fields took a long, slow swallow of beer. A sensual swallow. But I was more interested in her answer than the image.

"She hinted at an affair, possibly in the kitchen. God, it couldn't have been with the little guy at the washing machine. I mean, God love him, but that wasn't her style. She was driven, Skip. The girl I knew would do anything to get where she wanted to be. I was," she hesitated for a moment, "envious. I think most of the kitchen staff was envious. She worked off of, what appeared to be, very little creative talent, but she was always in the right place at the right time. When someone needed something done, Amanda was the go-to girl. Just like that."

"Who was she dating?"

"There were rumors. One that was pretty graphic, but—"

"Who? Who was rumored to be seeing her?"

"I'd rather not. But, it could have been almost anyone, even Chef Marty. And I know that she and Joaquin had a love-hate relationship."

"Yeah?"

She sipped at her beer. "Love may be too strong a word. He'd praise her and in the next breath scream at her. Fire-and-ice kind of a thing."

I made a mental note.

"I will tell you this. When Amanda wanted something, she went after it. She and I had a little problem with that."

"Oh?"

Her gaze shifted to the bar. Apparently there was no more to say.

"I heard that Sophia was trying to keep Bouvier's name out of the list of suspects. Could Amanda have had an affair with—"

"Oh, hell," she snapped. "Amanda could have had anyone. I

figured out six months ago that she got around. You know what I mean?"

I did.

"She was hot. Good looks, great personality, and guys were standing in line. So make a list of anyone who was interested and—"

She was silent for a moment.

"Drew, my husband, and I—we—" She went silent again.

"What about your husband?"

"Forget I mentioned it."

"I told you, my roommate went out with her twice. I know she was a friend of yours, but he wasn't that taken with her. He used the word several times. Clingy."

Kelly Fields stared at the table directly in front of her. With a bitterness in her voice she said, "She was emotional. Needy. She needed someone to affirm her worth."

I waited, drinking my beer, hoping she'd continue. She did.

"You know, she wanted it all. And I guess I somewhat admired that in her. But how she went about it, I'm not sure I could do that."

"What did she do?"

"I never verbalized this, Skip, but she was the kind of girl who would probably sleep her way to the top."

"She slept with Bouvier?"

"I didn't say that. I would have absolutely no knowledge of her relationships. It would be great gossip if I did. No, she never confided in me who she slept with."

She studied me for a moment, then looked away for a second.

"There was one story, but I never heard it backed up."

"And you won't tell me."

"No. But in the past, she gave me little inklings that she used people to get what she wanted."

"Kelly, you don't sound like someone who was her good friend. I mean—"

"I didn't approve of her methods. She only professed to be my friend."

Kelly Fields gritted her teeth.

"Methods? You just said Amanda Wright used people? Is that right? She used them?"

She straightened up and glared at me. "Tell me about your friend James."

"What?" I was taken back. The girl sounded like she was on the attack. "What does that have to do with anything?"

"Oh, I've been involved in some conversations, Skip." There was some fire in her eyes. "James uses people. With women, he can sleep with them and then walk away the next morning, never calling again. Your friend James uses people to get jobs, to make his money, and you, Mr. Moore, you ride on his coattails. You're his friend, just like I was Amanda's friend. So let's not make this a black-and-white case. There are gray areas, here, Skip."

She leaned back and watched me, waiting for my response.

Kelly Fields had nailed it. I was stupid enough not to realize that she and Amanda had shared some intimacy. Amanda had told her about James, long before Kelly had met the chef in training. Still, I had to ask.

"How do you know this? How much more do you know about us?"

"I know why you're asking these questions. Use your head. I was friends, I thought, with Amanda Wright and, as you know so well, she went out with your roommate."

It seriously hadn't even crossed my mind until now. James had told Amanda that he moonlighted as a private detective.

"And hey, it doesn't bother me. I would love for you to solve the murder, but honestly, Amanda never once told me whom she was seeing. Every time it came up, she backed off. The stories were just that. Stories." She squinted, her eyes narrowing as she said the word stories. "I've had a hard time finding middle ground, Skip. Her little dalliances became something I believed in."

I had no idea where she was going with that, but I did understand one thing.

"So you know that we are—"

"Private investigators? Yes. I'm brighter than most of the staff, Skip. I say that with all humility."

She was putting all her cards on the table.

"Do you know that they fingerprinted the staff tonight? I didn't see them print you or James."

I hadn't even thought of that. Who else on the staff would have noticed?

"The only two who didn't ink up."

All of a sudden I was very uncomfortable.

"I'm glad you are talking to me. You need to connect with everyone there, because I think Amanda's entire life was that restaurant, that kitchen. And someone from that life, they took that from her."

Again, the cover had been blown. But I felt we had an ally. Someone who wouldn't spread the word. It was probably a good thing to have someone on the inside of our inside.

"Did Amanda ever talk to you about a sexual harassment charge she filed against an instructor at her college?"

"I remember something like that. There are other things she told me but—"

"What other things?"

She raised her eyebrows. "Even though Amanda is dead, I'm not sure I should be mentioning this."

"Does it have any bearing on her murder?"

"Oh, God, I wouldn't think so."

"So, what was it?"

"Back in high school."

She was taking her time, stretching the story.

Toying with her rich auburn hair, she asked, "Skip, do you have kids?"

"No."

"I do. And I wouldn't trade them for anything. I love my kids so much."

"That's a good thing."

"Amanda didn't have kids."

"I assumed that."

"But when she was in high school, she had an abortion."

"Really?" Was that what Em was keeping from me? And, if so, why?

"She was dating some guy when she was like sixteen or seventeen. I really don't have all the facts, but she got pregnant and his dad paid for her to have an abortion."

I smiled. Not an appropriate thing to do at the moment, but I smiled.

"Do you find that amusing?"

"No." I found it astounding. I found it unbelievable. But I was putting some pieces in the jigsaw puzzle. "Did she ever mention that the boyfriend and the father were jewelers?"

"She just said that he had money."

"I don't know how it fits, Kelly, but I think you've just given me a link."

"I hope it helps. Now, I've really got to go."

"Hug your kids tonight."

"I always do," she said.

CHAPTER TWENTY-EIGHT

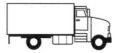

I was supposed to call James. He was going to drive over to pick me up, but instead I walked two blocks to The Grand Condominiums where Em lived. Nodding to the two uniformed doormen, I walked into the huge marble-tiled lobby. As I approached the desk, I suddenly stopped.

What was I going to say to her? Accuse her of not telling me something that might be important to the girl's murder? I wasn't sure what Kelly Fields had told me was tied to the killing. I was still filling in the blanks, still mulling it over in my mind.

I could ask Em what was the deal with the cop. Was she all of a sudden romantically interested in the guy who'd tried to prove she was guilty of grand theft? I wasn't sure I wanted the answer.

I turned, walked outside, and called James. I couldn't fault Em for getting tired of waiting. Waiting for me to get a little more focus. Waiting for me, as she sometimes put it, to grow up. To get out of James's shadow.

Kelly the baker had figured it out, and she didn't even know me. She'd said something about riding on James's coattails. And it was pretty much what I was doing. Pretty intuitive. Pretty sharp lady.

Thirty minutes later, as I sat on the curb, James pulled up in the white monster.

"Why so glum, chum?"

"Just thinking."

"Em's building. So you two talked?"

"Nope. We will."

I filled him in on most of the conversation with the Fields lady.

"Whoa. Amanda Wright is knocked up at sixteen, gets an abortion, then when she's twenty she files a sexual battery charge against a college instructor?"

"The kid's dad paid for the abortion. I was wondering if somebody paid her off to drop charges against the teacher."

"Skip, you're talking about Em's friend. You're making her sound like some sort of—"

"Wondering, James."

"And you can't go to Em and say something?"

I couldn't. Not yet. I wanted something tangible to present to her. What I wanted was to solve the murder.

"It's not our job to investigate this lady, Skip."

I'd thought about that, too.

"Our job, the reason we were hired, was to clear the restaurant staff. Bouvier wants to know if someone from L'Elfe was responsible."

"Yeah. Well, it seems to have taken on some other dimensions."

He nodded as he lit up a cigarette and was careful to blow the smoke out the window, not at me.

"I'm not saying don't go after it, amigo. I'm just saying that we need to concentrate on that kitchen staff. And so far, we haven't made much headway."

"There's a reason she was murdered. So, I'm thinking we find that reason, and we'll know if someone from the kitchen staff, the restaurant staff, was involved."

"Nothing wrong with approaching it from both sides," he said.

"One more thing, James."

"Only one?"

"When Kelly Fields said Amanda would sleep her way to the top, I think it adds another suspect to the mix."

"That's all we need."

"Jean Bouvier."

"Pard, I don't care how much she wanted something, can you picture her having sex with the elf?"

I didn't want to.

"So you're saying that Bouvier may have killed her because—"

"Maybe she was blackmailing him?"

"Only if she slept with him."

"And maybe Sophia suspects that Bouvier killed her. And that's why she is so insistent that we don't consider him. She's adamant that we don't go there."

He was quiet for a long time, and I reached for the radio. Then I remembered it quit working a week ago.

"I think it's a long shot, pard."

We drove in the warm humid night air, both windows down. Mainly because the air-conditioning didn't work and because my window wouldn't roll up.

CHAPTER TWENTY-NINE

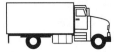

I heard James's phone ring at seven a.m. Rolling over, I pulled the pillow over my head and tried to ignore it. I could still hear him as he finally answered on the fourth ring.

The one-sided conversation was hard to follow.

"Hello?"

Silence, then, "The *L'Elfe Two*?"

More silence and, "You want me to what?"

Even though I prayed for quiet and another hour or two, I obviously wasn't going back to sleep anytime soon.

"Chef Jean knows this?"

Getting out of bed, I walked to the kitchen and grabbed the orange juice from the refrigerator. I checked the smell test to see if it was spoiled, then gulped a mouthful from the spout. Sitting down at the kitchen table, I reflected on what I'd learned last night. What about Amanda's sexual past could lead to her murder? I still hadn't figured it out.

"Hey, chief, you're not going to believe this." The hangover effect seemed to have left him and he was as chipper as usual. I, on the other hand, not so much.

"What? They're giving you the South Beach restaurant after just three nights on the job?"

"Not quite. But close."

"What's close?"

"Chef Marty pulled a little disciplinary action on our friend Joaquin. He pulled him from Bouvier's party boat detail tonight. Mr. Vanderfield will not be working this evening."

"Party boat?"

"It's a dinner cruise boat. He named it *L'Elfe Two*. Not very original, but apparently people pay a lot of money to eat his food on the water."

"Okay, what does that have to do with you?"

"Chef wants me to be the number two guy on the boat tonight. Number two, amigo. Pretty cool."

I shook my head. "Chef Marty doesn't know you're not really there to work the kitchen."

"No." James shot me a look. "What he knows is that Bouvier told everyone I was the heir apparent to the new place, so he's figuring, why not try me out on the boat. I'm sure Marty is going to watch me to see if I have the talent or the magic to make this happen."

James smirked. He was in on the joke.

"And I guess Bouvier approved it, so there wouldn't be any question about my ability and skills."

"And you don't really know what you're doing."

James opened the refrigerator and pulled out the orange juice. Without checking on the expiration date he slugged down two or three swallows.

"Skip, I've surprised myself. I actually am working almost up to speed. I've helped a couple of the cooks with their sauces, made some suggestions and decisions, and even got involved in baking some bread with Kelly last night."

"James, we're here to catch a killer."

"I'm supervising, advising, and last night I introduced my red wine plum sauce with cloves and Dijon mustard. Get it, dude. Bouvier's kitchen was serving my plum sauce. It doesn't get much better than that."

"You get it, dude. Play the role but keep in mind what we're here to do. Got it?"

"One night on the boat, Skip. There will be a couple of the kitchen staff, four from the waitstaff, and, get this, the group that hired the cruise have asked for Bouvier and Sophia to join them."

"High rollers."

"Very. I mean, in the food chain, you don't get much higher than celebrity chef Jean Bouvier."

"So, you're cooking for the boss and some big shot party?"

"Chef said you were invited."

I blinked and tugged at my boxer shorts. "As a member of the party?"

He smiled, rolling his eyes. "Hardly."

"What are they going to do without me back at L'Elfe one? I was beginning to think no one else knew how to run the damned dishwasher."

"Don't be bitter, son. We'll still be hanging with Chef Marty, two of the cooks, and four waiters. It will give us a chance to talk a little to Marty. You did say that Kelly mentioned that it was possible Amanda even had an affair with him."

"What the pastry chef said was that Amanda could have had her pick of anyone on the staff, even Chef."

"Skip, while we're one on one with Marty and two other cooks, Em can be working on the backgrounds of Joaquin Vanderfield and Juan Castro. We're still covering all the bases. I liked that line the cookie lady had about Vanderfield and Amanda. They had a love-hate. What do you make of that?"

"I don't know, but I'll check with Em and see how far she's gotten on her computer checks."

He had a point. Em could be doing some legwork while we worked the dinner shift. And working on a boat sounded like a lot more fun than spending another night in that hot pressure cooker of a kitchen.

"What the heck."

"Great. It's an easy gig. Most of the cooking is done at the restaurant. He says we simply warm, serve, and clean up."

I was pretty sure who was going to clean up.

"You call Em, I'll let Chef know we're on board."

"Literally."

I dreaded the call, not knowing what to say to her about my insecurities, but I plowed ahead. She picked up on the third ring.

"Skip."

"Can you talk?"

"Of course."

"I didn't know if you were busy."

"I'm not."

That was a positive sign.

"What's up?"

"Well, James and I have been invited, summoned rather, to appear on Bouvier's party boat tonight."

"*L'Elfe Two*? That's supposed to be quite a yacht." She was tuned into the elite, sophisticated scene. I'd never heard of the ship.

"Yeah. And Chef Marty is going to be there. Last night I had a chance to talk with the pastry chef, Kelly Fields, and she, in a roundabout way, suggested that possibly Marty or Joaquin may have had an affair with Amanda."

"Oh, really?"

"Yeah. And, of course, Joaquin Vanderfield is the guy who the kitchen staff thinks had a reason to kill her."

I didn't want to say that Amanda Wright could have slept

with the entire staff. That's not what Em would want to hear. Two of that elite kitchen staff didn't seem overwhelming.

"So, I wondered if you'd had a chance to look into Joaquin's background or if you found out anything about Juan Castro, the dishwasher? Excuse me, former dishwasher. You have intimate knowledge of the most current dishwasher."

Em didn't laugh. She didn't even pause. "I have information on the dishwasher and Vanderfield. Both of them have somewhat of a checkered past."

I had thought the same thing about the sous chef victim. Amanda. Definitely a checkered past.

"And?"

She was silent for a moment. A moment turned into sixty seconds.

"Em?"

"Skip, Ted has been pushing it a little bit."

I wasn't ready to hear this. Ted. I hadn't mentioned him. I had dreaded bringing it up, and here she was, volunteering information.

"He's called several times, and I've tried to keep it all business. We've had coffee, you know? But he wants it to be a little more friendly. He picked me up and took me to the lab. I couldn't lie to you about that. You knew it right away. And, Skip, I'm not sure how to deal with it."

"What about you? Do I even want to know how you feel?" She knew how I felt. There was no question. "Are you encouraging this guy? For God's sake, Em, help me out here."

"I'm flattered, Skip. Come on, you've met him. He's an attractive guy. Maybe a little old for me, but—"

"He does nothing for me, Em. Sorry."

In the silence that followed I remembered she had said "but."

"But what?"

150

She sighed. "By my staying close, he's sharing things with me about the case. Things he probably shouldn't be sharing."

"What's close, Em?"

"Not that close, okay? God, you're sounding like a sixteen-year-old high school boy."

"So what's he sharing with this closeness?"

"One thing he shared, someone has called the coroner's office several times asking if they've released the autopsy report yet."

"So?"

"I'm not sure of the significance," she said. "Ted just said it's unusual that an anonymous caller would make multiple contacts."

"Have they done the autopsy?"

"They have, but the results are still kept under wraps."

"So there might have been more than just a stabbing? That's what they're going for, right? That there might be another cause of death?"

"I don't know, Skip, but it might be important. And I don't know if you heard, but they printed the staff last night." Kelly had mentioned it. If I hadn't talked to her, I wouldn't have even known.

"They already have our prints. So what's this privileged information?"

"There seems to be at least one other set of prints on the knife."

"Whose?" This could be the key to the investigation. Marty, Vanderfield, or Castro? Whoever had left it in James's locker could be the one who stabbed Amanda. But I was certain the case was much more complicated than that.

"They didn't match anyone on staff."

"Somebody whose prints aren't on file anywhere?" My prints

were now on file. And if James hadn't had some bad luck in Islamorada, his wouldn't be on file.

"That's what it would seem."

"So where does that leave us?"

"James is a person of interest."

It was my turn to be shocked. "Get out." I was sure I hadn't heard her right. "Somebody actually called him that? A person of interest? I thought Conway was just running the idea through his head. Now they're on record as thinking James may have killed her? My God, Em, are they crazy?"

"Settle down and listen to me. They're looking into it. James comes up as someone they are interested in."

"Em, that's totally impossible."

"I know that, Skip. Believe me, I know, but they've got the knife, they've got the blood on the tang, they've got the prints, and they've got a relationship. Plus, he was home alone that night with no one to back up his story." She paused for a moment. "I wish I'd never set the two of them up on a date."

"What, are they going to arrest him? This is absurd." This was the best that Ted could come up with? What an idiot.

"It's a lead at this point, Skip. I don't think they are seriously pursuing it, but Ted did say those four famous words. *A person of interest.*"

James was going to be so happy.

CHAPTER THIRTY

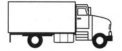

If I told him, he'd go crazy. If I didn't tell him, what kind of friend would I be? It was a dilemma I didn't want to face. James was doing early prep work for the boat party, so I dropped him off at L'Elfe. He phoned me three minutes later.

"Dude, Joaquin isn't speaking to me."

"Dude, I don't blame him. You're taking his place."

"Seriously, Skip," speaking in a hushed voice, "this guy is creeping me out. He's got that plastic holster with two knives in it and he glares at me every once in a while, right hand on the handle. Like a cowboy with his hand on his six-shooter. This could be the killer. I seriously feel it."

"The only motive we've got is Amanda being advanced to head chef."

"Love-hate affair, Skip. Kelly Fields said so."

"She was a threat to his career, James."

"And now it's me. I'm the new threat. I'm the decoy, bringing in the real ducks. This guy may be psycho."

"And you're taking his place on the yacht tonight. Which sounds like a plum job. Am I right?"

"Hey, the guy didn't show up for work one night. That's about the worst thing you can do in this business, Skip. They can't trust him." He paused. "Looks like you've been missing a lot of work lately." He waited for my comeback.

"I wouldn't say I've been *missing* it, Bob." A quote from that very funny movie, *Office Space.*

"If I don't make it to the boat tonight—"

"Check out Vanderfield's alibi?"

"He's pissed, Skip. And he's making me very uncomfortable."

"Duly noted, James, but as you pointed out, on the positive side he's one hell of a chef."

I hung up and drove to Kahn's Jewelers. Parking several stores down, I strolled by the plate glass window and gazed inside. A thin, balding man was waiting on a young man and woman as I opened the door. Walking in, I stood there for a second, and the guy looked up and smiled.

"I'll be with you in a couple of minutes, young man."

The son wasn't there.

Browsing the watch case, I glanced at the older man, showing diamond rings to the pimply faced kid and his pale girlfriend. The same thing that happened nine years ago, only it was his teenage son showing a diamond ring to two young girls. One of those girls, apparently knocked up by the kid. Was he trying to impress them with the jewelry? Showing off the expensive ring?

Seiko watches, Timex watches. With a look over my shoulder, I watched the pasty blonde girl try on one ring, then another. The engagement was going to cost the boy plenty. She held her finger out, studying the effect, then looked at the young guy for approval. He just looked scared.

I wasn't quite sure what I was going to do when they left. Confront the owner? Tell him I knew about Amanda and the abortion? And it still didn't tie in to the murder. James was right, I was chasing something that had nothing to do with our mission. We were hired to clear, or implicate, someone from the restaurant. I should let it go.

But Em was involved. She'd been accused of theft several years ago, and it happened right here. And the kid and his father were part of the case. And Em refused to say anything. My curiosity was getting the better of me.

These two kids were planning a life together, the ring, their symbol of—and then it hit me. Not a major revelation, but Amanda's boyfriend, this wet-behind-the-ears sixteen-or seventeen-year-old teenage Lothario, Kevin Kahn, had been proposing to Amanda. With a ring that he probably couldn't afford.

Amanda knew what was in store, or maybe she didn't. But she brought her friend Emily along. And Emily was excited to be a part of it all. So there she is, trying the ring on too. Both of them. Maybe the old man walked in and confronted them about playing with inventory. Or, maybe the kid was distracted by another customer, and the girls left the ring on the counter where someone could steal it.

Or maybe, and I was just thinking, maybe Amanda actually did steal it, or accepted it. If it was being offered as an engagement ring, why wouldn't she take it? But the kid was still trying to keep the pregnancy from his father, so he tells her to keep it quiet for the moment. It was all my demented imagination, but it seemed to make sense. Speaking as someone who was sixteen not that long ago, I know that there's a lot of confusion at that age. Oh, hell, what am I saying? There's a lot of confusion at *my* age.

Amanda takes the ring, puts it in her purse, the old man finds it missing, and he confronts his son. The kid confesses to showing the ring to the girls, protects his pregnant girlfriend, and says Emily must have walked out with it.

I'm making it up. Trying to find a theory that makes sense to me.

"Now, can I help you, young man?"

I look up from the Seiko Ladies Date dress watch.

"You've got good taste. The Seiko ladies watches are a great value."

He gave me a gentle smile. Someone who dealt with young couples on a regular basis most of his adult life. Only he'd had a problem with one young couple. He'd had to spring for an abortion, and maybe, just maybe, he'd forced the accusation of theft on my on-and-off girlfriend.

I studied him for a moment, hoping that if I became a father, I wouldn't turn out like him.

"Just killing some time."

Turning around, I walked out of Kahn's Jewelers, hoping never to go back.

CHAPTER THIRTY-ONE

The one-hundred-foot yacht accommodated sixty people, and we were easily at maximum capacity.

"You will bus the tables, relay any requests to me, and keep these customers happy. Is that understood?"

Chef was very matter-of-fact.

"I can take care of that. No dishwashing machine, right?"

"No." No levity, only a businesslike attitude. "However, you will scrape the remains off the plates and be responsible for getting all of the dishes and silverware to the kitchen when this cruise is over." The kitchen being the cramped closetlike space off the main cabin.

James came up behind me, his holster and chef knife strapped to his side.

"Dude, they brought Mrs. Fields on board. She's out there icing individual desserts. And listen to this. Lil Wayne is part of the party. More celebs on the horizon. How cool is this gig?"

"We're trying to catch a killer, James."

"No reason not to revel in the moment, Skip."

I didn't believe that Lil Wayne had anything to do with Amanda's murder. What I did believe was that James was too hung up on celebrity and was missing the focus he needed to solve this crime.

Peeking into the dining area, I saw the hand-rubbed cherrywood and polished brass trim. Fresh flowers graced each table and I wondered if the setup guy, Mikey Pollerno, had been aboard.

They stood in clusters, drinks in hand, and cigars lit, the tips burning brightly. Young guys and girls, whites, blacks, Hispanics, drinking colorful cocktails, sporting dress shirts, shimmering spangled blouses, some in tight jeans, girls in form-fitting dresses with flowing hair, and the largest diamond rings and earrings I'd ever seen. And those were on the guys.

"That could be us, amigo."

If I made that kind of money, I wouldn't blow it on rings and earrings. I'd already made that pledge to myself.

James watched from over my shoulder as we admired the DJ from Club Play South Beach seamlessly mixing the tunes with a heavy backbeat. An Hispanic bartender shook a silvery cocktail shaker over his head and one of his assistants popped a bottle of Bollinger Blanc, a champagne that supposedly is one of the best made.

"We're going to be there, pard. We're young, we've got time."

It was funny, but I didn't feel like I had time. I needed to put some focus in my life, make something happen. I needed to solidify my relationship with Em. And I needed to find out who killed Amanda Wright. If I figured that out, then things with Em could be normal again. Maybe normal wasn't good enough. Better than normal.

I saw Kelly Fields, complete with chef coat and toque, handing out fancy pastries in the shape of maybe seahorses. I couldn't tell. She glanced up and nodded at me.

James sauntered back into the kitchen, and I walked out into the party, tray in hand. Grabbing empty drink glasses, wine goblets, and delicate demitasse cups, I carefully stacked them. Napkins, small china plates with smeared sauces and pieces of sausage and breads were the remains of hors d'oeuvres that twenty minutes ago were spread in an elegant seashell effect on a sparkling glass buffet table. Meats and cheeses that would make a gourmet meal for working-class stiffs like James and me simply whet the appetite of these rich folks. There had to be an easier way. Playing busboy as a cover for undercover detective work, and making six thousand for two weeks. That was chump change for the assembled. My guess was they were all making six thousand a day, an hour, a minute.

I deposited the soiled plates and glasses in a tub in the kitchen and looked around for James. No sign of him. Chef Marty was barking orders, stirring a pot of something, and looking as sour as was humanly possible.

Walking back into the party area, I noticed the booze was flowing freely. One of the uniformed bartenders was making short work of a pineapple as he cut slices, fitting them perfectly on the rim of a dozen piña coladas. This is a bash that James and I and Em should have been invited to.

"Hey, man, pretty cool party, huh?"

I looked up, and up. Lebron James smiled down on me. I remembered the line from Wayne and Garth in *Wayne's World*. "We're not worthy, we're not worthy." Nodding, I wordlessly walked away. I sort of got what James had gone through with Lil Wayne. Heroes that you admire are even more imposing in person.

I made another sweep of the room, noticing that attendees were starting to sit at their assigned tables, entourages with their personal celebrities, producers, media giants, and hangers-on at their special tables. I only knew this because there were small place cards with names and titles. There was no card big enough for "Skip Moore, busboy, dishwasher, private investigator, personal security salesman."

"Hey, Moore."

I spun around and saw Chef Marty calling me from the swinging kitchen door. I put a final drink glass on my tray and headed toward the door.

"Where the hell is your friend Lessor?"

I had no idea.

"The guy gets a choice job, and then what? Hits it for a cigarette break?"

James wanted the gig. He would never take the break unless he had information on the case, and in that case he would cell phone Em and give her a heads-up.

"I haven't seen him. I've been a little busy picking up after your high-stake partiers. Maybe he's in the head?"

"If you see the son of a bitch, tell him he's about to be fired. I need some support back here and he decides to take a powder."

Just another reason our careers weren't going anywhere. Another reason I should unhitch my star from my roommate. James was totally irresponsible. And I wasn't far behind. Where the hell could he be?

I made my way to the upper deck, where a handful of partiers had congregated. The sun had set and the water was black, like shimmering coal. The ship was moving, but very slowly. Inches, almost like a slow drift. Standing at the brass railings, watching the lights of Miami in the distance, these people seemed to be a little more romantic, a little more introspective. Picking up the plates, the glassware, the utensils, and napkins, I scouted the area for James. No sign of my business partner. Upstairs, downstairs, he had to be on the ship. I'd talked to him ten minutes ago.

Trudging down the steps, I almost spilled my tray of remnants when a party of revelers came racing up in the opposite direction, screaming nonsensical words at the top of their lungs.

Dodging the herd, I flattened my back against the wall of the cabin, eyeing each one of them in hopes James was in the pack.

"Moore, in my office."

It was Chef Jean, whose only official function was to be host of the party. And as I followed the short, stout cook, I wondered how much smaller his office on this yacht could be than the size of his L'Elfe restaurant office.

Much smaller. The room was tiny. Postage-stamp tiny. Barely enough room to turn around. Chef sat behind the desk. I stood.

"I had to play along with having you and your partner work this cruise, but I thought Lessor would be professional enough to do the work."

"Chef Jean, he is professional. He's working on the murder case, but I know him well enough to understand that he takes his kitchen duties very seriously too. He's into the cooking thing. And I can't explain where he is right now. Believe me, he wouldn't blow this opportunity for all the tea in China."

My mother used to use that phrase. I have no knowledge that the Chinese drink that much tea or manufacture that much of the beverage.

"Marty wants him fired. Give me a good reason to keep him in the kitchen, Eugene."

"Because you want to know who killed Amanda Wright."

He sighed. "I do."

"Then let me find him. He may have a lead that had to be followed, but I'm sure I'll produce him in the next hour."

James didn't have a lead. He would have contacted me. Hell, he would have shouted it out to the crowd at the party. A smoke break? I don't think so.

"Find him. In the next ten minutes. Do you understand?"

I don't know where I got the guts to say it, but I did.

"Chef, I understand that Marty is pissed off. When someone abandons his post, everyone else has to pick up the slack."

He nodded his chubby face.

"But, you? You own this company, right?"

I sensed hesitation. He squinted his eyes and looked away from me, toward the door to his mini-office.

"Well?" I didn't really need the dishwasher gig. Confront the boss and take the chance of never scraping a plate again.

"I'll take care of Chef Marty." He studied the mahogany desktop.

"And I'll find James. But you've got to understand, everything we're doing is working toward closure. I'd love to report to you that your staff totally checks out, but they don't. There are a lot of problems with this staff. First of all you've got a setup guy who thinks that Amanda was pushy and self-serving, a missing dishwasher who had a crush on her, and a very disappointed sous chef who is not happy that Amanda Wright was promoted to head chef of her own restaurant. He's also not happy that you told everyone James was next in line. Plus," I finally took a breath, "there's a feeling that she was seeing someone on your staff. Your pastry chef, Kelly Fields, says Amanda hinted at a romantic fling. Amanda even told Juan Castro that she was seeing someone, but we have yet to figure out who that person might be."

He looked up at me and blinked. "An affair? Really? Someone actually believes that she was having an affair with someone from my staff?"

I just shrugged my shoulders. I'd gotten the impression it was almost common knowledge.

"I don't allow that in my kitchen."

"It's what we heard."

Bouvier let out a breath and pursed his lips.

162

"I'm not saying that it's not possible, but—"

And I wanted to tell him his wife was even involved, telling James that she feared her husband was a suspect in the murder. Which was suspect in itself, since we weren't aware anyone was even considering Chef Jean.

"I'll take care of my end." The little chef stood up. He pointed to the door and I exited. I'd bought myself a little time, but my roommate had better show up soon. James was once again the major thorn in my side.

Walking into the kitchen, I saw Sophia in a sparkling silver gown, her ample back to me, dressing down the guy who was making the salads.

"Two tomato slices, and they should balance the plate. I want a memorable presentation. Do you understand? *Two*, not three." She turned to me with a scowl, drink in hand. "And where's your friend the sous chef?"

I wondered who really did own this company.

I also wondered where James was. It didn't take long to find out.

CHAPTER THIRTY-TWO

The polished teak deck that surrounded the yacht was emptying as the revelers searched for their seats in the main cabin. I walked the deck to the rear of the yacht where there were no lights. The rising moon cast a golden shimmer that bounced over the rippling water, and I could barely make out what lay ahead. As I rounded a corner, I heard the voice screaming.

"Man overboard."

I froze. It had to be James. Not the voice, but the actual body. The man overboard was James. I knew it.

Sprinting toward the sound, I saw one of the uniformed deckhands toss something into the water. It settled on the surface as a floodlight flashed on the inky sea, blinding me for a moment.

I closed my eyes and reached for the railing. Opening them I could see someone flailing in the water, grabbing for the life ring buoy as it floated just beyond their grasp.

"Quick," yelled another deckhand, "toss another one. Somebody with better aim this time."

Through the air the round buoy sailed, this time hitting the bobbing body on the head. The swimmer appeared dazed, and I was afraid they were going to let this life ring move out of range. And as I watched, eyes wide open, the body went under. For a long moment there was no motion, nothing except two life-saving rings floating on the water and that brilliant light, bouncing off the shimmering surface.

"I'm going in," yelled a deckhand who was stripping off his jacket.

I should have. I'd been on the swim team in high school and the person wasn't that far out, but I think I was still in shock, realizing it might be James.

Then, with a lunge, whoever it was broke the surface and grabbed the second white lifesaver and hung on tightly as two men in white pulled on the rope, dragging my business partner through the water. No doubt about it, it was James.

There was applause from the assembled guests as they moved to the railing to watch the rescue.

He looked like a beached white sea mammal, dark hair matted over his face and his skin pale as a ghost.

As they pulled him from the bay, he grabbed the ladder and shakily climbed on board.

"What happened?" A man who appeared to be the captain of the vessel approached him.

James glanced at me, shivering as a deckhand wrapped a blanket around his shoulders. Still shaking, he shook his head slightly and said, "I tripped. I'm embarrassed to say, I tripped."

The captain pointed to the gate where guests walked on to the boat. "Was it unfastened?" Walking to the hinged metal gate, he grabbed it and pushed. It held firm, not moving an inch.

"I don't know." James brushed the wet hair from his eyes, as another deckhand offered him a large plush towel.

A crowd had gathered, guests from the party interested in

the latest diversion. It was probably a once-in-a-lifetime experience. I mean how many times in your life do you hear someone shout, "Man overboard?"

"There's a stateroom to your left," the captain took him sternly by the elbow and guided him away from the gathering. "We'll get you some dry clothes."

I followed close behind.

Once inside the room, the captain opened a closet with a wardrobe of white uniforms.

"You can shower there," he pointed to a bath area, "and change into one of these." He seemed to notice me for the first time. "You're a friend?"

"Yeah. Roommate."

Spinning back to James, he said, "Tell me what happened, young man. Accidents like this do not take place on my boat."

I sensed the hesitation in James's voice.

"I don't know. I came out from the kitchen for a smoke break, leaned against the gate, and it swung open and—"

"I thought you told me you tripped."

"Sort of. Look, I'm safe, and I'm sorry for any disturbance."

"Disturbance? I don't think you understand what's happened here. First of all, we have to file a report and there will be an investigation. This isn't simply a small accident." He wore a scowl on his face as he seemed to go over a mental checklist. "The Coast Guard, the Miami Police, they'll all have to be notified."

This was going to be a black mark on a ship's captain who apparently had a stellar reputation. And I gathered there would be paperwork. Lots of paperwork.

"Get your shower, change, and I'll be back." He turned with military precision and walked toward the door.

"Hey, Captain."

The man turned his head, pulling on the brim of his cap.

"I could have drowned."

The scowl was replaced with a serious frown. He paused as if waiting for the timing, then spoke.

"You didn't."

He continued out the door.

"What the hell, James?"

"I was pushed, amigo."

"No."

"Yes."

"You're positive." I was surprised to realize that I wasn't surprised. We both knew there were people who weren't happy with James working for Bouvier. Still, attempted murder was a pretty serious charge.

He glowered. "Somebody's hands at my waist, shoving me through that gate. It wasn't fastened, Skip, and when I hit the water, I think I blacked out for a second."

"How long were you in there?"

"I don't know. I don't swim well, but when you see your life leaving in the form of a large, white luxury yacht, you swim like hell and yell at the top of your lungs. A lesson in survival in case this ever happens to you."

I thought for a moment.

"My question should be, what the hell were you doing out there?"

He nodded, a knowing look on his face. "I was summoned."

"Summoned?"

"You and I were talking for a moment, and when I went back to my station there was a note from one of those sticky pads. Somebody'd stuck it on my cutting board. Just a scrawled message saying 'meet me on deck by the gate in five minutes. I have some information.'"

"Signed by?"

"No signature. I thought maybe Marty or the big guy himself."

"It couldn't have been any of the people we consider to be suspect. Juan Castro, Joaquin Vanderfield, they're not even on board. So who?"

James was dripping in the bathroom, taking off his clothes, and running the shower.

"You told me that Kelly Fields said Amanda could have been screwing Chef Marty. Didn't you say that?"

Sighing, I told him, "What I said was, Kelly simply alluded to the fact that Amanda could have had her pick of guys. Mrs. Fields didn't feel there was a real good chance that the sous chef was doing it with Juan Castro. I think she said the dishwasher wasn't Amanda's type. So she said that Amanda could have even been having an affair with Chef Marty. It was like, she could go right to the top."

"Well, Chef Marty is here. On board." He started to step into the shower, then stopped.

"You know, Skip, she was damned good looking."

"I agree."

"But getting her choice of men? I don't get it. I mean, I may not be the best judge of people, but I went out with her and I didn't see it. She wanted your undivided attention. It was almost her job to make you fall in love with her immediately."

"There are guys who apparently are looking for that."

"Guys who are desperate. Guys who aren't happy with their lives." He stepped into the steamy stall, and I walked outside. Chef Jean was rounding the corner.

"Jesus, what the hell happened, Moore?"

"An accident, Chef. That's all it was."

"Well, he's going to cause more problems than the two of you are probably worth." He turned and headed back to the main cabin. I watched him halt and look back over his shoulder. "This may have been a big mistake. Hiring you two."

Six thousand bucks, slowly sinking in the sunset. "Chef Jean,

I just gave you a damned good reason why we should stay on this case. We know who the players are. One of them may be Amanda's killer. Maybe none of them are. But, we're following every lead. We want this killer caught as bad as you and your wife do."

Bouvier and the captain of his ship, worried about the stain on the boat's reputation. Worried about the news that would by now be Twittered all over the world, and worried about its effect on business and the success of the restaurants, the spices, cutlery, and pots and pans.

I'd been worried about James's life. If there was one thing this case didn't need was another murder.

CHAPTER THIRTY-THREE

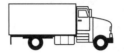

It was time to come clean. At least it seemed that way to me. I needed to confront Em about the jewelry store diamond ring heist, and the professor who had been accused of sexual battery. James and I also needed to tell Detective Ted Conway that James had been pushed from the ship. His life had been threatened. All hands on deck.

"Skip?" She picked up on the first ring.

"You heard?"

"Oh, my God. Apparently, the boat's gate wasn't secured."

"Apparently, he was pushed."

She was quiet for a moment. "So someone has tried to implicate him with the knife, and now they tried to kill him?"

"Either that, or scare the hell out of him. I think they may be trying to get us off the case."

"Are you really that close to solving it? I mean, we haven't got any solid clues. Why would someone try to kill him? Unless they thought he was a lot closer to solving the murder than he is."

I closed my eyes and pictured her face. Soft blonde hair framing her cheekbones and that wide-eyed innocent look.

"We need to talk."

"Great. I've got some stuff on Joaquin Vanderfield and Juan Castro. Where do we meet?"

"How about your place?"

"Maybe someplace neutral."

Either Ted was staying over, or she was afraid I would want to. Either way, it was not a good sign for our relationship.

We met at a small café four blocks from L'Elfe. Em had an iced vanilla latte. I had a coffee, black.

"Juan Castro lives in his car."

She cut right to the chase.

"What?"

"At least he did. He parked the car in the L'Elfe lot overnight. He'd sneak in when Mikey Pollerno would open to do the setup and he'd take a shower in the locker room. It was his home for several months."

"And you learned this from?"

"A little bit from Ted," she said sheepishly. "He let some of it slip. It seems they arrested him for vagrancy once after he started work there."

Cops had records of things like that. We didn't. But then, we had Ted. Or Em did, so we weren't totally in the dark.

"And I did a background check on our Juan. He's been in trouble for petty larceny, for peddling some grass, nothing serious. But his address always came back to the same address as L'Elfe. So I started checking around. He drove a beat-up 1996 Dodge Intrepid and it was always there."

"Really." I knew how it felt to drive a beat-up clunker. But Castro's car wasn't in the lot anymore so at least his vehicle ran. Mine was still waiting for a new battery.

"It turns out some of these restaurant guys are nomads, Skip. They move around a lot. I wouldn't be surprised if there wasn't at least one other person in that kitchen who's considered homeless."

"Do you think Chef Jean knew?"

"I would think that Marty knew. Bouvier, he is too removed from the day-to-day stuff, and he's got other restaurants to worry about. I don't get the impression that he's that hands on."

And I was immediately reminded of Sophia Bouvier, who was screaming at the salad guy on the yacht. That seemed pretty hands on to me.

"What about Joaquin Vanderfield? Anything on him?"

She nodded and sipped at her fancy latte. We hadn't decided who was going to pay yet, but her drink was around six bucks. Mine, a dollar twenty.

"Get this. He graduated from Le Cordon Bleu in Orlando."

"No kidding."

"He did. Near the top of his class."

"My God, Em, Le Cordon Bleu is a big deal. I mean, Amanda dropped out of a second-tier school after one year."

"Yeah. Don't let James hear you call his alma mater a second-tier school." She shook her finger at me. "Anyway, this guy is apparently a top-notch chef, but his attitude got in the way."

"With all due respect to your friend, Amanda, I would think that Joaquin had a reason to be upset." I would have been pissed off as well, but the idea that his anger led to her murder was stretching things a bit.

"It's worse than that." Em took another sip, set the cup on the table, and leaned toward me. Her voice was softer now. "He got into it with a sous chef in Sarasota at a place called Darwin's. The ruckus caused quite a stir."

"What happened?" I took a gulp from my coffee and felt the caffeine start to do its job.

"Darwin's apparently is a pretty good operation, and they had this sous chef named Andy Potts."

"Potts? Works with pots and pans?"

She didn't return my smile. "This Potts was the kind of guy who was very much a hands-on supervisor. Sometimes he'd take over a cook's station if he thought things weren't moving fast enough or if he thought the quality was suffering."

"And?"

She looked over her shoulder as if she was afraid someone was going to hear her. "Joaquin Vanderfield is known for his temper. He's the one in the kitchen who will throw a pan at the wall, or swear loud enough for the dining room to hear him curse." Em sipped her beverage. "Throwing a pan against the wall is not tolerated in a professional kitchen, at least that's what I've heard."

I was sure she was right.

"Anyway, Vanderfield became enraged when Potts called him out on a dish he was preparing. Apparently Potts didn't think a dish was prepared correctly and he announced it to the kitchen. Words were exchanged, along with some shoving, and Vanderfield went after Potts with a knife."

"No."

"Oh, yeah." She nodded emphatically. "According to reports, he pushed him against a wall, held the knife to this neck, and told him that if he interfered with his cooking again he was going to slit his throat on the spot."

"What happened?"

"Ten minutes later Joaquin was out the door, looking for another job."

We both sat there, letting it soak in. Here was a guy with some anger-management issues who had threatened someone's life when all they did was offer some constructive criticism. How would Vanderfield react when he thought someone was taking away a job that belonged to him? I flashed back to my first sight of the feisty cook, his dark brooding look, three-days' growth of beard, his knife strapped to his side, and his obvious contempt for Chef Marty. Yeah, this guy was one to watch.

"So what do you think?" She stared at me from across the table.

"We've got nothing."

"Yes, but we're starting to build a case. A little more about Castro, a little more about Vanderfield, and maybe we start seeing some progress."

"What's up with Ted? What else has he shared?"

"Not that much."

I paused. I didn't want to ask. Didn't want to sound like some college kid with his first serious girlfriend who was asking inappropriate questions.

"Em, you and Ted, have you—"

"Slept with him?"

I sheepishly nodded my head, hoping she wouldn't answer.

"No." She shook her head, seemingly embarrassed that I had even asked. "I don't go to bed with the first attractive man that asks. I would hope you'd know me better than that."

"I wasn't suggesting—I just thought—hell, Em, I don't know what to think. You and I are on two different paths and it's not always easy to—"

As I spread my hands on the table, she put hers on top of mine. "Skip, I think he's working toward that, but it's not going to happen. I am not going to let it happen. There are a lot of emotions going on inside, but I care for you more than you think I do. Let's not go there again."

I let out a breath. Inside, I was cheering.

"I needed some perspective, Skip. Sometimes this thing with you and me, it just seems to go nowhere."

I was afraid the next question would queer the relationship altogether.

"I've got another question."

"What? I just told you that I am not screwing around. That

should be enough questions and answers for one session, don't you think?"

"Under normal circumstances. But these aren't normal circumstances."

Em sighed, brushing at some imaginary speck on the tabletop in front of her.

"What's your question?"

"Before I ask—"

"Skip, ask the question. I don't need qualifiers. If you ask, then it must be important."

It was as if she already knew what was coming.

CHAPTER THIRTY-FOUR

"Who stole the diamond ring from Kahn's Jewelers?"

She shook her head. "I promised myself I wasn't going to revisit that story, Skip. Can't you respect that?"

I reached out and touched her hand. She immediately withdrew it, burying both of her hands in her lap.

"I think it's important."

"Well, I don't think it is."

A stand off.

Em looked into my eyes for fifteen, twenty seconds, studying them.

"How much do you know?" she asked. "Or I should say, how much do you think you know?"

"I talked to Amanda's mother."

"Oh, Jesus. No. She's vulnerable. How could you do this? She doesn't even know the story, Skip."

"I gathered as much."

Em grabbed for her purse, pulled out a ten, and laid it on the table.

"Let's take a walk."

She'd picked up the tab, so it was her call. I followed her out the door into the dewy Miami night.

We walked a city block. No words were exchanged. Dim streetlights highlighted a laundry, a boarded-up restaurant, and a twenty-four-hour FedEx business center.

"You see, it's not important who stole the ring."

"I talked to Kevin Kahn."

"What? You what?" She spun around and stopped in her tracks. Looking at me like she'd never seen me before, she said, "Do you have any respect for our relationship? Behind my back, you talked to these people?"

"He threw me out of his store. What the hell happened, Em? I thought I knew you. Apparently, I don't know you at all."

She covered her face with her hands.

"There's something in that story that is important. What is it?" I needed to know. Even if it meant a rift in our relationship. "If it reflects on Amanda, then maybe there's something there. Something that we can use to understand her better."

"Oh, I understood her." She said it in a sarcastic tone of voice as she turned and started walking.

"I thought she was your friend. The way you just said—"

"Do all your friends play by the rules?" Raising her eyebrows she looked at me in the streetlight. "I'm reminded of one of your best friends."

"Somebody else just asked me that. Kelly Fields. The answer, of course, is no. And you're right, James is a good example."

"Well, Amanda didn't always play by the rules. But she was a good friend, a listener, and loyal. So I let things slide."

"What things?"

"Her relationship with Kevin Kahn. His father did not approve. She was from the wrong side of the tracks, you know what I mean?"

I was from the wrong side of the tracks. Way down the

tracks. Of course, I understood. But I didn't want to bring up the abortion. That was up to Em if she wanted to go there.

"They were sixteen, and getting pretty serious, and his dad was ready to put his foot down."

"Come on, Emily. We're talking about kids. Sixteen year olds. I mean they were just kids. I had the hots for you back then." I still did.

"We weren't serious, Skip. You and me. At least I wasn't. As I recall, we weren't even dating then, were we? These two were inseparable."

"So what? They were going to get engaged?"

"He told her he wanted to show her something at the store. Kevin was working by himself on a Saturday and he invited her to stop by. I think she did that often, and when there were no customers in the store there was some fooling around in the back office. I'm pretty sure she told me that."

"Kinky."

She shot me a look.

"So, for whatever reason, she asked if I wanted to tag along."

"Well, obviously there wasn't going to be any fooling around with you there, was there?"

"I'm not sure that I wasn't supposed to be the lookout," she said sheepishly.

It sounded to me like she'd done that before. Another side of Em I hadn't seen. Helping young lovers with their sex lives.

"Anyway, we get there, no one else is in the store, and he opens up a case and pulls out this gorgeous diamond ring."

"You were right there?"

"I was. And he was showing off. A sixteen-year-old kid with access to this expensive piece of jewelry. He asked her what she thought of it. Can you imagine? She was wide eyed. So was I. And she was like—it's beautiful. You know, to two sixteen-year-old girls, any diamond was beautiful."

I nodded, not really knowing at all. I wondered if I'd ever be able to afford one for Em.

"He starts stammering a little, like he wants to say something. Finally, he blurts it out."

"What?"

"Will you marry me?"

"Sixteen?"

"He wants to put the ring on layaway. I know, it sounds idiotic. What guy in his right mind would consider this? He was—they were—so young. It was romantic, yes, but marriage? Come on."

"You said his father wouldn't approve. He was dead set against it. Even against them dating? Am I right?"

"He didn't approve. But Kevin didn't care. He was in a jam and only wanted to do what was right."

She paused, obviously not comfortable in telling me the rest of the story that I already knew.

"She'd told him she was pregnant, Skip."

I took a deep breath and nodded.

"And Kevin Kahn wanted to make sure that he was totally involved in her life. Her life and the baby's life."

So she'd confirmed Kelly Fields's story.

"I had a feeling that was the case." I shouldn't have admitted that, but I told Emily everything. I always had.

"Oh? You knew?" Em looked at me with the question in her eyes.

"When I talked to our pastry chef, Kelly, she'd said that Amanda told her some rich guy had paid for her abortion. I thought that it was probably—"

"Jim Kahn?"

"Yeah."

"Then maybe you can fill in the rest of the story, since you've apparently been looking into it since the beginning of this investigation."

"Em, I want to find Amanda's killer, just like you do."

She was quiet for a moment. Thinking the situation through. I'd shared my every thought with this girl for almost as long as I'd known her, and it was becoming obvious to me that she was reluctant to share hers with me.

"The ring came up missing."

"Missing?"

"When we left, the ring disappeared."

The rest of the story was about to be told.

"The value was well over two thousand dollars. Kevin Kahn told his dad that he thought I was the last one to hold the ring. This guy who was dating my friend told his father that I must have stolen the ring. Do you believe it? What kind of a person would put someone else in jeopardy like that?"

I had no answer.

"I was arrested at home the next day, and as soon as Amanda heard, she raced down to the police station and confessed to the theft."

"Really?" This story, that I thought I knew, was spinning out of control.

"Really. She knew I hadn't taken it. There was absolutely no way I would have even considered that."

"So she stole it? Amanda took the ring?"

"No. Kevin didn't want Amanda taking the rap, so he then claimed that he'd left the diamond ring on the counter. He told the authorities that he now remembered it was there when Amanda and I left the store, and he finally announced that a stranger walked in and probably walked out with it. There was a lot of confusion, but Amanda and I were both cleared."

"So, who stole the ring?"

"I told you," she had that exasperated tone to her voice, "it doesn't matter. That's not the issue."

"What is?"

"The fact that Amanda had admitted to being pregnant. And Jim Kahn, Kevin's father, wanted nothing to do with her or any baby that she and his son had made."

"So he buys the abortion."

"He gave her the money and told her in no uncertain terms that she was never to come back to his store or his son."

"Pretty harsh words."

"They were."

How could anyone consider killing off their unborn grandchild? I thought about the jeweler I'd talked to and his love-struck son. All of a sudden I had a different perspective of them. The kid, I could understand. He was head over heels in love with Amanda, but the father? A real piece of work.

"What did she do?"

"Oh, there was a tearful goodbye, and Kevin tried to talk her into keeping the baby, but she told him she didn't want the wrath of his father, and she impressed upon him that they were probably too young to get married anyway. And then she walked away."

"And she got the abortion."

"No."

"She had the kid?"

"No."

"Em, you're not making any sense."

"She was never pregnant, Skip. She made the whole thing up just to snag Kevin Kahn. When the father paid her off, she put the money in her pocket and walked away."

"You knew? Back then?"

"No. I didn't have a clue."

I breathed a sigh of relief. I couldn't believe that Em would have bought into this kind of deception.

"I assumed she got the abortion and so I kept it all quiet because she was my friend. I even volunteered to take her to the clinic."

"I didn't see that one coming."

"Neither did I, Skip. We were having a talk one night when she mentioned something about ripping off Kevin Kahn's dad. When I asked her about it, she laughed and said she'd never been pregnant in the first place."

"Damn."

"Yeah. I know. She was devious."

We headed back to her car.

"Why couldn't you tell me this?"

"I was arrested for theft."

"You didn't have anything—"

"And Amanda confessed so I could walk away."

"Still."

"Skip, I was embarrassed, not only because of the arrest, but embarrassed to be friends with Amanda. Yet she stood up for me. I didn't ever want to visit this story again, okay?"

"Em, she put you through all of this."

"She put Kevin Kahn through all of this."

"Did she steal the ring?"

"No. I'm certain she didn't."

"How do you know?"

"Because I know who stole it."

"*Now* you're going to tell me?"

"Kevin Kahn. He offered it to her a year later. He was still passionately in love with her."

CHAPTER THIRTY-FIVE

We slept late. James was the first up and I heard him making coffee in the kitchen about ten feet away from our bedroom in the cramped quarters we called home. It was time to make some money and move.

I struggled to my feet, pulled on a pair of jeans, and walked into the living room. "Are you okay?"

Standing there in just a pair of cutoffs, he handed me a cup of milky looking coffee and I inhaled the aroma. Some cheap instant, but caffeine nonetheless.

"Room service. Really good, isn't it?"

I sipped it and it tasted like bitter dishwater. "Very good," I said. "You went through a lot last night. How do you feel?"

Throwing himself down on the threadbare sofa he said, "A little rough. I've got some sinus problems and—" he hacked long and loud, "cough. Some water still in my ear, but other than that, you know—"

He'd actually finished his shift on the boat. Here was a guy who would skip on a regular job if he had the chance, but he went back and finished the gig. James was actually showing a little responsibility.

"Lil Wayne actually walked into the kitchen and shook my hand. Pretty cool, Skip."

"James, it's getting personal. Now someone is trying to take you out."

"Tell me who pushed me. I'll be happy to agree with you. Whoever did that, that's the killer."

"It's very possible. Maybe this whole thing that Chef Jean came up with will actually work. We'll flush the killer out because Bouvier told the staff you were a new sous chef in training."

"Joaquin Vanderfield." James closed his eyes for a moment. "I would have bet on him."

And I told him what Em had discovered about the surly sous chef.

"He threatened another sous chef with a knife, man. Over in Sarasota. Violent kind of guy."

"Dude, he wasn't there last night. On the boat."

"No. Not that we know of."

"What, you think he was a stowaway?"

"Stranger things have happened," I said.

"What about the dishwasher?"

"Castro? Em doesn't hold out much hope. She thinks he moved on to another job. I guess dishwashers don't last too long at any one place."

He smiled as he sipped the coffee. "You, my friend, may hold the record for moving out faster than any of them."

"Look, I want to get this killer. Then I'll retire my wrinkled hands from the steamy, soapy water."

"Pally, I'm going to do some research on Chef Marty. He was obviously on board last night, and if Kelly Fields says that Amanda could have been sleeping with him, I want to know if it happened. Executive chef had the perfect opportunity to sneak out and push me overboard. Let me work on that today."

"And I'm going to find another Amanda Wright conquest."

"Yeah? Who's that?"

"Someone who I'm sure will not want to revisit the past. Nathan Brandt. The guy she accused of sexual battery."

James smiled and nodded. Draining his cup of lukewarm coffee, he said, "I always thought that was what powered a vibrator. A sexual battery. But I could have been wrong."

James isn't always the funniest guy in the room.

CHAPTER THIRTY-SIX

I didn't figure a phone call would get me an appointment, especially if I told him what I wanted, so I visited the campus of Sam and Dave University. A cold call was worth a try. Ever since the sixties, the school had been nicknamed Sam and Dave, and every student at Samuel and Davidson had to know the melody and lyrics to "Soul Man," the song made popular by the vocal duo Sam and Dave. Even as a joke, it was a prerequisite.

James was busy on the Internet trying to find a little background on Chef Marty, and he'd gladly handed me the keys to the truck. I say gladly because the white monster needed gas.

"Needs a couple quarts of oil too, amigo. Oh, and Skip, while you're buying the gas and oil, get some WD-40. Those doors are going to work a lot better."

I had about fifteen bucks on me, but I filled up with enough to get me a round-trip.

Nathan Brandt's schedule was online, so I knew where he'd be. Samuel Hall was a building where I'd taken most of my business classes, and the old stone steps leading up to the heavy, paneled glass doors were familiar. We'd had some good times while we were there. Maybe we would have done a little better if we hadn't had such a good time.

Having seen his picture online, I knew what to look for. Late thirties, shaved head, about six feet tall. He was the last one out of class and he was accompanied by a mousy brunette wearing tattered jeans and a T-shirt announcing her affection for Velveeta processed cheese. There was the familiar yellow box pictured on her chest with simply the word "Cheesy" underneath. I thought it was.

The short girl was looking up at him, possibly pleading her case for a better grade. As they passed me in the expansive, marble-tiled hall, I turned and followed at a respectable distance. I hoped the conversation would be brief. It was.

"Professor," I stopped him, "can I have a word with you?"

Never having had him in class, and not really knowing much about the man, I'd decided not to pretend I was a student or to manufacture some lame excuse to talk to him. Either he would agree to discuss the charge of sexual battery or he wouldn't.

"What can I do for you?"

"Give me five minutes of your time."

He glanced at his watch, and I realized the age difference. I didn't wear a watch. Neither did James. We used our cell phones. A lot more accurate and a lot more convenient. Em wore a watch, more as an accessory, jewelry, than anything else. This guy still used his wrist.

"Okay, five minutes. Are you in one of my classes?" He was studying me, trying to figure out if he knew who I was.

We continued walking, I assumed to his office. He must have thought I knew where we were going.

"No. Not at the moment. I was a student here about three years ago."

He did a quick turn and there we were. Inside his tiny cubicle.

"Now, what did you want?"

"Professor Brandt, I'm Skip Moore."

I stuck out my hand, but he made no effort to shake it, so I withdrew the offer and concentrated on my short speech.

"I am a private investigator looking into the murder of Amanda Wright. I would like to ask you a few—"

"Get the hell out of here."

I hadn't expected the interview to be this brief. But I'd seen the interview with Kevin Kahn cut short when I mentioned Amanda's name, so it didn't totally surprise me.

"Professor, this is simply—"

"I'll call campus security."

I wondered if there was such a thing. If there had been when James and I were students at the school, we would have been arrested a number of times.

"Look, I'm not here to open any wounds. Okay?" Poor choice of words. "Amanda was murdered several days ago and I'm simply trying to—"

"What are you insinuating?" He was ghost white, his hands clutching at the desk calendar in front of him.

"I'm insinuating nothing." I wasn't sure that I shouldn't put this guy on the front list of suspects. He was paranoid from my opening statement.

"Then why are you here?"

"I want to find out who killed Amanda Wright. And you have a history with her."

"Oh, yeah. A history, you call it? Kid, you can't imagine what kind of history we have."

"Well, I wanted to explore that."

"Let me be very brief about your exploration. The girl is, the girl *was*, serious trouble. And now, after she's gone, I still have to deal with her?"

188

Brandt spread his large hands on the wood-topped desk in front of him.

"She ruined my life. She lied to authorities, and damn it," he pointed his index finger at my head like the barrel of a gun, "she should have been prosecuted for what she claimed. But for all the fairness in our litigious society, she remained above the fray. What are you even doing here? Are you suggesting I had something to do with her murder?"

Both of us still stood, Brandt on his side of the desk, me still in the doorway. I was afraid the guy might come over the top to get me.

"No. Nothing like that. I'm trying to figure out what she was like. I thought if you'd talk to me maybe I could understand her a little better. Get into her head and possibly that would help me find her killer."

Finally, he sank into the swivel desk chair, staring at his hands.

"It doesn't matter anymore." His voice had gone from combative to subdued.

"What doesn't matter?"

"The whole thing."

"You're still here, still employed. You're doing seminars, I even saw where you recently had a book published on business ethics. I mean, it doesn't sound like your life is too bad."

"Ever been accused of something you didn't do?"

Almost everything I'd been accused of, I'd actually done.

"We had an affair." The fight seemed to have left him and he let out a slow breath.

"She wanted it to continue and I called it off. I've admitted all of that."

"So this was the way she paid you back? Accusing you?"

He nodded.

"She got mad, furious is more like it. Threatened me, told me she'd ruin my career and it came down to a matter of he said-she said. She couldn't prove the charges and as there were no witnesses—"

"It just went away, or did she drop the charges?"

"Why should I tell you this? You're a detective, go look it up."

He looked up at me and shook his shaved head.

"All right. You want to know what happened, it's there for anyone to see. She dropped the charges and dropped out of school. I have not seen or heard from her since then. Of course, I was surprised at the news about her murder. I hated the girl, but I wouldn't wish that on anyone."

There was not much more to ask, but I needed his answer to get this thing straight in my head. "One final question."

"That's it."

"I know. This is the last one. When she dropped the charges," I wasn't sure I could go through with it, but it seemed like the logical conclusion, "was there any compensation?"

He stood up and came around the desk as I backed out of the cramped office.

"I think it's time for you to leave."

"If there was even a request for money, it might follow a pattern. Just a yes or no and I'll never bother you again."

"Damn straight you won't. Get the hell out of here. Leave. Now."

I started down the long corridor, hearing my steps echo off the walls. The hallway was eerily empty, and I figured everyone was in class. I hadn't really found out what I wanted to know. Either he was never going to tell anyone, or I just hadn't asked the right questions.

"Kid." I turned, and he was still in the doorway watching me, the scowl etched on his face. "Don't come back."

"I won't. You won't hear from me again." I had no intention of visiting this place again. I didn't need this kind of aggravation. Maybe I'd find a job as a retail clerk or insurance salesman, but I didn't need this kind of pressure.

"Kid."

"Yeah?" I didn't want to hear any more. I felt certain the guy had been set up, and I was just picking at old wounds.

"It's complicated."

His voice was barely above a whisper. I had to strain to hear him.

"When something as meaningless as that happens, when you are just having a fling with someone of the opposite sex, and then you realize it's not only a mistake, but that fling is going to cost you everything that's important in your life, you'll do just about anything to make it go away. Almost anything."

"Did you make it go away?"

There was a long pause as he took a deep breath.

He nodded. A confession that he'd kept bottled up inside.

"I did. I did."

CHAPTER THIRTY-SEVEN

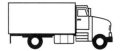

With my last couple of bucks I bought the cheapest WD-40 I could find and sprayed it heavily on the door hinges. It made the inside of the truck smell even worse than it normally did, but I was amazed at the difference. The doors weren't that much easier to open, but there were almost no squeaks and squeals.

As I walked into the apartment, James was scowling.

"Why didn't you tell me?"

"What? What did I leave out?"

"That the cops were seriously looking at me as a person of interest."

I had left that out.

"It didn't seem that important, James. Em said that Ted Conway mentioned it to her, but she didn't think they were serious."

"Well, they're on their way over to sweep the truck."

"You're kidding, right?"

"No. They found some fibers on the body, and they can't identify them. Hell, it couldn't possibly be anything from the truck."

"No, no way."

Now I felt like shit. I should have told him.

"Listen, James, I saw Amanda, I talked to her that night. But even then, Em drove and I didn't do so much as shake her hand. There's no way any fiber, or whatever was at the scene, came from our vehicle."

"Well, they're apparently not having much luck with the case if they're down to vacuuming my truck. I mean if that's the best they can do—"

"Did you pick Amanda up in the truck? When you took her out?"

He hesitated for a moment. "Yeah, but that was months ago, and I can't believe she still had fibers from a three-month-old date."

"Stranger things have happened."

"Em stopped by. I told her about the truck and that's when she told me that the cops considered me a person of interest."

"Listen, there's no way you're going to get implicated. They're just covering bases. What did Em want?"

"Wanted to talk to you. She said there was some friction between the two of you and she was hoping to talk it out."

I let out a deep breath.

"What I learned today isn't going to make it any easier." I needed to debrief him on my meeting.

He leaned back on the sofa and I eased onto the recliner. "Amanda Wright had an affair with Brandt. When he tried to break it off, she filed charges of sexual battery. He fought it."

"Dude?"

"His story. She can't very well refute it at this time."

James folded his hands. "You know, that doesn't surprise me. I told you she was a needy little girl. The woman was out on a limb."

"Charges were dropped, James."

"And you found out why?"

"First of all, Brandt said there was no proof. But she could have kept it alive and done even more damage to his reputation. Instead, she dropped the charges."

"I'm waiting for the payoff, amigo."

"Surprise, James. That's what it was. A payoff. Brandt pretty much told me he'd paid her to go away."

"Wow. And how close were Amanda and Emily?"

"She's admitted that Amanda wasn't the nicest girl in the world, but I don't think Em knows all there is to know."

"And if you tell her—"

"It just strains our relationship."

"So, you're going to keep it quiet?"

"Nope. You just got pissed because I held back the thing about person of interest. I'm going to be open with her. No more secrets."

They showed up twenty minutes later, two gloved officers with forceps, tape, and an official search warrant. I'd never seen one before, so I examined it thoroughly, then passed it to James while one officer tapped his foot and kept looking at his watch.

"We don't have all day, guys. And we do have the official warrant."

"Signed by a judge and everything," James said. "It says here you can only search our truck, am I right?"

The impatient one nodded.

"And you're going to vacuum the floor? Because," he said smugly, "it needs a good cleaning."

"There you are out of luck. A vacuum picks up too much extra stuff. We use tape and forceps. That's it."

The cop opened the door to the truck and sniffed. "What, you sprayed WD-40?" He spun around and stared at me, his forehead creased with a frown.

Standing on the blacktop, James looked at me and smiled. "You did it, pard. Lubricated the doors."

"Look, you probably know that the lubricant will hydrate the fibers in the carpet, but if these fibers match the ones on the body, we're going to know it." The cop smirked. "You can't mask it, pal. We'll know." He turned to his task.

Pressing the tape to the floor, the officer then lifted the sticky cloth and deposited the gray tape in a paper envelope. His partner pulled fibers up with his forceps. In a matter of minutes they were done. As the two of them climbed into their car, the driver turned to us and said, "Nice try, guys. But seriously, we'll know."

I couldn't believe it. They thought we were trying to mask the fibers in the carpet with a lubricant. Maybe they really were going to make a case against James. With me as an accomplice.

CHAPTER THIRTY-EIGHT

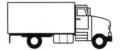

"I've been doing a little research on stab wounds," James commented as we drove to L'Elfe.

"What did you learn?"

"Men stab overhand. Women stab underhand."

"Bullshit."

"No, no, Skip, there's a reason."

A breeze was blowing through the open truck windows and I could smell the salty fish odor coming from the bay as we drove down the road.

"What's the reason?"

"Guys are taller than women. It's that simple. Guys are stabbing in a downward motion." He took his right hand off the wheel and made a downward stab. I was glad when he put it back on the steering wheel as the truck swerved.

"Because the woman is shorter than he is. And because he is going for the heart."

"God, I wish I didn't even know this."

"Women, when they are stabbing a guy, are stabbing upward. Toward the heart. Therefore, underhand."

"The heart is most often the target?"

"It is. The heart and the neck. Most killers know that the heart will bleed out, that, and severing the carotid artery can also cause massive hemorrhaging."

"How do you find the heart?" I knew it was on my left, and if I concentrated I could hear it beating—sometimes—but I would have been guessing if I was trying to identify it with the point of a knife.

"Doesn't matter, Skip." He stared straight ahead, one hand on the steering wheel, one hand out the window, the ashes of his cigarette blowing behind us. "Anywhere in the chest can cause someone to bleed out. Big thoracic blood vessels cover almost as much area as the heart."

I was impressed. James had gotten to the heart of the matter, so to speak. But I wasn't quite sure what it all had to do with our murder investigation.

"But we're not worried about that. We're not worried because our killer stabbed Amanda in the stomach and abdomen."

"And that means what?"

He tossed the cigarette and we pulled into the parking lot. I looked around for a '96 Dodge Intrepid, hoping that Juan Castro had come back to wash dishes. That didn't seem to be in the cards.

"I'm not sure what it means. It could have been, like, a guy who kept the knife in his hand, arm distended, and he just walked up to her and stabbed her from that position. I mean, I can picture that. Arm hanging down, you just walk into someone."

Again, something you don't want to imagine.

"Could have been a woman. Stabbing up, this person might have been a short woman."

"Like Sophia Bouvier."

"Bite your tongue. That's the hand that feeds us, pal. But yeah, someone of that stature."?

"What about depth of the wound?"

"We don't know how deep the wounds were. And apparently it's hard to tell, because the skin and other organs compact and contract as soon as they are invaded." James reached across the seat and grabbed his chef's jacket.

"Think about a five-inch knife. Five inches, and you stab someone. As you push into their abdomen, you can probably feel the cavity give another three or four inches. Maybe more. So," he paused, probably for dramatic effect, "you could get a nine-inch-deep cut on someone's torso with a five-inch blade. And apparently there is so much blood, that until the body is totally drained, the actual length, depth, and other damage done by the stabbing is almost impossible to decipher."

"You've really done your homework."

James smiled, proud of himself. "I'm not sure it does us any good. I still think Joaquin Vanderfield is the prime suspect. And I go for the knife hanging below the belt, and just pushing it in."

Vanderfield was easily six foot or six one. I was trying to picture how low his hand would have to be to stab someone almost a foot shorter below their stomach. I knew it could be done, but it almost felt unnatural. And here I was, thinking that stabbing a young woman was unnatural? Duh.

"What kind of knife does the pirate wear?"

"Pirate?"

"Never mind. Just this kind of fantasy—" I was somewhat embarrassed. "Vanderfield. What brand, style of knife?"

"Same as I do. A Wüsthof."

A very popular brand and style of knife.

"Tell you what, Skip. We need to contact Cheryl Deitering, the knife lady from the lab. Get her take on this. Seemed like a pretty sharp woman."

James opened his door, leaning into it a little.

"Hey, pardner, no squeaks. No groans."

"But we are minus some of the carpet fibers. That's going to hurt the truck's resale value."

James laughed as we walked toward the kitchen door. Turning to me, he suddenly stopped.

"Oh, I got some information on Chef Marty."

"Anything we can use?"

"He's been sued a couple of times for firing people, and he's written several articles about his cooking style. Oh, and Bouvier has had him on The Food Channel show four or five times. Not much there, really."

"Married?"

"Yeah. One kid. So if he did have an affair, that could cause a problem. But the thing that I found interesting? Before he went to The Illinois Institute of Art in Chicago, before he got his culinary art major, he worked for a slaughterhouse. Right outside of Chicago. Butchering hogs and cows."

I winced as James opened the door and we walked in.

"Think about it, Skip." He turned to me, his eyebrows raised.

"About starting out as a butcher?"

"Yeah, but I'm talking about appearances on The Food Channel."

"What about it?"

"If I play my cards right, amigo—"

Two cooks and Marty were already working prep. One guy with a green headband was stirring soup and Kelly Fields was busy putting dough in the oven.

I offered my services to Chef Marty who seemed genuinely surprised to see a dishwasher volunteering to do anything other than their mundane task of scraping and washing.

"Sure. Help with the baked goods. Kelly can tell you what she needs. Special dessert tonight. Okay?"

I walked up to the attractive brunette, tapping her on the shoulder.

"Skip?"

"Chef said you could use some help. And since I don't have dishes until we open, just tell me what to do."

She studied me for a moment, and even in the L'Elfe kitchen with its smells of onions, carrots cooking in the soup, garlic, and savory sauces, I detected the gentle floral tones from her perfume. If she wasn't married, if I didn't think things were back on with Em, I'd have been tempted.

"A caramel frosted cupcake is on the specials tonight." All business.

"And what do I do?"

"The big mixer over there, you're going to mix butter, brown sugar, milk, and confectioner's sugar."

"A couple of cups?" The few times I'd helped James make anything, a couple of cups was quite a bit. "That's a pretty big mixer."

She laughed. "Lots and lots of butter, brown sugar, milk, and sugar, Mr. Moore. We are going to serve a lot of cupcakes tonight."

Handing me the recipe, she glanced around the small kitchen.

"Skip," she was almost whispering, "There is something I didn't tell you when we talked."

"Yeah?" Now I glanced around. Still Marty, the green headbanded soup guy, James at the stove, and me and Kelly.

"I heard this thirdhand, and I'm not sure even now I should mention it. It could just be like an urban legend. It has to do with the other sous chef."

"Vanderfield?"

She looked me in the eyes. "Keep it down. I told you there was a love-hate relationship between the two of them."

She pounded dough with her fists on a long stainless table, her piercing eyes still focused on mine.

"Please, understand, you can't tell anyone this because it may not be true."

"I'll keep it quiet." I wouldn't. Not if it meant solving the murder.

"I'm certain that this meant nothing. I really believe that, if it did happen, it was a one time thing, but supposedly Marty caught the two of them taking a break together one evening."

"That was it? A break?"

"Behind the Dumpster."

"And?"

"The story that got back to me was that neither was wearing anything below the waist."

CHAPTER THIRTY-NINE

Halfway through the evening, James and I passed each other.

"James, Kelly Fields says Amanda and Vanderfield were doing the nasty one night out by the Dumpster."

He paused, a pan in his hand with some sort of hot liquid still bubbling.

"Could be." He glanced over at Kelly, busily applying my frosting to her cupcakes. "Also, it could be that Mrs. Fields was interested in Joaquin's actions and she was jealous of Amanda. Maybe we missed something on our list, Skip. Suppose Kelly Fields had it in for Amanda Wright?"

"Why?"

"Think outside the box, amigo. Why would someone feed us false information? Not that I'm saying it's false. It's just that, we need to be looking at every angle."

Short girl, accomplished cook, probably owned a knife, although what a pastry chef was doing with a Wüsthof I couldn't imagine. Damn, instead of eliminating suspects, we just kept adding new ones.

The evening was slow, good for me, bad for the business. I

asked for a smoke break, and Chef Marty grunted. I took that as a yes and walked outside, immediately calling Em.

"Hey, Skip. Any more news?"

"Lots of news, Em. We need to meet."

"Ted wants to talk, too."

"About?"

"What do you think?" She sounded peeved. "About the case. He wants to know what you've found, and he's got some interesting information to share with you."

"When?"

"Tonight. When you get off."

I heard a voice in the background.

"Is that the TV?"

She was quiet for a moment. "Can you and James come over here?"

"Sure."

"Ted's here right now," she said.

Taking a deep breath and closing my eyes, I said nothing.

"He's leaving at this moment and he'll come back when you guys get here. Okay?"

I couldn't talk.

"Skip, he stopped over to ask for the meeting. He's not staying. The four of us will talk in a couple of hours."

She hung up the phone and I concluded my smoke break with an uneasy feeling.

CHAPTER FORTY

We met at Blue Moon, one of the restaurant-bar establishments in Em's building. The food wasn't that great, but it was a sports bar and grill, open until two a.m., so the timing was perfect.

"I understand someone pushed you off a boat."

Conway started the conversation. At the four-top, he was to the right of Em, I was to the left and James was across the table. I wasn't certain who Em was with, but the cop and I were both close enough to vie for her attention.

"Yeah. I was pushed."

"And this Joaquin Vanderfield wasn't on the yacht? He's the guy you've been leaning toward implicating?" He sipped on his black coffee.

James glowered. "And I'm the guy you've been implicating. Am I right?"

Conway shot Em a quick look, surprised at the accusation.

"I'm not sure what you mean."

"You told me yourself, my alibi might not hold up. The fact that I claimed to be watching TV by myself. Since then, I've heard the same thing from others." James glanced at Em. "And then," he paused for dramatic effect, theatrics being a part of James Lessor's persona, "and then you have a team come out and sweep my truck?" He was way up at the end of the sentence. "For fibers that had been found on the body."

Righteous indignation. James was at his finest.

"Seriously? Sorry to bust your bubble, Lessor, but we're not that interested in you. You're way down on a long list. But, if it makes you feel any better, that list is narrowing."

"So why the truck sweep?" Which hadn't actually been a sweep at all. More of a tape and forceps.

"Settle down, guys. It's simply an elimination process."

"The two officers who did it—"

"Overzealous perhaps?" Conway smiled. "Don't take it personally. It's simply what we do." He watched James for a moment. "And, the way that we do it."

I decided it was a lesson learned and good to know. As new private detectives we needed to learn a lot about police procedures.

"So who else would push James?" I asked the question.

"We're working every possible angle." He leaned in, running a hand through his salt-and-pepper gray hair. "Even if it was an accident, as you told the ship's captain, we get involved, the Coast Guard gets involved. It gets complicated."

Complicated seemed to be an understatement. My best friend almost lost his life, and this cop didn't seem to understand the gravity of that situation.

"This Chef Marty. I understand you've had a conversation with the pastry chef about him? What's her name? Kelly Fields?"

I nodded. "Nothing serious. She thinks Amanda could have—" I'd pledged to give every question from this point forword an honest answer, despite how it might affect my girlfriend. If she was still my girlfriend. If she would be my girlfriend from this point on.

"Let me lay it all out on the table. Kelly Fields thinks Amanda Wright could have slept with everyone in the kitchen."

There was total silence at the table. I could hear Dick Vitale in the background, his annoying voice announcing an Ohio State –Purdue basketball game. The big-screen TVs at every angle showing the fast-paced game.

"Except," I added, "for the dishwasher. Kelly feels that would have been beneath Amanda."

"So, according to one of the staff, there may have been sexual tension with the kitchen help?"

Em was looking at me, her eyes wide open in surprise.

"You didn't share that with me."

"From now on," I said, "I'm sharing. Em, it's what one person said. I'm not sure she knew what she was talking about, so I was sort of filtering what I thought was important, and—"

"No more filtering. Okay?" Em was as firm as I'd ever known her to be. She was obviously upset about my disclosure.

"No more."

Conway was busy taking notes. James, Em, and I had no paper or pens. No iPads or laptops. We'd have to rely on memory. Another thing to remember: always carry something to jot down notes.

"Kelly Fields thinks that, despite being a friend and a confidant," I glanced at Em, knowing she would understand, "Kelly felt that Amanda would sleep with anyone who could help her get ahead. Sorry, Em. It's what she said."

Again, there was no conversation. No comment. Finally, Em pushed her chair back and announced, "I'm going to the restroom. Normally at a table of friends I'd ask if anyone wanted to join me. In this case," she glanced around the table at Conway, James, and me, "I think I will refrain."

"She doesn't seem to be comfortable with the conversation." Conway watched her as she walked away in her tight jeans.

"I think it's three guys talking about her girlfriend's sex life that is a little uncomfortable."

"You want to make it more uncomfortable?" James asked.

"What?"

"When she comes back, tell her about your trip to Sam and Dave."

"Oh, shit."

"Honesty, pardner."

Ted Conway looked back and forth at James and me.

"Anything I should know?"

I shook my head. "Nothing to do with the case." And to be totally honest, I'm not sure it did. Maybe I could keep some things to myself. Total honesty was already becoming a problem.

"The idea that it happened in a close proximity to the restaurant, the fact that a kitchen knife was used, I think we've narrowed our search down to people in the restaurant that evening. Customers and staff." Conway's eyes swept the large room, focusing on windows that looked out at the bay.

We'd pretty much come to that same conclusion, but from there the narrowing got a lot harder.

"So now, we start looking at everyone who was in the place, and that's why what you boys see and hear is critical."

Em walked back, pulled out a chair, and sat down quietly. I really hated to bring up my next discovery.

"No more filtering." I looked directly at her.

"Go ahead. How much more can there be?"

I looked at James, Conway, then back to Em. "The runner, Carlos, told me Amanda admitted to the dishwasher she was seeing someone in the restaurant. He admitted that Juan Castro thought it was just a way to get rid of him. To stop him from being encouraged to ask her out."

"And," James said, "Chef Jean made it clear to Skip that there was a rule about no dating staff."

"Like those rules ever work." James chuckled. I assumed he was thinking about his romantic liaison with his boss at Cap'n Crab.

"So Kelly, the pastry lady, had one more story about Amanda and her possible sexual hookups with the staff at L'Elfe."

Em let out a big sigh. "Go ahead, Skip. Let us have it."

"She admits it's a rumor. Understand, she said it was third-hand information."

"Get it over with, already. God, you drag these things out."

"The rumor is that Chef Marty caught Amanda and Joaquin Vanderfield going at it out by the Dumpster one night."

"This is the guy who threatened the life of a sous chef in Sarasota? Held a knife to his throat because he criticized Vanderfield's cooking?" Em shook her head, her blonde hair flying. "Oh, my, God. Tell me you're done with these stories. Please tell me."

I wasn't done, not yet, but I certainly wasn't going to mention the Sam and Dave story right now. I'd already killed any buzz this party had.

CHAPTER FORTY-ONE

We set up a second meeting with Cheryl Deitering, hoping to find out more about the knife wounds. Driving to Doral, I asked James about Marty. He was definitely a player in our investigation.

"Chef Marty started out as a butcher. A guy who killed livestock for a living. He really knew how to use a knife. Does that have any bearing on the case?" It was a new wrinkle.

"I keep wondering about him. If he was having a fling with Amanda, and he really did catch Vanderfield and her screwing by the Dumpster, maybe he went nuts and decided that if he couldn't have her, nobody could."

"And he'd killed before." Cows, pigs, I could eat the meat, but I didn't like to think about them being butchered.

"Not a human being, Skip. And not with a knife like that. The guys who gut the cows and pigs, they use a small, four- or five-inch knife. It's kind of like an extension of their hand. They're doing a lot of close-up work."

"You learned this in school?"

"I did."

"I thought all you ever did in school was hang out with me, drink beer, and pick up girls."

"There was a degree of formal education as well. I guess you never got the hang of that." James playing the grown-up for a change.

"Marty or Vanderfield."

"If we had to narrow it down, it would be between those two. But I can't figure out which one."

James pulled into the parking lot and we got out, the doors practically squeak free. WD-40 actually did the job.

Cheryl was waiting for us in her office.

"Guys." She nodded.

"You said we'd been cleared to get information."

She gave me a gentle smile. "Actually, you've been given clearance to ask me any questions."

"And the difference is—" James trailed off.

"I don't have to give you the answer."

We both nodded.

"First of all, we heard that someone has been calling and asking for the autopsy report on Amanda Wright."

"That's true."

"Is that unusual?"

"Not necessarily." She sat behind her desk, dressed in her white smock with her hands neatly folded in front of her.

"So who calls?"

"The detectives who need immediate information. The press. My God, they call ten times a day. Sometimes the relatives call."

"And in this case?"

"The detectives, the press—ten times a day."

"And relatives?"

"No."

She was giving us short answers. No lengthy explanation

like the last time, but Conway wasn't present, and I had the impression she was guarded.

"You haven't released the autopsy report yet?"

She shook her head.

"Is there a reason? A surprise? Maybe she didn't die from the stab wounds?" James was pressing.

"The reason is that Detective Conway has asked me not to release the results, except to him."

"And why is that?"

"Because we've been getting anonymous calls two or three times a day, asking when we're going to release the report."

"I don't follow," I said.

"Mr. Moore, I'm not sure I do either. I guess I'm not giving anything away to say that the detective feels it's highly unusual that a stranger is calling with such frequency. He feels that it may be the killer, and he's not going to release any information until he tries to source the call."

"Male or female?"

She smiled again. "Yes."

James looked at me. I looked at James.

"You're right on both counts. Sometimes it's a male, sometimes a female. They refuse to identify themselves."

"I thought you guys could trace any calls," James said.

"You probably watch too much television," she responded. "There are still such things as pay phones, disposable cell phones, and blocked numbers. We're not nearly as successful as you would think."

I thought for a moment, trying to figure out who would be calling. Amanda was dead. How she died was pretty much, pardon the pun, cut and dried.

"What are your thoughts?" James was asking for her opinion.

"Mr. Lessor, I deal with cold, hard facts. My job here is to lay out the details and let someone else put the puzzle pieces together. The simpler I make it, the easier it is for the puzzle solvers to do their job."

"The pieces of the puzzle are?"

"Elementary, Mr. Lessor. Depth of the cuts, damage to various organs, establish if there were multiple weapons used, determine, if possible, which incision was responsible for her death."

"How deep were the cuts?"

"We're not sure. There was compression of the organs."

"Nine inches?" A Wüsthof nine-inch knife had been involved.

"At least."

"Were there multiple weapons?"

"No."

"So there was only one attacker."

"All indications are that this was the work of one person."

I realized this was getting us nowhere, but I had one more question for her.

"You don't make guesses, obviously, because your job is to just keep things simple, like you said."

Coldly, matter-of-factly, she said, "I have three dogs at home, Mr. Moore. A golden retriever, a fox terrier, and a miniature Pomeranian."

"And?"

"I go home after work, they're all waiting at the door for me. They want to be petted, walked, and fed. I like it like that. No major complications. No guesswork. There's an order to things. That's the same reason I like my job."

"But if you had to make a guess as to the sex of the killer, if you had to make that call based on your knowledge of knives and wounds, what would you guess?" I felt certain she wasn't going to

212

answer me, but she surprised me with her response.

"A female may have killed Amanda Wright. Because the wounds were made low. In the stomach and the abdomen."

James had been right. He was grinning, nodding his head up and down.

"Or a male. A male could easily have killed her, hiding the knife down by his side, walking right up to the victim and shoving the blade into her." Cheryl looked at me, then glanced at James.

"Good luck, boys. Don't hesitate to call. But, I've made my point. Don't expect magic. You get what's there. No spin, no guesses. It is what it is."

Again, James had been right. And we were walking out with not a whole lot more than we'd walked in with.

CHAPTER FORTY-TWO

"The funeral is supposed to be on Saturday. But they can't have it until they release the body, and since they haven't—" I could hear Em choke up on the phone. She paused, her voice cracking, "They won't release her because Ted doesn't want the autopsy report out. So now they may have to postpone the—"

"Funeral?"

She was silent on the other end.

I wanted to be as supportive as possible. I also wanted to know if there was something being released in those reports that would influence the investigation. If there was another cause of death besides the knife wounds or if the Deitering lady had lied to us, then we were looking in the wrong direction. We'd been guaranteed two weeks. Maybe we could stretch it to three. And I was sure of one thing, I did not want to be washing dishes for another week. No way.

"So there's no indication when they will release her?" Pretty much what Cheryl Deitering had told us.

I could hear the break in her voice. "No. I don't know if

there's something else, Skip, but how long can they keep this up? She was killed with that knife and why isn't that enough?"

She was the one with access to the lead cop. Apparently, he wasn't telling her everything he knew.

"Have you talked to Amanda's mom?"

"She's not handling it well. Wants to constantly know if you have any new information. She told me about your visit, and now she prays for you, hoping you give her some closure. She loses it from time to time, Skip."

I was certain that was the case. The lady, Amanda's mom, seemed very fragile. I wasn't surprised.

"You and me, are we going to the funeral together?" I still couldn't tell. Maybe she wanted Ted involved. "I just wondered how you wanted to handle this."

There was a long pause on the other end of the line.

"Of course. Of course, we go together. We were the last of her friends who saw her alive. No, we go together. Maybe James should go and—"

"Maybe he shouldn't. Maybe I shouldn't."

"Why, for God's sake?"

"Because we weren't supposed to have a close connection with her. Because as far as the staff is concerned, we are new employees who don't have a history with Amanda. And there's a good chance that there will be employees at that service."

As soon as I said it, I had second thoughts. I was reminded of the people who weren't exactly her friends. Kevin Kahn, the jeweler; Juan Castro, the dishwasher; Joaquin Vanderfield, the sous chef; even Kelly Fields, who sounded like someone who wasn't as close to Amanda as she had pretended to be.

"I didn't even think of that, Skip. Doing this undercover thing can get a little confusing, can't it?"

"Okay. We're going to get this thing figured out, Em. Let's

give it some thought." I filled her in on the visit to Cheryl Deitering.

"It sounds like you're no further ahead there."

"No. She was very clear about her role. She didn't have any
guesses. She would present all the evidence, and it was up to
someone else to tie it all together. She did say there was only one
attacker. Anything else from Ted? Any confidential information
he's been willing to share?"

"It's not like we talk all the time, Skip. I told you, this thing
isn't going anywhere. Okay?"

"So he hasn't leaked any more information?"

She hesitated. "Well, maybe we did talk briefly. On the phone.
He said that he'd reviewed the security CDs from that night."

"Oh, my God. Those cameras. Outside the walk-in cooler."

Again, a stupid oversight from a detective firm that was still
green.

"Yes. And there's a camera outside the back door. Did you
know that?"

I didn't.

"But they didn't show anything unusual."

"So the camera focus wasn't on the murder."

"He didn't show me the videos. He just mentioned that they'd
reviewed them and they didn't show anything out of the ordinary."

"So, they're at the police station? The videos?"

"They made copies."

"The originals?"

"In the restaurant, I would guess."

CDs? I almost laughed. Selling security systems for a living,
I knew nobody used CDs anymore. We sold Drop 'n' Lock, a
cloud-based service to upload and store security videos.

I looked at James, sprawled on the couch. "Hey, roommate,
you and me, we've got to find the CDs that go with those
restarant security cameras."

Glancing up from the *Ellen DeGeneres Show*, he nodded. "Hadn't thought about those."

"Skip?"

"Yeah, Em?"

"I told you. They found nothing." She hesitated. "So I asked him if we could view them."

"Great. Maybe we'll pick up something that they didn't see."

"Nope. Ted said they were not going to release them."

"You just said there was nothing on them with any relevance."

"I think they want to see them again, fresh eyes."

"Why not ours?"

"Skip, he's feeding us some information, but there's not a lot of trust built up."

"So we'll get them from Bouvier."

"Good luck. They've given Chef a written notice that no one is to view those videos until they clear them."

"What? That makes no sense. We're fresh eyes, and we are getting to know the staff. We could—"

"I get the impression that if someone voluntarily lets us see those videos, they could be breaking the law."

I didn't think Bouvier was above breaking the law. But if he refused to show them to us, then we had no recourse. If, on the other hand, he didn't know that we'd found the CDs, then he couldn't be held liable. My twisted logic coming into play.

"Maybe he didn't know what to look for." I would love to find something on those recordings just to rub Ted Conway's face in it. To walk into his office and say, "Hey, Conway, look what you missed." It would be total satisfaction. I know, I tend to be full of bluff and bravado, but I wanted to squash him as much as I wanted to solve the murder.

"Skip, are you thinking what I think you're thinking?"

She was like James. She usually knew what I was thinking.

"Don't even tell me," she said. "But, if you do stumble on them, if you're going to view them, I want to be there." Em was once again energized.

"If I find them tonight, and if you view them with us, aren't you breaking the law?"

I could hear a soft laugh. "Tell me it's some soft porn. What a surprise when we find out it's not."

"Could be sex in the walk-in cooler? Maybe a waitress and the dishwasher?"

James's head spun around.

"Better not be the current dishwasher," her voice had an edge.

"No."

"Skip, if you're thinking about taking those CDs, please, be careful. Please. Do you hear me?"

"We will."

"You bring them to my condo. We'll view them as soon as you get off work."

"Oh, so you think I'm going to go back and wash dishes again? Tonight?"

She sounded much brighter than she had at the beginning of our conversation. "I think it's in your blood, Skip. You are just starting to realize how much you like it."

"I don't live out of my car."

"Your car would be a step up from that ratty apartment you and James live in. Am I right?"

I knew she was right. We said our goodbyes and hung up.

"Dude," James gave me a nod. "I only got about half that conversation, but we're going to solve this murder. Before the cops. And, when we do—not if we do, but when we do—we'll have a pot full of moolah. We'll be the investigation team that everyone will be calling. We are going to make a shitload of money. Do you understand me, amigo?"

CHAPTER FORTY-THREE

Walking up to the pastry station, I touched Kelly Fields on the arm and she turned away from a large bowl of butter.

"Skip. I wanted to talk to you."

"And I wanted to talk to you."

"Listen," she wiped her hands on her apron and furtively glanced around her, as if to make sure no one was within hearing range. "I hope you didn't say anything to anyone about our stopping for a beer."

Only James, Em, and the detective.

"I may have said something to James."

"I know it was just a meeting to get information, but it was after work, and it was for a drink and—"

"That's all it was. A meeting."

"Yes. But it could be construed as a date and I really can't have anyone questioning that."

"Kelly, it wasn't a date."

"I'm getting back with Drew. I think I told you that we'd separated, briefly, and I just don't want anything to go wrong."

I nodded, as if I understood what the problem would be. Actually, I did. It wasn't as if Em and I hadn't broken up numerous times over the years.

"I'm glad you're getting back together."

"We are, Skip. Everything is going to be fine."

"And I would ask the same favor. Don't mention our meeting to anyone, okay?"

She nodded, and I knew the conversation was over.

The evening rush started late, and I could see James working side by side with his nemesis, Joaquin Vanderfield, the two of them pouring white wine into sizzling pans, deglazing as my friend called it, after searing pork loins. Flames leaped around the skillets, steam from the hot metal and the wine was sucked into the stainless steel hood, and I could have sworn they were in competition with each other as they worked their craft, sprinkling seasonings and spraying some sort of marinade on the meat. I had no idea what it all meant, but I did know that James was a pretty good cook. Apparently, he could hold his own with Joaquin Vanderfield.

"Hey, my boy, you chattin' up the pastry lady?"

Mikey Pollerno stood there watching me, his hands in his pockets.

"Chatting up?"

"You know, you seem pretty friendly with her and all."

I wondered if he knew we'd gone for a beer.

"You got to be careful of that one."

"She doesn't seem to be that dangerous."

"She thought the lady sous chef was after her husband."

"What?"

"Just sayin', the Wright girl makin' eyes at Kelly's husband didn't sit well with her."

"So?"

220

"She thought maybe the husband was interested back. Just sayin'."

With that, he walked away.

The clanking of dishes, the clinking of silver in the runners' trays let me know that the crowd was picking up. As they slammed the plastic trays down on my stainless counter, I scraped, rinsed, and shoved the plates and utensils into the steamy machine, realizing how much I hated the task. If I hadn't had another purpose, if I wasn't playing mind games with the working staff, I think I would have gone insane. On the flip side, playing mind games with the staff was probably going to drive me insane. I was screwed either way.

Halfway through the evening, I glanced up and saw James standing by my side and staring down the hallway that ran to the locker room.

"Those security videos, they're in Bouvier's office?"

"They must be."

"It's locked."

"I assume."

"Pard, we've got to look at them."

"And for some reason, Chef can't show them to us. The cops have told him to keep them private."

"Yeah, well, something like that shouldn't stop us."

"It shouldn't."

He glanced back down the hallway once more. Reaching into his jacket pocket he pulled out two thin rods of metal.

"Large paper clips, my friend."

"James." He could be such an idiot at times. "You're crazy. We're not picking locks with paper clips."

He held the bent metal pieces flat in his palm. "This one I bent in the shape of a tension wrench." He pointed to the L-shaped bend. "And this, with the wavy end, I made as a rake."

"What are you talking about?"

"YouTube, pardner. This guy went through the entire process. You make these tools out of large paperclips and when you use them in tandem, voilà. The lock opens."

"You got this off of YouTube?"

"Me and four hundred thousand other people. Do you believe it? There are a lot of dishonest people out there, Skip." He smiled, a mischievous grin on his face.

"Let's say you can make it work."

"I tried it, dude. On our apartment door."

"I would guess that those locks were made in the eighteen hundreds. A bump on the mechanism would probably open our door."

"It worked. And the guy in the video, who appeared to be a total doofus, even he opened his lock."

"We've still got another problem."

"What's that?"

"Three cameras that catch all the action in the hall."

"Yeah, I've thought of that."

"And?"

"In my locker. Two hoodies."

"As I said, and?"

"After work, we go back to the changing room, put on the sweatshirts, pull up the hoods, and come back to the office."

"Are you out of your mind?"

"Skip." He shot a quick look at the prep table. "I've got to go, but here's the scenario. Nobody is expecting a break-in. Am I right?"

"I guess."

"We have to cover all bases so we disguise ourselves."

"If you can call that a disguise."

"Once we get in—"

"Assuming you're successful."

222

He squinted at me. "Once we get in, we simply remove the CD from the recorder. There's no record we were ever there."

"And they won't miss that CD?"

"Sure. But they won't have any proof of who took it. And, hey, maybe Marty or whoever is in charge forgot to put it in. Could happen. They'll just think it was an oversight."

"And if you can't get in? If your locksmith talents fail you and me?"

"It won't matter. They're only going to review the CDs if something happens. Like someone walks out with a dozen steaks or lobsters."

"Or if someone breaks off a paperclip in the lock."

"Mmmm," he nodded. "You know, the guy in the video did say that could happen."

"I hope you know what you're doing."

James dropped the clips back into his pocket.

"So do I, amigo. So do I."

CHAPTER FORTY-FOUR

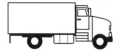

"Where did you get the idea of hooded sweatshirts?"

"YouTube. One of the best ways to hide from surveillance cameras. You can learn so much shit on there, man."

We walked the hallway, tossing stained aprons into the laundry hamper.

"So now we live our lives by what happens on YouTube?"

"Let's give it a try, Skip."

"YouTube. Mostly made up of stupid people doing stupid stuff!"

"Brian Gurney's movie, *Phase One*. Paul Rudd says it to Cecil Jackson. Don't try to fool me with movie quotes, amigo."

I knew he'd recognize it.

"One, two," he was gazing up, "and three." Red lights on the cameras were blinking. "And unless someone does something really bad tonight—"

"Like killing a sous chef in the alley?"

"Something like that. Unless that happens, no one is going to go looking through those CDs. And they recycle them after four weeks. So pray that no one steals food, tries to have sex in the walk-in, or, as you pointed out, Skip, kills someone. With just a little luck, we should be home free. No one is going to see us on any video surveillance. Okay?"

Reaching his locker, James unlocked the padlock and slowly pulled open the thin metal door. He seemed to steel himself for the possible shock of another macabre surprise.

There was nothing. Just his civilian clothes and two rolled up hoodies on the upper shelf.

"All right, Tonto, most of the crew is gone."

The waitstaff, dining room manager, and Marty never visited the locker room. They exited as soon as their shift ended, hurrying out the back door.

"Who locks up?"

"The manager. Tara. She's in her own little office across from the pastry station, tallying the night's receipts."

"How much does a place like this make in a night?"

"Not as much as you think. This place probably grosses eight grand."

"That sounds pretty damned good."

"Skip, they're lucky if they net eight percent."

All of a sudden it didn't sound so good.

"It's enough to say that this guy, Bouvier, doesn't worry about the gross or the net on this establishment. He's making his killing on TV, on pots and pans, on spices, and all the other stuff. Give it to him, Skip. The guy is a marketing genius."

"Or, he's the chief cook and bottle washer, but his wife is the brains behind the organization."

"Could be."

We pulled on the sweatshirts and started back down the hall.

"Put up your hood."

Feeling extremely silly, I did just that. "They're going to know it's us, James. This is crazy."

"We're going to take the CD, Skip. This is strictly precautionary."

"Talked to Kelly Fields tonight. Or rather, she talked to me."

James stopped and looked at me through the opening in his shroud.

"About what?"

"She asked me not to mention the conversation we'd had. The night we went out for a beer. Didn't want me to tell anyone."

"After you've shared it with everyone you know?"

"Sort of."

"And?"

"She's getting back with her husband. Didn't want our meeting to appear as anything it wasn't."

James laughed. "Dude, you are the least likely candidate to be the 'other' man in a married woman's life."

I didn't know whether to be offended or complimented.

"Anyway, Mikey Pollerno comes out of nowhere, and tells me the reason for the breakup was that Amanda Wright might have been making a play for Kelly's husband. And maybe this husband didn't discourage the advances."

"Dude."

"I know."

"When did this chick ever have time to work?"

"Just out of curiosity—" and I was curious, "did you ever—"

"No. Never. We've been over this before."

"It wouldn't be beyond you to—"

"Skip, let's get to the matter at hand. I've got two pieces of metal in my pocket. I've had some success with opening at least one lock, and I'm hoping I can do it again. I need you to keep an open eye, be a lookout."

If James was caught, I was caught. As usual, my best friend was putting me in a very vulnerable situation.

Pulling the paper clips from his pocket, he looked back at the kitchen. No one was in view.

"This is the tension wrench," he said as he gently inserted it into the lock. "And this is the rake."

Slowly, carefully, he pushed the bent metal into the upper portion of the slot. Then he started wiggling it.

"You have to apply the tension, then get the tumblers to fall. You jiggle, put some tension on the wrench, jiggle some more—"

He was reveling in the method, when all of a sudden he stopped.

"Tara's office door." He was whispering. "I think it just opened."

"Shit."

We both pressed up against the wall, holding our breath.

Ten seconds went by and there was no more sound from the kitchen office.

We stood perfectly still. If someone walked down that hall, we would have some explaining to do.

I could hear fans in the kitchen and a faucet being opened. Water splashed in a stainless sink. Someone started whistling off key, and the water stopped.

"How the hell are we going to explain what we're doing?" I barely mouthed the words.

James motioned toward the locker room.

"We go back there. We were just getting cleaned up and lost track of time."

A door slammed shut, and I froze.

"She's back in the office. We've got time. She's doing the books and that's a long process."

I wasn't so sure.

"Skip," he whispered again, "this means that Kelly Fields is a primary suspect."

I was quiet. I really liked her. However, her relationship with Amanda Wright didn't seem to be symbiotic.

"Think about it, man. Amanda was hitting on her husband. She had the perfect motivation. And, she was on the boat that night."

"I know, James. But she's getting back with him. Nothing happened. So it makes no sense that—"

"Dude," he was slow and deliberate, "Amanda was hitting on Kelly's husband. In a brief, unguarded moment, in a moment of passion, of unbridled violence, she stabs the girl. Repeatedly. Picture it, Skip, she wants to save the marriage. She's got kids, she's got—"

"Pick the damned lock. If you're that good, prove it to me."

CHAPTER FORTY-FIVE

He wiggled the rake. This wire of a paper clip, bent out of shape, he moved it rapidly inside the lock, all the while holding the tension wrench, another paper clip jammed into the bottom portion of the slot, to the left, putting pressure on the mechanism. Back and forth he jiggled the rake as I continually checked down the hall, keeping my hood pulled tight around my face.

If we got caught or if Tara came back out, holy hell would break loose. Pretending to be kitchen personnel wouldn't sit well with the staff, but breaking and entering, stealing CDs, there had to be a penalty of several years in prison for that. My guess. I hadn't had time to research the sentence.

"Hurry up."

"It's going to take a minute or so."

"Longest damned minute I've ever experienced."

"Minutes are minutes, Skip."

The temperature in the building must have gone up ten degrees or those hoodies were warm, because I was sweating and I saw perspiration on James's forehead. Jiggling that piece he called the rake seemed fruitless. It was only a matter of minutes before Tara or some other employee would wander down the hallway and see us breaking the law.

"James, let's go. Screw the CDs. We cannot get caught doing—"

"It's open, amigo. Quick. Inside."

Opening the door, he stepped inside and I followed.

James gently closed the door, and we stood in the dark office, lit only by the lights in the hallway shining through the small window in the office door.

"Where are the CDs?"

"Right there, beside the monitor and the recorder."

"Five of them. These must have video from the night in question."

I grabbed the plastic discs and stuffed them under the sweatshirt. James opened the door, glanced in both directions, and we exited.

"Take off your hood. Hell, we look like thieves," James said.

"Take off the shirt," I replied. "It's eighty degrees in here and probably eighty outside."

"Good point."

I wrapped the CDs in the cloth as we headed out through the kitchen. Tara walked out of her office, startling us both.

With a questioning look she said, "Getting out a little late, aren't you?"

"Just talking back there." James pointed toward the locker room. "Taking our time, you know?"

She studied us for a moment.

"Anything in the shirts?"

We both shook our heads. Maybe she thought we had food.

"Nothing, just heading home."

She nodded to us and walked back toward Bouvier's office.

"Thank God we got out of that one." James watched her walk away, obviously admiring her butt.

"Let's just hope these are the right CDs."

"We'll know in about fifteen minutes. Em is waiting up for us."

Stepping out into the humid Miami night, I took a deep breath. The pungent odor of saltwater and seaweed permeated the air, fresher than the mixed smell of grease and food inside.

"Skip, it looked like Tara was going down to Bouvier's office."

We walked to the truck.

"Yeah?"

"The door to the office is open. I forgot that it only locks with a key."

"James, she'll think someone forgot to lock it."

"Maybe. But we also forgot something else."

"What?"

"The CD in the recorder." He stopped, staring back at the building. "The one showing us breaking into the office."

CHAPTER FORTY-SIX

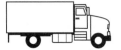

Em has this seventy-inch Samsung 3D television screen that is unbelievable for sports shows. We saw the Super Bowl on her TV last year, and it was almost as good as being there. Actually, I have no frame of reference.

"So you just waltzed in and took the CDs?"

We were sitting on her balcony, looking out at the lights from Star Island and farther to South Beach. The water in Biscayne Bay was inky black and the half moon cast a lazy, wavy pattern to the marina directly below.

James and I sipped our beers. Em had a white wine, something I'd never developed a taste for.

"James went on the Internet and found a video on how to pick a lock."

"With paper clips," James reminded me.

Em shook her head. "Paper clips?"

"Hey, I was skeptical too. The proof is right there." I pointed at the five discs on the coffee table inside.

"Make a bomb, rob a bank, pick a lock—it's as easy as logging on, am I right?"

She was.

"Five discs. Are they labeled?"

I hadn't even looked. They appeared to be rewritable.

"They aren't labeled."

"Why wouldn't they label them?"

"Because they can use them over again."

"Ah."

Em eased out of her chair, and we followed her into the condo. James and I sat down on the butter-soft leather sofa.

"So how do we know?" She slipped one of the discs into her player. The date immediately displayed on the lower left of the screen.

"Question answered."

The date was two days before the murder.

"Try this one."

I handed her the disc that had been two down in the stack.

"Perfect," she said when the video started. "This is the night."

The video started with a timer. Five p.m. Again, the numbers occupied a small section of the screen in the bottom left. The digits rapidly increased in fractions of a second. Thirty seconds later, with four different pictures on the display, nothing had happened.

"Man," James was frustrated, "we could be here for five or six hours."

Em turned her attention from the screen to the two of us sitting on her brown leather sofa.

"We don't know what we're looking for."

"People walking in and out of the shots," I suggested.

"People taking breaks outside," Em said.

"Do we have a time of death?" James asked.

I looked into Em's eyes. "Did Ted share that with you?"

Scowling, she said, "Yes. As a matter of fact, he did."

"Well, maybe we can fast-forward to five minutes before and see if there is any action that happened at that time."

"Time of death was, within half an hour, eight to eight thirty." We'd first seen her body closer to nine p.m., within ten minutes of discovery by the waiter.

"So," Em walked to the player, "I'll set this for ten till eight. That gives us at least ten minutes ahead of the possible killing."

Em fussed with the player, advancing the CD back and forth until we could see the on-screen timer as it registered 7:49.

I concentrated on the whole monitor. There were four separate grainy pictures on the screen grouped in a square, the numbers increasing at a dizzying pace in a small space on the bottom left of the television.

"This is going to be strange. Four cameras, four things happening at the same time. Hard to follow."

Watching the top left video I would see anyone walking from the locker room, restrooms, and showers toward the walk-in cooler and Bouvier's office. There was no one. The top right picture was directed at the cooler entrance. Anyone walking in or out would be pictured. And they were. One of the Spanish-speaking cooks, Adelpho I believe, walked in, and almost immediately walked back out with a pan of what appeared to be chicken parts. The video was black and white, and blown up on Em's screen, it was pixelated. I'd sold security systems for my company that were a lot higher tech than L'Elfe's.

My eyes drifted to the lower right picture, where traffic headed from the kitchen down the hall could be seen. An employee walking toward Bouvier's office, the walk-in, or the locker room, restrooms, and showers would be picked up on this camera. Also, anyone walking from those areas to the kitchen would be visible. Adelpho was in that shot as well as he carried his pan of chicken to his cooking station.

Finally, on the bottom left, was a view of the outside. The camera was mounted above the door and seemed to show a fairly wide angle of the parking lot. However, the green Dumpster was not visible and neither was the fire hydrant where they'd tied the yellow crime-scene tape the night of Amanda's murder. Without a picture of that specific area, there would be no view of the killing. It would have been the perfect shot, but I was somewhat relieved. That image was something I really didn't care to see.

A minute passed and still there was no activity.

"The outside camera," Em pointed to the screen. "If Amanda exited through the kitchen door, we should be able to see her, right?"

As she spoke, almost on command, someone opened the heavy steel door and walked outside.

"Oh, my God. There." Em stood up and moved closer for a better look.

The harsh glare from a mounted floodlight blurred the upper body and by the time the person could have been identified, they were off camera.

"Damn." I frowned.

"Maybe this is why Conway said there was nothing conclusive on the CD," James said. "I mean, this could be a futile exercise."

"He also refused to let us see the CD," she reminded him. "I'm not at all sure we should trust the detective."

I much preferred her tone now to the times she called him Ted.

Em stopped the CD, reran the scene, but the upper torso was nothing but a blur of diffused light.

"You know, it's just like the security system on the kitchen door. That's a cheap version that could be bypassed in seconds. And whoever installed this video system used the cheapest thing they could find and did a piss-poor job." I didn't understand kitchens or cooking, but I did know security systems. "They should have taken into consideration that light, and either—"

"Skip, look."

The door opened a second time as another employee walked out. This person was a little shorter where the light didn't catch the head and shoulders. There was less glare, but it was still hard to identify the worker as the camera was focused on their back. We saw the person, black jacket and white pants take about five steps into the parking lot.

"Obviously, we're not going to have much luck," James said.

Then, while the shorter body was still in frame, the door opened again. This time no one walked out, but the body still on screen turned around as if to say something.

The three of us stared intently at the monitor, concentrating on the grainy, somewhat blurred face.

Blurred as it was, there was no doubt of the identity. It was Chef Jean Bouvier.

CHAPTER FORTY-SEVEN

"So we're not quite forty minutes before the latest time of the knifing and we've got somebody and Bouvier outside. Means nothing," James said.

Em nodded, making notes on a yellow legal pad. "There may be more of an exodus. We've got a lot of time left, guys."

"And," I reminded her, "the killer could be someone who was never inside the restaurant. Someone who came off the street."

We watched in silence, as if we were sadistic voyeurs waiting for a grisly killing. Actually, we were.

"It's like a really bad reality show." James watched too much TV.

There was a gentle breeze off the water, drifting through the open door, and outside we could hear the sound of a speedboat, running across the bay in the pitch black. I could hear soft conversation on the patio next door, and hoped they didn't hear us. Commenting on property that we'd stolen.

"Em, we've got another suspect." I needed to bring her up to speed.

"Where?"

"Not on the screen. Somebody we uncovered today."

Turning to me with a surprised look she said, "You waited until now to tell me this? What's that all about?"

"Look, this only happened this evening. Frankly, breaking and entering and stealing the CDs sort of overwhelmed me."

"So? Who is it?"

"Kelly Fields."

"The baker?" I could tell she was more than surprised. The Fields girl had never been on the radar. "The one you had a date with?"

"It wasn't a date."

"After work, a beer—"

So maybe I wasn't the only one who had a jealous streak.

"Anyway, she came up to me tonight and said she was getting back with her husband. She asked me not to mention our little rendezvous to anyone."

"Which you'd already done."

"Yeah, but—"

"Go on."

"Mikey Pollerno, the setup guy, told me why the Fields separated."

"Oh?"

"Kelly thought that Amanda was hitting on her husband."

"Hitting on her husband? You know, you guys have been making Amanda out to be a pretty awful person. She wasn't perfect, but she wasn't that bad. Damn it, she was a friend and I—"

James spoke up. "We haven't been making her out to be anything. We're hearing it from the inside, Em. It's not like we're making this shit up."

"Here comes someone."

The lower right corner had movement. Someone was walking toward the locker room.

"Sophia Bouvier," I said. The short, squat, waddling woman was moving down the hall.

We watched as she stopped halfway down to the locker room and opened the office door. The same office door that James had unlocked with paper clips. The door that had the jammed handle on the inside.

"Not locked." James studied her as she disappeared into the office.

"Not locked?" I shook my head. "Would have been a whole lot easier if we'd lifted the CDs during regular hours."

"And there's someone leaving out the back door," Em said.

Again it was impossible to tell who it was. The bright floodlight mounted on the building was creating an almost halo effect on the person from their shoulders on up.

"Damn, we lose many more, there will be no one else running the kitchen," James quipped. "Everyone is headed outside."

A minute later, give or take one hundredth of a second, Sophia exited the office and walked back toward the kitchen.

"Her husband left, and how much do you want to bet she's the next one out?"

James called it. The outside door opened and the short woman stepped into the parking lot. We assumed it was her. She was far too short for the floodlight to halo her head, and she didn't wear the black-and-white cooking garb.

"You two didn't tell me there were parties going on outside. Does this happen every night?"

"Someone's coming back in." I pointed to the screen.

As the figure got closer to the camera, I could barely make him out. It was Joaquin Vanderfield. Em scribbled something on her tablet.

"So, was he the first person out the door? And now he's done smoking his joint or using the cell phone?" James was watching intently, a brown bottle still in his hand but the contents a distant memory.

"Or was he busy banging one of the waitresses up against the Dumpster?" Em had that sarcastic tone in her voice.

"Or did he even show up for work until now? Maybe," I said, "he just walked in."

Em looked at me, throwing up her hands in frustration. "In order to find out, we'd have to watch the tape from zero."

"We'll be up half the night." James stood up and walked to Em's kitchen. "You mind if I have another beer?"

"Would it matter?"

He brought two Yuenglings out for himself and me and we continued to watch the screen.

"Here's what we have so far, boys." Em referred to her notes. "An unidentified person walks outside. The light and the rear view make it difficult to decide the identity of said person."

"Said person?" James mocked her.

Ignoring him, she continued, "Chef Jean Bouvier walks out."

"So far, so good," I said.

"Unidentified person walks out, followed shortly by Sophia Bouvier."

"We've lost four people," James commented.

"Joaquin Vanderfield walks in. Could have been unidentified number one or two or could be that he walked in off the street."

"This is confusing as hell," I said.

"That's why we're making the big bucks, Tonto. If it was easy, anyone could be doing it."

It's why I was washing dishes and getting damned tired of it.

"Someone heading toward the walk-in."

Vanderfield, wiping his brow, came walking down the hall. He glanced at the camera with a look of hesitation on his face. It was as if he didn't want to be recognized, but could see no way to avoid it. James could have told him about the hoodies.

I fully expected him to walk to the locker room. Instead, he stopped short of the hallway's end and opened the door to Bouvier's office.

"Shit, what business does he have in there?"

I had no idea. The workings of a professional kitchen were foreign to me, and I was simply an observer.

Vanderfield walked out within twenty seconds and proceeded down the hall to the kitchen. We were not privy to Chef Marty's tirade when his number two sous chef finally showed up back in the kitchen.

"Movement," I motioned to the screen. "Bottom left."

Someone walking out, the glare of the light destroying any chance of recognition.

Then there was no action. Everyone was either outside the building or in the kitchen whipping up wonderful creations for the well-to-do diners.

I picked up my beer and walked to the patio. The video wasn't getting us anywhere.

"Skip, get back in here," Em called, urgency in her voice.

"What?"

"Look who's walking in."

Bottom left screen, a cook with their head down. As the person approached the door, she lifted her eyes as if staring right into the camera lens.

"Kelly Fields."

CHAPTER FORTY-EIGHT

"What we're missing is Amanda." James pointed at the screen. "She may have been one of the people exiting, or maybe she was already outside."

"And we won't be able to tell due to that damned floodlight."

"Kids," James stood up, grasping his bottle, "we're missing something."

"No shit," I muttered.

"Maybe Conway and company are missing it, too."

Em smirked. "And you know what this missing component is?"

"We know Chef Jean walked outside. Where had he been?"

"In the kitchen," I ventured. "He had to be in the kitchen to reach the door."

"Where before that?"

"His office."

"Exactly."

"James, it is his office."

"Who else was in that office?"

"We saw Sophia go in," Em said.

"We did. And Joaquin Vanderfield."

"And who knows who else during the course of the evening."

He nodded, watching the screen.

"I think we're onto something."

"What?"

"There's something in the office that the killer wants."

I pictured the cramped space. A desk, one chair, a file cabinet, badly framed photos on the wall, the monitor and recorder—

"The tool chest."

"Tool chest?" Em hadn't been there.

"Exactly." James was waving his beer bottle like a conductor waves his baton. "The tool chest where he keeps his knives."

"So what are you suggesting? Everyone who works there has a knife. Their own knife. Or knives."

"And they apparently still have their knives. Yet one showed up in my locker, and we found that one in the garbage truck."

"So the killer had an extra knife."

"Maybe. But I think we need to check out the tool chest."

"You're crazy."

We had no idea what was in those drawers. Bouvier had told us it was his personal collection of knives, but we hadn't seen them. I agreed with Em. James was crazy.

"Do you remember how many knives he claimed were in those drawers?"

I did not.

"Thirty-seven, Skip."

"He told us that?" I was trying to remember.

"He did. I remember thinking how much it would cost to replace mine. Over one hundred dollars. I was doing the math in my head. I thought there could be almost four thousand dollars' or more worth of cutlery in that red chest."

No one spoke. James walked to the open balcony door, staring out at South Beach and beyond. There were parties going on, wild, drunk fests. Tourists and locals were eating and drinking at all-night venues, having the time of their lives. And here we were watching a silent black-and-white video, trying to make some sense of the whole thing.

Finally Em asked the question. "So what do we do next?"

She usually had all the answers.

"I say we open the chest. We see if there really are thirty-seven knives in there."

"And I say that's the dumbest idea yet."

He turned and gave Em a benevolent smile.

"Do you have a better one?"

"What's it going to prove?"

"Maybe nothing. But isn't this job about the process of elimination?"

"Enlighten me, Mr. Lessor. Exactly what are we eliminating."

Pausing for a moment, he drained his second beer.

"Bouvier told Skip and me that he believed in going with your gut instinct. I'm inclined to agree with him. My gut instinct is to open the chest and see how many knives there are."

"What are we eliminating?"

He took her hand and she took it back rather quickly.

"Em, I think one of the staff walked into Bouvier's office and took a knife from his tool chest. I think the murder weapon came from that chest. If I'm right, then we see who was in the office. So far we saw Sophia and Vanderfield, and we can assume that Bouvier himself was there."

"Chef Bouvier gave you a knife. Remember?" James had been surprised. "You told me that Chef Marty handed you a knife after yours came up missing. He told you that Bouvier wanted you to have it."

"So that brings the count down to thirty-six knives. If there are fewer than thirty-six knives, there's a possibility the knife that

Cheryl Deitering has came from Bouvier's chest. And I would guess there's limited access to those knives."

"So what now, James? You're suggesting we count knives?"

"It may prove nothing. Maybe he gave other employees knives."

"It's worth a look."

"Everyone in on this?" I looked at Em.

Throwing up her hands she said, "On what? On agreeing that you two are idiots?"

"Play nice, Emily," James said. "I've got a way to do this."

"How?"

James reached into his pocket and pulled out his two misshapen paper clips.

"Your friendly locksmith is ready and willing."

"Honest to God, James," Em picked up the empty Yuengling bottles and took them to the kitchen. "Why don't you just ask Bouvier if he'll show you the knives?"

"Two problems with that, Em. Number one, what if he says no? Then we're right back where we are now. And number two, we think there's a possibility that Jean Bouvier may be a suspect."

"A suspect?"

"Kelly Fields says Amanda slept her way to the top. There is no further to go than Chef Jean. And what if she was blackmailing him?"

"James, I'm going to say something that I've thought for a long time. Sometimes I don't think you've got a brain in that handsome head of yours."

CHAPTER FORTY-NINE

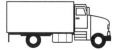

I still wasn't certain what we were going to prove, but James was bound and determined that the answer to our case was in Bouvier's tool chest.

I'd bought into this thing from the start, so I agreed to go with him. Em had never bought into James, even though she was responsible for our current position, but she refused to be a part of another breaking and entering.

We departed with the five CDs and two former paper clips.

"Let's say we find the thirty-seven knives—"

"Thirty-six. Chef Jean gave me one of his, remember?"

"Thirty-six. It means nothing. Any one of those people we saw going into the office could have picked up a knife."

"But I'm guessing only one did."

I had James stop at the all-night Walgreens on Biscayne Boulevard and I bought a small magnet, the kind you stick on the refrigerator to hold a bill or important piece of paper. We had several bills on ours, at all times. Electric, water, cable, Internet, all at least two months old.

"You can bypass the security system with that?"

"This one I think I can." I'd seen the contacts several times and they weren't installed very well. Usually, the installation requires someone to hide the magnetic contacts between the door and the frame. The installer will put putty or some covering over the small metal contacts. "The contacts are out in the open on this install, so we'll know where to place the magnet."

We reached the restaurant in fifteen minutes, and James pulled into an apartment complex across the street.

"Don't want to be too obvious."

"So you really think you can pick the lock on this place?"

"Pretty sure. And I've brought along a man who knows security systems."

It was one thirty in the morning, and fortunately the moon was behind a cloud bank over the bay. James pulled out his tools, as they were, and proceeded to wiggle the rake. It sounded like a new dance craze or something dirty you would do in bed.

"Once it's open," he said, "are you ready with the magnet?"

"You just get it open."

He moved it back and forth, up and down, all the time applying some pressure with the other clip.

"You just put another magnet over the one in the frame?"

"I explained it to you. This system isn't a sophisticated motion detector. It's simply two magnets that make contact with each other. When they are separated, the circuit is broken."

He continued working the metal rods.

"So, when you open the door, the two magnets are no longer together and the alarm sounds."

He nodded his head, concentrating on his motion. A circular pattern, then up and down. He would end with two diagonal movements, moving the metal pieces quickly to the right and down to the left, then left to right.

"Once you get the door open just wide enough to see the contact, you quickly put another magnet over the one mounted in the door frame. That will be the wired connection. You trick the system into believing that there's still a connection and," I hesitated for effect, "voilà. No alarm sounds."

"You've learned your trade well, Grasshopper."

"On the other hand, if the magnet isn't strong enough, or is too strong, it could send the wrong signal and we could be in some deep shit."

"Not much chance of that happening, right?"

"Actually, there's a good chance."

"Well," he pulled the thin rods from the lock and shrugged his shoulders, "time to test your theory. The lock is officially picked."

I'd read about it. I'd never done it.

"How much time after you open the door before the thing goes off?"

"Half a second. Maybe less."

"It's like when you watch a college basketball game and they make the last second last for five minutes?"

"Actually, James, it's not like that at all. When I open that door, I've got to place this magnet on the mounted contact immediately. And the polarity has to be correct. If it's wrong, they push against each other and we're screwed."

"I thought you said this was a piece of cake."

"Never said it, James. I simply said it could be done."

We both pulled on latex gloves, and I reached for the handle. My hand was actually shaking, and I took a deep breath to calm myself. I started over, both hands now down at my sides.

"Gloves, dude." In the dim light I saw James smile. "Should have worn them when we found the knife in the locker. You see, we've come a long way."

I didn't think we'd come nearly far enough.

Holding the magnet in my right hand, I reached for the handle with my left. If the polarity was wrong, maybe there was still a chance I could turn the piece of metal over and quickly place it against the contact. The chance of that success was almost zero percent.

"You gonna do it?"

I nodded.

"Then let's get it done."

"James, seriously, this might not work. That alarm may go off immediately."

"Skip, in the scheme of things, it's not that big a deal."

"You think the answer to this case may be in Bouvier's office?"

"I do."

"Then I want this to work."

He reached out and touched my left hand.

"Skip, if it doesn't work, if the alarm goes off, I've got a solution."

I'd learned over the years that his solutions are often worse than the problem.

"What's your solution?"

"Run like hell, amigo. Run like hell."

CHAPTER FIFTY

There's something about James that makes me somewhat okay with risk. Part of it is that my best friend has my back. Part of it is that with his bravado, his brash give-a-damn attitude, it's hard not to buy into what he's doing. And then I was reminded about what Kelly Fields said, how James uses people and I was pretty much riding on his coattails. In this case his coattails could drag us both off to jail.

I turned the handle, taking deep breaths, and letting them out slowly.

"You gonna be okay?"

I didn't answer. Feeling the perspiration on my forehead running down into my eyes, I reached up to wipe my face with my right hand. Wiping with latex gloves just smears the sweat. It doesn't help at all.

I kept pressure on the handle, careful not to move the door. James had, in fact, picked the lock and now all that was left was for me to pull the door open and place the Walgreens magnet on the door-frame contact. In half a second. And make sure that it fit snugly against that contact with the right polarity. What the hell, there was a fifty percent chance I'd get it right. Probably less than a fifty percent chance that I could do it quickly enough to bypass the alarm.

My roommate was strangely quiet, and when I glanced up at him, I could see his concentration. He was pulling for me; we both wanted everything to work perfectly.

Easing the door open, pulling it toward me a fraction of an inch at a time, I steadied my right hand, ready to position the magnet as soon as the contact in the frame became visible. Slowly, I moved it. James was right. If I screwed it up, we would simply run for the truck. It was going to take the cops at least a couple of minutes to get here.

"Dude, a cop car just drove by."

"Are you sure it was a—"

"No question. Lights on top, the whole thing. They were moving very slowly."

And there was the metal contact. With my right hand, my thumb and index finger, I pushed the magnet in place. It almost snapped. The polarity was perfect.

Holding my breath, I waited, expecting to hear the wail of an alarm siren at any second. There was nothing. I gently pulled and the door swung out into the parking lot, the magnet holding firm. The floodlight mounted above the door threw our shadows onto the asphalt, and I quickly stepped into the kitchen. James followed.

Closing the door almost all the way, I let it rest against the magnet, making sure the thin piece of metal stayed in place. If the door closed all the way, the circuit would still be complete, but then I'd have to repeat the process to get out of the restaurant. This way, when we exited, I would just push the door tight, the magnet would slide off the contact and the door and frame contact would once again make a seamless connection.

The atmosphere was eerie. There were three faint security

lights illuminating the kitchen, but the brilliance of work lights on a nightly basis was burned into my brain, and to see the broiler, stove, the bulky dishwasher, and other features in the hazy shadows of these dim bulbs was strange, to say the least.

"Cheap security system, James. We should have been detected by now."

"Shut up, amigo. Be thankful that you know that, but Bouvier apparently doesn't. Or he doesn't think anyone would ever break in."

I thought about it. We were seriously in violation of any number of laws. If we were caught, there was probably jail time coming. Unless Detective Ted would stand up for us. And if he didn't, with me away, and Em available, well, I didn't want to think about it.

"The faster we get this done, the faster we can vamoose."

I followed him, walking over the rubber mats through the kitchen as we took a left down the hall.

"We're going to take that CD this time, pard. No reason for the hoodies. Please, do not let me leave this office without taking the CD out of the recorder."

There was no way we were going to make that mistake again.

He tried the door to the office, but Tara had apparently locked it on her way out. She had probably assumed Bouvier had forgotten to lock it. Once again, James pulled the misshapen paper clips from his pocket and worked them into the mechanism. He seemed more confident this time and within three minutes he pushed it open.

Stepping into the tiny office, James flipped on the lights.

"If this detective thing doesn't work out," I said, "we can always go into B and E."

Walking to the recorder, James popped open the plastic door and removed the CD. He put it in the back pocket of his jeans and turned to me with a smile.

"We didn't do it, pard. No proof that it was us."

He still had to open the tool chest. A different type of lock, smaller and more fragile.

"How are you going to do this one?"

"YouTube, Skip."

He walked back into the kitchen and came back with a sheet of thin metal.

"A pan from Mrs. Fields's station. This sheet of steel will open the chest."

"You knew this before we got here?"

"Be prepared, Skip. The Boy Scout motto."

"You were never a Boy Scout."

James wedged the thin pan into the slot between the top of the chest and the first drawer, then slowly, he shoved it farther into the tool chest. When he'd finished, there was barely any of the pan showing, the metal hitting the back of the box.

"Now, if this works according to plan—" he pushed down on the metal pan and pulled on the first drawer as it effortlessly came forward.

"And that's how it's done, amigo."

I had to hand it to him. He'd pulled everything off perfectly. I should have been frightened, but then I'd beaten the security system. No easy task. We were getting good at skills we shouldn't even have.

"So now we count knives?"

"Look."

I glanced into the drawer. There were seven knives lined up evenly on green felt with one space next to them. The empty space had the perfect imprint of a nine-inch kitchen knife.

He shut the drawer and opened the second one. Eight knives lined up evenly.

And the third, and fourth. The bottom drawer had five knives.

"Room for thirty-seven, Skip."

"Yeah. And one removed to give to you."

We stood there staring at the red chest with the metal baking pan shoved into the top.

"Damn. I was sure the murder knife came from here. I could feel it."

"It would have been convenient for the killer."

"I've got a gut feeling, Skip. We're missing it. Right in front of us."

I heard the bump out in the kitchen and we both froze.

"Maybe a rat," James whispered.

"Vanderfield?"

He smiled.

"None of the staff is going to come in here at this hour of the morning."

We stood still, straining to hear another sound. There was nothing.

James stuck his head out the door, glancing toward the kitchen.

"I don't see anything."

We were both talking in hushed voices.

"We know that the Wüsthof was used as the murder weapon, and in the top drawer," he counted down the knives, "four of these are nine-inch Wüsthofs. Number five would be the one he gave to me."

"Pretty risky venture to find nothing." I was speaking in my lowest voice.

"I'm sorry man, I put us both in a spot. I just thought that—"

"Oh, my God. Oh, my God." I felt my heart jump in my chest.

"What?"

I wanted to scream, but ground my teeth instead.

"The knife on the end, just before the blank spot."

"Skip," his raspy whisper, "it's just another nine-inch knife."

"No, it's not."

"What is it?"

"Look. Carefully."

Leaning over, he studied the German steel knife.

"Holy shit, Skip. It's got the nick in the blade. That's my knife, amigo. My damned knife."

That's when we heard the bump again, coming from the kitchen.

"Somebody is out there."

"Shit, we are going to have so much explaining to do."

The office door was open, and James reached over to close it.

"You need a key to lock it."

I turned the lights off and we were left in almost total darkness. I could barely make out my surroundings from the faint light that came through the small window in the door.

We could hear footsteps coming down the hallway, the sound of someone's canvas sneakers slapping the concrete. Then silence.

Closing my eyes, I took a deep breath and held it. It was supposed to be a relaxation technique, but it wasn't working very well.

We were startled when the doorknob turned, James and I both pressing our backs to the wall. We could leap out and attack the person, we could immediately start making excuses, although I had no idea what those excuses would be, or we could just be quiet and let the scene unfold. I don't ever remember being in a situation like this, and James and I had been in some pretty stressful situations.

Even in dim light I could see the fear in my roommate's eyes.

Whoever was in the hall let the doorknob go and it flipped back to its original position. There was another moment of silence, then a click, and footsteps retreating toward the locker room.

"Oh, shit, Skip."

"Are you thinking what I'm thinking?"

"That jammed handle."

"Whoever it is just locked us in."

CHAPTER FIFTY-ONE

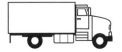

It's hard to tell how much time passes when you're in the dark and in panic mode. I'd have guessed fifteen minutes while we stood in silence, once in a while whispering an idea to each other.

"Worst case scenario, we break the door down."

"If we're able."

More silence. Then James spoke.

"Who was it? Did they know we were in here?"

"James," I'd pretty much gone over the whole thing in my head, "there was a magnet wedged between the door and the frame. The kitchen door was unlocked and whoever came in figured out the alarm didn't go off. I think they pretty much knew that somebody had broken in."

"Maybe they don't know we're in the office. I mean, whoever it is may have just checked the door, found it wasn't locked, and locked it."

More silence.

"Where did they go?"

"You know, whoever this is has a key. Who's got a key?"

"Bouvier."

"One."

"Chef Marty."

"Two."

"Tara."

"Three."

"Oh, and probably Vanderfield."

I was surprised. "Why?"

"He's a sous chef."

"So are you."

"He's the *real* sous chef." James spoke in a coarse whisper. "When Marty isn't here, he takes over. I'm certain he's got a key to the building, the office, and the walk-in. And I'm positive that Amanda Wright had the same access."

It could have been any one of them. Obviously not Amanda, but we had no idea what we were up against.

"Skip," he was looking out through the small window, "what if he called the cops?"

"I've already thought of that. We just try to get Conway to stand up for us."

"Skip—"

"Yeah?"

"You've got your cell phone."

"Yeah."

"Call Em."

"And tell her what?"

"See if she's got any ideas."

I couldn't believe that James was making a plea to solicit Em for a way to get us out of this jam.

"She told you she thought you were an idiot. Now you want me to call her and admit it. That we both got caught with our pants down?"

Silence.

Then I heard it. The faraway sound of those rubber-soled shoes marching back down the hall.

"Maybe he's leaving."

"Maybe."

A pause right in front of the door. We heard the click, then nothing. Now it was unlocked and someone appeared to be outside waiting for us to make the first move.

We waited, maybe two minutes, it might have been three. Neither of us moved an inch. Just as I was about to open the door, just pull it open and step into the hallway, someone pushed on it hard. He stood there, a sneer on his face, a knife in his hand.

"It's too bad I had to come in when I did. You broke in here to steal something out of the office." He glanced at the chest with its open drawers. "What? Knives? And I catch you in the act. Boys, I'm pleased to say I don't think you're going to be working here anymore." He gave James a cheesy smile. "Much less heading up the South Beach operation."

Vanderfield the pirate, a three-day stubble on his face, stood there, tapping the silvery blade in the palm of his hand.

"You didn't even know we were here."

"I did not. I was going to do some research on a new menu item, but let me say it's a pleasant surprise."

He ran his tongue over his lips, as if in anticipation of what was to come next.

"So are you going to kill us? Like you did Amanda Wright?"

"Oh, you think I killed the lovely, talentless Amanda. She wasn't bad in the sack, but couldn't cook her way out of a soup pot."

"You couldn't take the fact that she was getting the promotion and you weren't."

The sous chef gave us a grim smile.

"You've got this whole thing figured out, don't you?"

I was staring out into the hall, wondering if James kept him occupied, I could go around Vanderfield and head for the open door. But that left James with the knife-wielding cook.

"We were just leaving," James's voice was a little higher than normal. Higher with a slight quiver.

"Oh, I don't think so." He took two steps toward us, and that's when I saw the flash as a cast-iron skillet came crashing down on his head.

CHAPTER FIFTY-TWO

"Maybe I killed him." Em stood there shaking, the iron weapon balanced in her hand.

James was pale and I'm not sure I was any darker.

"God, James, you almost kill a cop with a truck door, and now I'm facing possible manslaughter charges for killing a sous chef. I'm not sure we're cut out for this stuff, guys."

"What the hell brought you here? How did you get in?"

"The door was propped open. And I thought about your situation and was feeling pretty bad that I'd kind of talked the two of you into taking this job. Then I refused to back you up. I got worried, having you here by yourselves."

I took some offense at the statement. "You didn't think we could handle it by ourselves?"

"Was I correct?"

"What do we do now?"

She pulled out her cell phone.

"Call Ted."

"It's three in the morning."

"He said twenty-four-seven."

"Maybe he had something else on his mind."

"Grow up, Skip." But she knew it wasn't going to happen.

Em called and he answered on the third ring.

"Ted, we've got the sous chef Vanderfield here at L'Elfe. He was attacking Skip and James with a knife, and I hit him pretty hard with a skillet."

I could hear his voice through her receiver.

"Jesus."

"Do you want to come over here?"

She switched the phone to speaker.

"Let me think. How many laws have you guys broken?"

She studied James and me. "Probably several."

"I think the guy is alive." James was on his knees, listening to Joaquin Vanderfield breathe.

"He's alive, Ted. But he'll have one hell of a headache to-morrow morning."

"Did he confront you?"

"No. He didn't know I was here."

"So, he's coming at Lessor and Moore with a knife and you think that proves he's Amanda's killer? Is that your jumping-off point?"

Again she looked at us, and James nodded.

"He had a knife in his hand, Ted. I assumed, as did the boys, that he was going to use it. That's all I know."

Once again, "Jesus."

"Do you want to come over?"

"No. Should I? Yes."

"We'll wait."

It took him twenty minutes and he arrived alone. I expected the cavalry.

"Where do you get off breaking into someone's business?"

James looked at the floor.

"My God, do you know that the police have to get search warrants? And even then we've got to have a lot more to go on than a hunch."

"In our defense—"

"You have no defense." Conway looked me straight in the eye.

"We needed to get confirmation on the knives."

He just shook his head and walked over to the chest.

"So, hot shit, what did you learn from your break-in?"

I shrugged my shoulders. "We may have learned nothing." I had yet to absorb the impact of James's knife in Chef Jean's drawer.

"So my entire jaunt out here at whatever god-awful hour this is, is for nothing?"

He leaned against the door frame of the office, leaving us to stand and take his criticism. "I've never had use for private investigators, they're more trouble than they're worth. And you two? Rank amateurs."

He pulled on Kelly Fields's shiny pan, still wedged in the top of the open chest.

"Where the hell did you get this idea?"

"YouTube," James said sheepishly.

"Not bad."

"Thanks."

"Does this guy," he motioned to Vanderfield who was still out cold, "have a key?"

James nodded. "Probably."

Conway studied the fallen sous chef, kneeling down and checking his pulse.

"So, even if he's the killer, he has every right to be here."

None of us said a word.

"I'm in a real mess here, kids." He squinted his eyes, looking at James, then me, finally coming to rest on Em. "If I cover this up, and I get found out, it's my job. It's a criminal act."

"And if this guy is the killer?"

"Based on what? He's got a key to the place?"

We did have a very lame premise.

"He came at us with a knife," I ventured.

"You just broke into his employer's business."

James studied the chest. "Did you fingerprint the guy?"

"They fingerprinted everyone in the—"

"He skips nights, shows up late on other nights. Maybe your guys missed him."

"So you're suggesting that if we didn't print him, then those prints we can't identify on the knife handle might be his."

My roommate nodded, a smug look on his face. He'd bet on Vanderfield from the beginning.

Taking a deep breath and gritting his teeth, Conway looked out into the hallway at the comatose body. "You three, take a hike. I'm going to talk to the sous chef and get another handle on what happened here tonight."

"Detective, there's one more thing."

His lips pursed, he frowned. "There's always one more thing."

I pointed to James's knife.

James was shaking his head, as if to say "Don't give that to him. No."

"The knife, with the slight nick in the blade, I'm pretty sure it's the one that was stolen from James's locker."

He looked confused.

"You're talking about the knife that was stolen from the locker the same night someone took the murder weapon and— Oh. What you're insinuating is—"

"I think the murder weapon came from this chest. And whoever killed Amanda Wright replaced that murder weapon with James's knife thinking no one would notice."

Em smiled, looking impressed with my deductive reasoning.

"Bouvier." James and Conway said it together.

"I don't think we have his prints on file." The detective studied the knife lying on its bed of green felt.

"What if they compare the unknown prints on the murder weapon with those on James's knife and they both match Jean Bouvier or Joaquin Vanderfield?"

"Could be a logical explanation."

"Maybe. But would you look a little harder at that person?"

He thought about it for a second. "It's not conclusive by any means, but it would warrant a harder look at one of them, I suppose."

"So you're going to print Bouvier."

"And Vanderfield, if he isn't already on record. Get me a kitchen towel. I'm wrapping up the evidence."

"No search warrant?" James had to push it.

"I now know how to break into this tool chest, Lessor. If I get a positive on the prints I will replace this knife and get the warrant. Don't lose too much sleep over it, okay?"

I got the impression that Ted Conway could do just about anything he wanted to do and get away with it. Sort of like James.

"Ted," Em put her hand on his arm, "thank you for—"

"No. You're not out of the woods on this one. Not yet. I'm covering all bases, and I'm covering my ass. You tried to kill the guy out there. Your two friends," he waved his hand in our direction, "they did exactly what I was afraid they'd do. They went over the line, they interfered with this investigation, and they were about to withhold information that may very well have led us to the killer."

It was even worse than I thought. There seemed to be nothing good coming out of this scenario.

"We'll be in touch." James was already headed toward the kitchen and freedom.

"Yes, we will. You can count on it."

Out in the parking lot, I said it for all of us. "We're in some deep shit, my friends."

"If we flushed out the killer, all will be forgiven," James said. "Furthermore, there's no evidence we were ever there."

I glanced back at the kitchen door, the security camera pointing at me, recording nothing. The CD was in James's back pocket.

"Not the most efficient police work."

"What do you mean, pard?"

"James, he doesn't know if they printed Vanderfield, and they didn't even bother with Bouvier."

"This would not be a good time to tell him how stupid we think he is. He's a little pissed at us."

Em kicked at a piece of gravel, sending the stone out into the alley.

"Yeah, and I guess my dream of being Mrs. Ted Conway is never going to happen now."

CHAPTER FIFTY-THREE

Em called at nine. I was passed out, hoping for a long sleep, but I knew she had to have some news.

"Vanderfield was printed. Those aren't his on the murder weapon. And Ted ran some serious interference to get somebody at the lab to run James's knife early this morning. Guess what? Your roommate's prints are on his own knife."

No surprise.

"They ran it for all the chemical tests and, thank God, there was no human blood. Traces of this and that, but nothing to raise a red flag."

"How much trouble are we in for the break-in last night?"

"Vanderfield was going to file charges, get Chef Jean involved, until Ted confronted him with the fact that there was no proof anyone had entered. It seems the CD that records all the security cameras was missing. He's got nothing."

I breathed a sigh of relief.

"Ted told him if he pursued this in any way, he'd be interfering with an ongoing investigation."

"So our cover may be really blown this time."

"Maybe, but hang on because here's the real news."

I hung on.

"Two unidentified prints on James's knife are identical to two unidentified prints on the murder weapon. It's a match." I could sense her smile over the phone. "You guys did it, Skip. Congratulations. Do you hear me? You hit a home run."

What is it they say? Even a blind squirrel finds an acorn? That's us.

"They're bringing in Jean Bouvier for fingerprinting later this morning."

"How much do you want to bet?"

"That he did it?"

"Em, I think she was sleeping with him. I know you don't want to hear it, but I believe he gave her the job to keep her quiet."

"Boy, Skip, you keep pushing my buttons." The smile in her voice was gone.

"Are you aware of a Professor Brandt at Sam and Dave?"

"Changing the subject? Oh, that's good."

"No. Actually, reinforcing a point. Em, I'm trying to figure out why she was killed, and I think I've done that."

"Suppose you tell me exactly what you think."

"I think that Amanda used people even more than you know. Brandt was a professor when Amanda and James were in school. He had an affair with her—"

"*Everybody* had an affair with her." She practically took my head off.

"Yeah, well, he did, and when he tried to break it off, she accused him of sexual battery." I was yelling back.

"Are you sure it wasn't?"

"No. But I talked to him. She agreed to drop the charges, and I get the impression it cost him a lot of money."

There was nothing on the other end of the line.

"Em?"

She was quiet.

"I think Bouvier may have killed her because she was blackmailing him."

Nothing.

"Em? She had a history of doing that."

Silence.

Finally, I ended the call.

CHAPTER FIFTY-FOUR

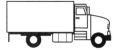

"Bouvier called." James stood in the doorway, boxer shorts and a Mötley Crüe T-shirt, holding up his cell phone.

"Yeah?" That couldn't be good.

"I was asleep, I mean in fog land, and he calls and says he needs to see me. Right now."

"According to Em, he doesn't know about our break-in last night. Conway threatened Vanderfield with interference in an ongoing investigation. Plus, he pointed out that there was no proof we were there."

"Why does he want to see me, then?"

"James, they're printing him this morning."

"What?"

"Em called." I told him about the knife and the unidentified prints.

"Oh, shit. And he wants to see me? Now that Vanderfield is in the clear, maybe Chef Jean is going to make some excuse, like he found my knife back in the locker room, assumed it was his, and just dropped it in the drawer. That's how his prints got on it."

"Actually, James, that excuse works."

"He killed her, Skip. It all makes sense."

Last night we were ready to hang Joaquin for the murder. Today it was Bouvier.

"And it goes back to your jeweler, the sixteen-year-old kid. Amanda basically blackmailed the kid's old man. Got a nice pay-day for that, didn't she? I'll bet she was trying it on the short chef."

"You're admitting that my background check of the kid is going to lead to the solving of this case?"

He nodded affirmatively.

"Then you buy beer for a month, James."

"Oh, yeah," he said sheepishly. "But the verdict isn't in quite yet."

"So, are you going to see what he wants? He couldn't tell you on the phone?"

"Had to be in person. What the hell, I'll drive over there, and if he gets crazy on me, I'll walk out."

"If he's the killer—"

"Skip, I've been with the guy before. I don't think he's going to come after me. If we're wrong and I blow him off, we may never see our six thousand dollars, and right now I could use the money, pally."

"I don't believe I'm saying this, but let's call Conway."

"Give me a break. I can handle the little guy. I could take him down if it came to that. Let me see what he wants."

"Not a good idea, James. Let me go with you."

"I can handle it, Tonto. I'm intrigued. Especially because he has no idea that we know about the knife drawer."

"Drop me off at Em's. She's pissed again about my allegations regarding Amanda. Time to make amends."

Half an hour later I got out at The Grand. I pressed Em's bell and she buzzed me in.

"I'm sorry about being so sensitive, so anal about this thing, Skip. It's going to stop. Right now. I promise you. I can't defend this dead girl anymore. Amanda was not a nice person, but I just didn't realize how conniving she apparently was."

I didn't push it.

"And do you really think it was a good idea to have James go down to the restaurant? If Bouvier had something to do with the killing, he might be feeling the pressure. I mean, with the cops fingerprinting him at this late date?"

"James is a big boy. He can probably take care of—"

Just then the phone rang, the Springsteen ballad at full blast. It was James.

"Skip. You're not going to believe this, amigo."

"What?"

"I think we've figured out who the killer is. And I believe Bouvier agrees with me. He's offered us a bonus of another three thousand if we can wrap this up."

"Who is it?"

"Just get down here. Bring Em and don't say anything to anyone. Seriously. Just the three of us, okay?"

"Got it."

I hung up.

"What?"

"Apparently James has figured it out."

"Who killed her?"

"I don't—" It hit me. Like a ton of bricks.

"Bouvier knocked her up."

"What?"

"Em, she blackmailed him to get the chef job. She was having his kid. And he stabbed her in the abdomen."

"To make sure the fetus was killed."

We were both silent for a moment.

"It's preposterous, Skip. Your imagination is over the top."

"She did it before."

"I don't believe it."

"Bouvier was on the boat. He pushed James into the water."

"Your friend Kelly, the baker, was on the boat. And Chef Marty."

"Okay, James is waiting for us. He claims he knows who the killer is. Drive me down to the restaurant. They want to see you too."

"Should I call Ted?"

"The Bouviers don't like cops. If James has it figured out, let him call Conway and rub it in later."

"Let me get my keys," she said heading for her bedroom.

When she emerged her face had a bound-and-determined look on it.

"We're going to actually find out who killed her? Let's go."

The morning was overcast, the smell of rain in the air, and I was glad James had the truck. The windshield wipers didn't work on his vehicle, but on Em's new car they came on automatically at the hint of moisture. Pretty cool.

Pulling into the lot at the rear of the restaurant, I glanced at the truck and Bouvier's black Escalade. Em's brand new Jag, the elf's shiny Cadillac SUV, and James's truck. What's wrong with that picture?

Pulling the back door open I saw only the security lights on, the same ones we'd viewed last night. As the door shut behind us, I was again caught up in the shadows and the almost ghostly look of shapes and objects that looked much different in the harsh light of an evening rush.

"Where are they?" Em talked in a hushed voice, feeling the eerie sensation that I did.

"James?"

No sound.

"Maybe we should leave, Skip."

"Come on, they're here. His truck is out back, the door was open."

I motioned to her and we walked out into the dining room. Tables were stripped bare, chairs turned up so cleanup could vacuum the carpeted floor. The bar was dark, no light behind the colored bottles of alcohol.

"This place is giving me the creeps."

"Let's try the office." I led the way, walking down the narrow hallway. The door was closed and the light was off. We continued to the locker room, with no lights at all. I flipped a switch but nothing happened.

"James?" my voice reverberated off the cold tile.

"Skip, seriously, we need to get out. There's no one here."

"Where the hell would they have gone?"

"I don't know and right now I don't care." She tugged my hand, pulling me back toward the kitchen.

"Hold on. Let me see if the office door is—"

I pushed on it and it opened. There, in the dim light, was someone sitting at the desk. I flipped the light switch on the wall, but again nothing happened.

"James?" It looked like him, but there was little light from the kitchen and no light from the other end of the hall.

Walking up to the chair, my eyes adjusted. It was James. A rope wrapped around his chest, tied to the desk chair. His mouth was stuffed with a piece of cloth and his eyes were wide open in fear. It made no sense. He was trying to shake his head, and as I reached to pull the gag from his mouth the lights came on. Brilliant, starry lights, flashing in my brain and I remember the sharp pain in my head as I passed out from the blow.

CHAPTER FIFTY-FIVE

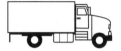

I could sense somebody before I saw them. And when I glanced up from the floor, there he was. Chef Jean Bouvier, the elf, in T-shirt and jeans.

"I'm somewhat sorry it will end like this. It was never my intention. Believe me, this has all gotten out of hand."

I tried to rise then noticed my hands as well as my legs had been duct taped together.

"What was your intention?" My voice sounded out of body, a little strangled, every word punctuated the sharp pain in my skull.

"My intention was to find who killed Amanda Wright."

"James," I twisted my head back to see James sitting up in the chair, watching the proceedings, "James said you know who killed her."

"I think I've known for some time. I just refused to believe it." He stared down at me.

There was a stirring next to me and I turned, seeing Em wrapped in the duct tape as well. Her eyes fluttered open.

"Are you the one who hit me? Us?"

"No. I couldn't do that."

"So who could?"

"Chef Jean?" Someone was calling him from the back door, and I wanted to shout, to alert someone that we were in serious trouble. Bouvier shook his head, putting his foot on my chest and I held my voice.

"Chef?"

Kelly Fields. I could hear her footsteps coming down the hall. Then the sharp voice of Sophia Bouvier.

"What are you doing here?" Came Sophia's voice from the kitchen.

There was a slight hesitation, then, "I had some prep work to do for tonight and—"

"No prep work today. We're doing maintenance this morning. There's a gas leak."

"I wouldn't be in the way, and—"

"Did you hear me? There's a gas leak. Go. Now."

The footsteps retreated.

"She's not right, you know." Bouvier stood above me, watching down the hallway.

I assumed he was talking about his wife.

"Ever since our child, my son was killed. She obsesses."

Em, in a weakened voice, spoke. "Why are we here? Tied up?"

"She has decided the charade must end." He pointed toward the toolbox. "Someone took a knife from my drawer. I'm afraid it was the murder weapon, and now they are asking for my prints."

"But you didn't kill Amanda Wright."

"No. I'm afraid my wife did that. And it's only a matter of time before they print her as well."

James mumbled through his gag.

"When you walked out that night, Amanda was already outside, wasn't she?" I wanted to keep him occupied, but I also wanted answers. "You went out. We saw the video, Chef. Then you turned around and spoke to someone in the doorway. I assume it was your wife. She told you she'd just be a minute, then you walked away. I suppose you were getting your vehicle. We saw Sophia go into your office, come out, and leave the same way you did. So what did she do? Take a Wüsthof knife, walk over and kill Amanda before the two of you left?"

He squinted his eyes. It appeared as if he might cry and his voice choked. "I didn't know. I really didn't know. It never occurred to me that she had the time, and I'd been with her almost all evening. She was only gone for a minute."

"And that's all it took."

He nodded, and I could see tears on his cheeks.

"Actually, I thought she was getting used to the idea."

"That you were sleeping with Amanda Wright?"

"He was." The short, squat woman walked into the doorway, a deep frown on her face. "I caught them in the shower one night after we had closed."

Bouvier bowed his head and nodded.

"Keep an eye on them, and I'll take care of the burners."

She walked toward the kitchen.

"What are you planning to do with us?"

The little guy opened his knife chest, reached inside, and pulled out a Wüsthof nine-inch knife. Studying the blade for a moment, he approached Em, reclining on the floor.

"No, it does you no good to kill us. They're still going to print you and Sophia, and they'll know."

"I'm sorry. About everything. This has to be done, and I should have done it half an hour ago."

With a flick of his wrist, he cut the tape on Em's hands, then her legs. Moving swiftly, he sawed at the thin cord holding James, then cut me loose.

Standing there with knife in hand he motioned to the doorway.

"Go. Now. Get the hell away from here."

"And what happens to you?" I wanted to escape with my life, but I needed to know.

"She killed my child. She said if her child was dead, I could not have one either."

Em stepped into the hallway. "Your child?" She glanced at me, her eyes wide open.

"Amanda was carrying my, our child."

The brutal stab wounds to the abdomen. The calls for reports on the autopsy. I was right. It had all been about Amanda being pregnant. I just had fingered the wrong Bouvier.

"Get out. Before she comes back."

I could smell the gas, the sulfurous rotten egg odor they add to natural gas. As we stepped out of the office, I heard her coming.

"What have you done?" She stood there screaming at Bouvier, waving her hands in the air. "No, no, go back."

James was running and the two of us were right behind him. This was crazy town. I looked over my shoulder and caught Bouvier shoving Sophia into the cramped office. He pulled the door shut and appeared to lock it.

She was screaming at the top of her lungs.

"What have you done? What have you done?"

With long strides for a short-legged man, he followed us to the door.

"Drive. As far away as you can."

We didn't have to be told twice. James and I jumped into the truck, Em got into the Jag and we drove out of the lot, two blocks before she called me on my cell and said to pull over.

"I called Ted again," she said when we were all standing in the 7-11 parking lot.

"Again?"

"I called him from my condo, Skip. I told him that something was going on at the restaurant, but he was on another call. Somebody has to go back in there and—"

"And what? They're crazy people."

"Did you smell the gas?"

We'd gotten out of our vehicles and were looking back at the catastrophe we'd avoided.

"Hell, yes." James was looking back down the road toward the eatery.

"She was going to blow the place up."

"Chef Jean locked her up in the office," I said. "I think he's got it under control."

The explosion rocked the block, shaking the very foundation we were standing on. A huge ball of flame shot into the sky, and we could feel the blistering heat from where we stood. Within seconds ashes and soot came pouring down, small pieces of metal and debris raining from the sky.

I think all three of us were numb. We stood there and watched the fire spiral higher and higher as the blaze found more fuel to feed on. Thirty-foot plumes of black smoke billowed from the restaurant and the roar was almost deafening.

An old Dodge came wheezing down the road, and the driver pulled over, window rolled down.

"Is that L'Elfe?"

"It was," James said.

"Damn." The dark-skinned man watched with us, his car still running and sputtering like it needed a tune-up.

"You know the place?" James asked.

"I do, man. I was just on my way to see if I could get my old job back. I was a dishwasher there."

We'd finally met Juan Castro.

CHAPTER FIFTY-SIX

"We'll never know. They're both gone, and the bodies incinerated. We can only guess what happened." Conway sipped his coffee, gazing out at the bay from Em's balcony. He'd called the meeting to finalize the information we shared. It was difficult since there was no corroboration.

"What appears obvious is that she replaced the murder weapon with James's knife before Chef Jean missed it."

"What a waste." James shook his head. "The man had an empire, he was the king."

"Who couldn't control his kingdom." I stated the obvious.

"When he picked Amanda to run his restaurant, Sophia knew that she was not right for the job." Em had finally rationalized her feelings about Amanda Wright.

"Everybody else thought the same thing, but Chef was a big celebrity and he carried the big stick," James said.

"He also signed the paychecks." I waved the envelope. A check for six thousand dollars, this one signed by Bouvier's accountant. Don't ask me how, but we'd been one of the first in line to be paid.

"So Sophia starts snooping." Conway's manufactured story. "She shows up one night when they are in the locker room, showering. That had to be a shock. Anyway, she waits until he comes out and they have a real blowup. How long has this been going on? How could you put our business relationship in jeopardy? She probably told him to fire Amanda and never see her again. Somewhere, Bouvier gets some backbone and tells her that Amanda is going to be the mother of his child. She's pregnant."

"That didn't go over so well." It wasn't the first time she'd made that claim.

"So," Conway continued, "I'm guessing she has this epiphany. She's lost her kid to violence, her last shot at an offspring, and she certainly wasn't going to let Jean have another child."

Em jumped in, "Amanda was being paid off with a fabulous new job, and when Sophia called her out to the parking lot she obviously was worried. After all, she told her it was a matter of life and death. Remember? She told me that on her voice message just before she was killed."

"So," Conway went on, "she went out to meet Sophia, but Sophia wasn't there. The chef's wife had told her to wait by the Dumpster. Very ominous. I find it hard to believe Amanda didn't tell Chef Jean. And maybe she did. We saw him leaving on the security camera so we know he had been in the building."

"And, we saw Sophia leave shortly thereafter," James said.

"It turns out he was getting the car. Sophia knew how long that would take, and we'd already seen her enter his office, where she probably had taken the knife from the chest. She walked over, said 'hello' to Amanda and stabbed her in the stomach."

"Over and over and over." Em was dealing with it.

"The object wasn't just to kill the home wrecker," Conway pointed out. "The object was to kill her unborn child, just like the one that had been stolen from Sophia."

"Only Amanda had been up to her old tricks."

"She wasn't pregnant," Em said. "She was going to tell him that she lost the baby, but not until the head chef job was solid."

"Sophia then hid the knife, maybe in her purse, got in the car with Jean, and they left. He had no idea. If there was blood on her, it was dark outside, and he'd never see it. If he did, she'd tell him she cut herself somewhere. The timing was such that it was almost seamless. Bouvier got the car, she came out, and got in with him. Only she took maybe ten, fifteen seconds to kill someone first."

We all knew that the Bouviers had an aversion to organized law enforcement. So it made sense they would hire an outside firm.

The detective kept going, "Sophia embraced the idea of hiring you guys because she could keep tabs on the investigation. We weren't going to tell her anything."

"But she didn't. I mean, she didn't really keep tabs on us." The lady had very little interaction with James or myself.

"She did. In her own way. She probably had her husband grill you, and then she'd check with him. She did confront you guys a couple of times, trying to see if anyone was investigating Bouvier."

She had. Telling James that Chef Jean couldn't possibly be the killer, when she was really fishing to see how James would respond.

"Purely speculation here, but I'm guessing this lady didn't think the chef had paid enough for his indiscretion. So the next day, after James was hired, she walked into the locker room, did the simple combination, and staged an apron with some catsup from the laundry basket. I think Sophia was going for the drama here, and she stuck the murder weapon through the apron. She wanted someone to find that knife with Jean's prints and Amanda's blood down the tang."

"Why James's locker?"

"I don't think it had anything to do with James. He was using a house lock, and she could get the combination for that one. Everyone else had their own locks. Makes sense to me. As much as any of this makes sense."

"But her prints would have been on it too."

"She may have worn gloves. We don't know. We're dusting their home, and maybe we'll pick up identical prints, but we certainly can't print her now."

"Why didn't you print her in the first place?" James asked.

"In hindsight we obviously should have, but there was really no reason. She came and went as she pleased, and she was under everyone's radar. Technically, she wasn't an employee of the restaurant."

"So she wanted Jean to get arrested for the murder."

"I think so. One minute she did, one minute she didn't. She was hot and cold, drunk and sober. She had second thoughts. She was throwing away everything she'd worked for, and she must have decided that was a bad idea, so she goes back to the locker, takes the apron and knife and hides them in the Dumpster."

"Did she know that the bin had already been searched?"

"Maybe," he said. "But she lucked out, because we searched every bin in the neighborhood the night of the murder. Not the second night."

"She thought she'd taken care of the evidence, underestimating James's determination to find the knife." He lucked in to almost everything that happened to him.

"She was so irrational." Em stood, and walked to the railing, staring out at the cruise ships docked half a mile away.

"You think? What's that line, hell hath no fury like a woman scorned. A cold, calculating killer would have been methodical. She was anything but methodical. She took James's knife out of his locker while she was there, to replace the one she stole. Bouvier didn't check his knives every day or probably even every week. So her goal was to slip it back in the red tool chest when she was alone. Bouvier would assume it was his. And apparently he did."

"James." I nodded to him. "If you hadn't pushed the idea of opening the knife chest, we'd never have figured out where your knife went. Em, I think an apology is in order."

She gave him a thin smile.

"All right, you're not an idiot all of the time."

"There were little things," I said. "Like when you were pushed, James, you said someone put their hands on your waist. It hit me that a guy or even a taller woman would push you at the shoulders. Now I get it."

"But, Skip, why was Sophia trying to kill James? She was in the clear at that point."

Conway weighed in. "Again, we have no way of knowing, but I think the constant presence of the two of you reminded her that someone was possibly going to figure it out, and in the end she decided that killing you was one way to avoid that."

We were quiet for a moment.

"Oh, yeah, we finally got a trace on those autopsy calls. They came from Bouvier's home and the restaurant. Both of them thought Amanda was pregnant, and both of them were calling to see if there was any mention of the fetus. That's the best guess we have."

Conway stood up, put his cup on the counter, and walked to the door.

"What was Vanderfield doing at the restaurant when we broke in?" I never had figured that one out.

"He said he couldn't sleep and he was going to experiment with some sauces."

"And why wouldn't you let us see your copies of the video? We knew the players, yet you refused. We had to steal the originals."

"Some evidence has to go through a procedure before it's released. Just one of the processes that sometimes slows down an investigation. You guys found a way around it, didn't you? At the risk of being arrested for breaking and entering."

"So much of it doesn't make sense," Em said.

"In crimes of passion, it seldom does," he replied. "Give me a planned, calculated murder every time. Point A leads to point B to point C. In matters of the heart, anger issues, the killer is all over the place. We got lucky on this one, if you can call it luck. The killer confessed before we solved the crime. It happens. Thank God, it happens."

His eyes locked on Em.

"So, I probably won't see you again."

"No. I don't think so."

She walked over to me, putting her arm around my waist.

"Stay away from jewelry stores and restaurant parking lots late at night, okay?"

She smiled.

Conway walked out of the condo, and I was never so happy to see someone leave.